"Oh, love me,"
she whispered.
"Love me...love me...."

But even as he gazed at her, tender and beautiful to him now, he could not forget how she had looked the day before. For that one moment she had made herself alien and hateful to him, and one moment was long enough for him to see himself separate from her.

PORTRAIT OF A MARRIAGE is a novel to touch everyone's heart. Probing, deeply sensitive, it tells of two passionate people caught by love and stirred by its meaning.

PORTRAIT OF
A MARRIAGE
was originally published by
The John Day Company.

Pearl S. BUCK

Portrait of a Marriage

PUBLISHED BY POCKET BOOKS · NEW YORK

PORTRAIT OF A MARRIAGE

John Day edition published November, 1945
A *Pocket Book* edition

1st printing...........June, 1953
8th printing........October, 1968

This *Pocket Book* edition includes every word
contained in the original, higher-priced edition. It is printed
from brand-new plates made from completely reset, clear, easy-to-read
type. *Pocket Book* editions are published by Pocket Books, a division
of Simon & Schuster, Inc., 630 Fifth Avenue, New York, N.Y. 10020.
Trademarks registered in the United States and other countries.

L

Portrait of a Marriage

⋙⋙⋙⋙⋙⋙⋙⋙⋙ PART I

THE June landscape of Pennsylvania was full of pictures. Young William Barton, surveying it from under an ancient ash tree upon a low hill, could not make his choice of which one he would paint. He sat upon the grass, his arms clasping his knees. There to the right of him was the Delaware River, a smooth flow of silver between green banks. To the left of him was a valley and in it a small town hidden except for church spires and sloping roofs set in trees. Below him was a farm, cows in the meadows and waving wheat and a red barn and an old stone farmhouse. In a field of red-brown earth a farmer was ploughing for corn.

He looked at the richness about him and asked himself if it were perhaps too rich and the beauty too lush for a canvas. Did such plenteousness also contain monotony? It needed an accent.

As if in answer to his demand he saw the accent appear. The door of the farmhouse opened and a girl in a blue dress and a white apron came briskly out into the sunshine. She had a bell in her hand and she rang it with a wide sweep of vigor. The sound came up the hill, clear and full.

"Can it be noon already?" he asked himself. He had no watch because he always said he did not want to know time when he painted. But if it were already midday, then he had let the morning pass without any work done. He looked up through the leafy green above him. The sun was

1

poised at the zenith above the top of the trees, and moreover, he was hungry. The morning was over.

Feeling slightly ashamed of himself, he rose, took up his knapsack of paints and folding easel, and went down the hill toward the farmhouse. He would ask for a lunch and then perhaps, his conscience salvaging, he could find in the closer perspectives of the farmhouse the picture he wanted and had not been able to see in all the variety of the plenteous landscape spread about him.

He walked across a meadow and by a narrow lane between low hedges of uneven yew he approached the door into which the girl had returned. As he drew near he smelled meat roasting and he was suddenly ravenous. Certainly he must have food whether he had worked or not. He knocked at the Dutch door, whose upper half was open, and stood waiting, hatless, because he never wore a hat when he was walking in the country. Someone came toward the door. He could hear quick, firm steps upon a bare floor, the sort of steps a strong young girl would make. Then she came into his sight in the shadowy hall and then she stood in the half-open doorway.

"What do you want?" she asked him.

It was the same girl. He recognized her blue dress, her white apron. But now, close to her rosy face, he saw that she had blue eyes and brown hair and was very pretty. Her eyes, wide and quiet, looked at him with directness as she waited for him to speak.

"Could you—" he began, "I mean, I hope it doesn't seem rude for a complete stranger, but I happened to see you ring the bell and suddenly I was hungry. Would it be possible for you to let me have something to eat?"

Her rather resolute young face stayed grave. Not a tramp, her candid eyes were reflecting, because his clothes were too good, and he did not talk like a tramp.

"We don't give meals out," she said doubtfully.

William laughed. He had seen her clear little thoughts.

"I'm quite respectable," he said. "I happen to paint pictures, and I'm on a painting trip, that's all. And I will pay for my food, please."

Her red and white skin flushed. " 'Tisn't that," she said.

"It's just that—wait a minute, and I'll go speak to Pop."

She disappeared and William waited, looking about him with pleasure. The house was made of fieldstone, brown and dull red and streaked with weathered gold. In the chimney there was an oval of white marble inscribed, T. H. and M. H. 1805. Over the porch a trumpet vine climbed in full leaf but not yet flowering.

"Come in!" a man's voice shouted.

William turned with a slight smile. A grey-bearded farmer was coming toward the door. "Come in and have some dinner!" he shouted. He threw the lower door open and stood, shortbodied in his blue jeans. His shirt, opened at the throat, showed a mat of reddish hair.

"May I?" William said gratefully. Tonight when he reached home this would be an experience to tell his parents.

"How charming," his mother would say.

"Quite European," his father would agree.

They both knew the peasants of Europe better than the farmers of their own state. The irritation of a discussion about this with his father only a few days ago had been the spur that had driven him to a painting trip. He had argued that good pictures were waiting to be painted of American countryside, the more hotly because he knew it was partly because he did not want to go to Europe again this summer.

"The countryside here is raw," his father had said with his usual gentle certainty on any subject concerning art. "There is no depth. It has not been lived in long enough."

"I'd rather like to show you, sir," William had said. His father's unbelieving smile had compelled him to it. William had a deep stubbornness of his own—had to have it, he thought, because of his mother.

Now he entered the shadowy hall. The stone house was as cool as a cellar.

"Come right in," the farmer said heartily. "Harnsbarger's my name—and Harnsbargers' is the house. Four generations of us lived here, and my children'll be the fifth. We eat in the kitchen—straight ahead down the passage and then turn left."

"Thanks," William said. He felt quite at home with this sort of man. He liked simple people; they gave him a chance to be himself.

They were in the kitchen now, a big stone-floored room, and in the middle of the outer end wall was a wide fireplace in which a cook stove had been put. Above were great oak beams, smoked to a dark brown. By a window the table was set, and beside it a woman in a full-skirted brown dress was cutting bread. The pretty girl stood waiting at her own place.

"Ruth, put another plate," Mr. Harnsbarger ordered her. "Sit down," he said to William.

"You are Mrs. Harnsbarger," William said with his quick smile to the woman.

She nodded, too shy to smile or to speak.

"And you," William said to the girl, "are Miss Ruth Harnsbarger."

"Yes," the girl replied calmly.

They sat down and ate. The food was plain and delicious. No one spoke until hunger was first appeased. It was the way people should eat when they were hungry, William thought, the good food absorbing every hungry sense. He was often weary of the polite necessities for useless conversation at the meals in his parents' house where food seemed held unworthy of notice for its own sake. He liked the dishes set upon the table before his eyes instead of at his elbow upon a silver tray. His hunger quickened as he helped himself.

"You from around here?" Mr. Harnsbarger said suddenly. His plate was soon empty, and he passed it to his wife to be filled again.

"My home is in Philadelphia," William replied.

"Folks in business there?" Mr. Harnsbarger asked again.

"My father owns a railroad," William replied. He had not in years seen his father do anything that could be called work.

"Business good?" Mr. Harnsbarger went on, taking up a leg of chicken with fresh zest.

"It seems to be," William replied. He had never asked his father the question. From railroad dividends, he supposed, must come the money which kept the great house and gardens so beautifully neat and quiet, which paid for the pictures his father bought, and for his own years in Paris and his sister Louise's music. Louise had been married last winter, and the railroad, too, must have provided for her trousseau and wedding.

"Don't know nothing about that sort of business," Mr. Harnsbarger said frankly. He was gnawing the chicken from the bone, and William turned his eyes away.

They chanced to fall, quite naturally, upon the face across the table. A wonderfully pretty face, he thought again, and then it occurred to him that here was his picture. Why not? Here in this dusky old kitchen, with the dark, wide fireplace and the chimney piece for a background, he saw a picture Dutch in its light and dark interior and yet with that peculiar tridimensional depth he was beginning to develop as his own technique, which critics were already saying would be his peculiar gift to American painting. He hated the ordinary pretty girls with whom his world seemed surrounded, but this face was not ordinary in its prettiness. There was firmness in the way the red lips pressed each other, and a clear, warm determination shone out of the calm blue eyes. The combination of rounded pink cheeks and a smooth, full chin, broad forehead and straight nose was perfect in itself, and though there was nothing extraordinary in these features, yet there was character behind them. He made one of his impetuous decisions.

"I would like to paint your picture," he said warmly, leaning upon the table toward her.

They all looked at him, startled. Mr. Harnsbarger put down the chicken leg.

"I'd paint it here in this kitchen—" William went on.

"The *kitchen!*" the girl exclaimed. She was mortified, he could see, and he hastened to explain.

"It's a beautiful room to paint. The light from these small windows makes good shadows, and there is the black fireplace and you in that blue and white—"

"You wouldn't take her in her old clothes, yet," Mrs. Harnsbarger said. It was the first time she had spoken.

"I can't imagine anything better," William replied.

They were doubtful but flattered, he saw, and he pressed them, wanting the picture more earnestly each moment.

"Please!" he urged. "I have been looking everywhere to see what I could paint, and here it is. I won't disturb you— not much. I'll paint you while you work."

"I don't know as I'd want that," Ruth said doubtfully.

"Then you shall say what you'd like," William said eagerly. He leaped up and pushed a small, heavy old table to the window by the fireplace. "There, you could stand and put daisies in a jar—no, you must cut a loaf of bread!"

She hesitated a little, pleased, but looking from her father to her mother.

"I don't care," her father said in his loud voice. "Give the women their way is my motto. I got to get back to my field. Well, good day, mister!"

"Good day," William replied joyfully. The women he could persuade. "See, like this," he said. He took the girl's round, bare arm and led her gently to the table. "Like this," he said, posing her with quick touches upon her shoulders, her head, her hands.

From the table Mrs. Harnsbarger stared at him speechlessly. But he did not see her. He was watching something in the girl's eyes, a shy, dawning self-consciousness that made them liquid, that curved her sweet mouth and made her lips tremble.

"Why, you—you lovely thing!" he whispered. He rushed to the door and fetched his paintbox and easel and fastened his canvas. "Don't move!" he begged her, "don't change!" And he began to paint.

. . . He noticed suddenly and with unwillingness that the kitchen had begun to grow dim. He had painted all afternoon forgetting everything, even the girl standing before him. Twice Mrs. Harnsbarger had come to the door and stared in at them and gone away again. He had not spoken to her. But he was stopped now only by the fading of the colors in the twilight. He put down his brush and then he remembered the girl.

"Oh, how careless of me!" he cried. He saw her now, still patient in her pose. "How tired you are!"

She moved. "Seems a body shouldn't get tired just doin' nothin'," she murmured. She stood waiting, not knowing what would come next.

"Oh, but to do nothing is very wearisome," he said quickly. He was peering at his canvas, examining it minutely. It was good, he thought with rapture, very good. He would be proud to show it even to his father. But he would not risk those critical eyes until it was finished.

"May I leave my picture here overnight?" he asked. "I don't like carrying it back and forth when it's wet."

" 'Twon't do no hurt, yet, if you do leave it," she said.

"Then where shall we put it out of the way?" he asked.

"I reckon the parlor'd be best," she said. She moved with a sturdy grace across the uneven floor and led the way while he followed, across a narrow passage into a square room whose blinds were drawn. She lit a candle on a table and he saw heavy, dark furniture and on the walls crayoned ancestral portraits. "Nobody comes here," she said.

"I'll be back tomorrow," he replied. He glanced swiftly about the incredible room as he set up his easel. He would describe this tonight at dinner, too.

But the kitchen, he thought, as he entered it again, was beautiful. That was because it was lived in. When people shaped a room to daily use, it became beautiful beyond their planning.

"I like this room," he said as he wiped his brushes. She stood watching him and at his words she lifted her eyes to his.

"This old kitchen?"

"This old kitchen," he repeated. He smiled as he put his paints away. Would it be worth while to explain to her the reasons for beauty? He decided it would not. Besides, why explain what she herself possessed in such abundance? He looked at her face with fresh appreciation and smiled into her eyes. Then he took up his knapsack and slung it over his shoulder.

"Good-by," he said.

She gave him in reply the smallest of smiles, and when he saw it he realized that it was the first time he had seen her face change its pure, grave tranquillity. He stopped, held by that change.

"Until tomorrow," he said.

She did not speak, but stood there, the smile upon her face. He went away, the look of her in his mind as clear as the picture he had half finished. All the way home he pondered that smile. Should he have put it upon her pictured face? He decided against it. No, lovely as the smile had been upon her lips, her gravity was lovelier.

So deep was he in his pondering that his father's house when he entered it seemed unfamiliar and remote. Yet this was the hall which he had entered year in, year out, of his whole life. A door opened and the butler came in noiselessly and took his knapsack and stick.

"Shall I do your brushes, Master William?"

William hesitated. He was always lazy about his brushes. Long ago he had taught old Martin to clean them. Now tonight, he wanted, without reason, to clean them himself.

"Thanks, I'll do them. I want to look at one or two of them."

"Very well, sir. I'll take them up."

"I'll take them up, thanks."

He took back the knapsack and mounted the stairs that swept in a great curve up three flights. At the top were his bedroom and his studio, hung with the pictures he had painted since he had first begun at eight. He kept them here, sensitively aware that his father thought none of them good enough to be hung in the gallery in the south wing. His father, as sensitive, said now and again, "Someday, my boy, you'll do a picture for me."

"I don't know if I ever can, Father."

"Of course, of course you can," the old gentleman insisted. To his wife in private he murmured doubtfully, "William has technique, Henrietta, but he has not found his inspiration."

Mrs. Barton had replied with her usual firmness, "I only hope that when he does find it, it will be a true one."

In his room now, William was aware of a curious feeling of daze. He was very tired. He had never before painted steadily for so many hours. Nothing before had been able to make him forget time and weariness. "I was inspired," he thought, wondering and half excited. Was this, he asked himself, the beginning of something new in his work, something for which all he had done as yet was only preparation? He had the feeling of power about to begin in him. Perhaps at last he had found his own material. Certainly he had painted today with swift ease and sureness. But was it good? He wished now he had brought the picture back with him. He was eager to examine it and see if it was really good. Or had he been deceived merely by the simplicity of his subject? He began to be impatient for the morrow, fearful lest he had been deceived.

In his uncertainty he decided to say nothing at all at the dinner table. He would not speak of his experience. He could not bear to speak of it, he decided in one of his characteristic impulses toward self-doubt. What if it were nothing?

He was glad he had so decided. When he went downstairs he found his sister Louise and her husband, Montrose Hubberd, unexpectedly in Philadelphia. That they were back in New York from a long honeymoon in Italy he had known, but their first visit had been arranged for the end of June, so that his parents could go back with Louise to Bar Harbor. On the stairs he heard Louise's high voice.

"Yes, we loved Italy, didn't we, Monty!"

A murmur signified Monty's reply. William disliked his brother-in-law without troubling to discover why. A tall, conventionally well-dressed figure, Monty was always a decoration to the background of any picture, but he never came out of that place. Thinking occasionally of the pale, flat-cheeked face with the dark mustache, William had wondered about the honeymoon. Could a woman honeymoon with Monty? But then, could a man honeymoon with Louise? It was difficult to imagine and smiling, he avoided it.

He entered his mother's white and gilt drawing room in a mood of irreverence. The moment in all its setting seemed as trivial as an eighteenth-century water color. Then his mother spoke and the triviality ceased.

"William, you're late!"

"Sorry, Mother!" William bent over his sister's cheek and gave Monty a nod. "Well, Louise! How are you, Monty!"

Monty inclined his smooth black head, and Louise fluttered her handkerchief. She was looking almost pretty, her slightly sallow pallor relieved by her dark crimson gown. Mrs. Barton rose from her chair.

"William, your arm, please," she said. They moved toward the door. "Where were you, William?"

"I was working, Mother." Instantly he regretted the words. Why had he told his mother he was working? Now she would ask where he had been and what he had been painting, all that he did not wish to tell.

"Working? Where?"

"Oh—out in the country."

"You won't find anything there."

He was nettled. "I did, though."

"What?"

"An old farmhouse."

"Pah—a chromo!"

"No, Mother, it was good stuff."

She did not answer, for she had reached her chair and stood directing the seating. "You, Louise, at your father's right, now that you're a married woman! William, sit beside your sister, and Monty, you are alone on the other side of the table. Harold, mind you don't touch the red wine. I see Martin has put a glass at your place—though I told you distinctly not, Martin!"

"Yes, Madam." The butler removed the glass and Mr. Barton sighed and sat down.

She had forgotten him, William thought with relief, through soup and fish. She threw her questions at Louise and Monty like darts, prodding with delicate persistence until she had the answers she wanted.

"Louise, did you go to St. Mark's in Venice? On Sunday, I mean—of course any other day it's simply a center for tourists. But for worship— I always say one cannot get the real flavor of a church unless one worships in it. Well, I'm a religious woman and you're not, Louise. You miss a great deal. I hope your influence won't make her worse,

Monty. What's that? No, I disagree with all that. Sermons and stones have nothing to do with each other, I'm afraid, and woods are apt to be damp. You must find a spiritual home in New York, Louise."

They listened to her as they had always listened to her, he and Louise, two rather pale little children, very well bred in the handsome, quiet home. He had never been able to find out whether Louise was bored as he had often been. There had been days when he had stood looking out of this tall window into the square full of spring sunshine and had felt the heart in his bosom a creature separate from himself. It would spring straight out of him some day, he used to think, and go off without him, leaving him behind like a shell. What color was a boy's heart and what would be its shape?

Then his mother remembered him. "By the bye, William, what did you say you painted this afternoon?"

"I didn't say, Mother." He helped himself to roast duck and apple.

"Well?"

"I think I'd rather wait until I've finished, Mother, and then show it to you."

"Nonsense, William!"

"I really mean it, Mother." That he surprised her into faint anger he saw, and was ashamed that he felt a quiver of his old childhood fear of her.

"Very well, William—though it's odd of you."

Before he could answer, Louise began to speak—quickly, he knew, to smooth the moment between her mother and anyone else.

"Oh, Mother, Monty and I were wondering—what would you really think if we should get one of the new horseless carriages?"

Mrs. Barton forgot everything else. "I should consider you both extremely foolish," she said severely. Her grey eyes lifted their heavy lids at her son-in-law. "Surely, Monty, you weren't considering anything so foolhardy for Louise."

Monty sipped his wine before he answered. "You hear a lot about them nowadays," he said evasively.

"That's no reason for joining the company of fools," Mrs. Barton retorted. Her ringed left hand, clasping the stem of her wineglass, was thin as a sinew and as strong, though with it she had never touched anything coarser than the washing of her Spode tea set.

Monty smiled and did not answer. Since he had come to see his father-in-law about investing some of his millions, he knew better than to antagonize the old lady. From Louise he had learned a good deal about her mother.

In the silence Mrs. Barton returned to her son. William, feeling the cold grey light of her eyes upon him, braced himself. "I will not tell her about Ruth," he thought. But before she could speak, she caught sight of her husband lifting a filled wineglass to his lips.

"Harold! What are you doing?"

Mr. Barton's hand scarcely faltered. He gulped heavily twice and set the glass down. "Merely tasting Louise's wine, my dear."

Mr. Barton's voice was gentle and his eyes were as bland as a child's.

"You shouldn't," Mrs. Barton said severely. "Harold, I speak for your own good."

"I know you do, my dear, and I won't touch it again." He glanced at his two children, and all three of them bent their heads to the blanc-mange now served. As well as though he had seen it did William know that Louise had, when she lifted it, set her glass on her left, where if luck pursued, her father could sip the wine. But luck had not pursued, and they let it pass as they had done so many times.

But William, thinking it over as he idled about his room before he slept, was uncomfortable. His mother had forgotten him after the wine. If she had not, could her or could he not say that he would not have told her about Ruth? He would never know.

. . . Ruth lay awake, and for the first time in her life. She lay quietly, wondering at herself. She felt no pain and no distress, nor was what she felt excitement, but she could not stop thinking about him—the young man. She did not even know his name. They had not asked it, and he had not spoken it. She had not thought of this in her daze at the whole afternoon until at the supper table her father had asked, "Did he tell you his name, a'ready, Ruth?"

She had said, surprised, "I didn't think to ask him, yet."

"I thought of it," her father said, "but I said to myself, I said, I won't ask a man's name if he don't give it. I told him Harnsbarger's my name and he didn't say nothin'. Does seem as if a body would answer back his own name, but he didn't."

She had not replied to this, in secret dismay. Suppose he never came back and she never even knew his name? But of course the picture was still in the parlor.

"He finish the picture?" her father asked abruptly after supper.

"No, he's coming back tomorrow," she said. She began lifting the dishes from the table to the sink.

"Take it with him?"

"No, it's in the parlor."

"Then I'll have a look at it." Her father lifted the oil lamp from the narrow mantel shelf and went toward the parlor, his stockinged feet noiseless upon the boards. She followed and her mother behind her, and in the parlor the three of them stood staring at the painting.

"The tablecloth come out nice," her mother said.

"It don't hardly look like you, Ruth," her father said.

" 'Tis too pretty, ain't?" she said despondingly.

" 'Tis," he agreed. "But then, maybe that's how he seed you."

They had gone back to the kitchen, and after yawning a while her father had gone to bed. In their usual silence she and her mother had washed the dishes and cleaned the kitchen and set the table again for breakfast. Only when her mother was ready to climb the steep stairs did she pause.

"Reckon we'd ought to make soap tomorrow, Ruth. The fat jar's full a'ready."

"Oh, Mom, not tomorrow!"

Her mother gazed at her heavily and was about to speak. Then she did not. She turned her head and began to mount the stairs slowly. And alone in the kitchen Ruth had finished quickly. She was not tired. She was never tired, but tonight her body felt full of strength and power.

"I wisht I could make the soap now," she thought, and had longed for the task. She opened the door and stood there for a moment, looking out into the night. Had there been a moon, she would have been tempted to go over to the wash shed where the lye and fat were kept. The stars were large and soft but the night was dark. She hesitated, and closed the door, and went up the stairs to her own room. By candlelight she had washed herself and put on her sleeved cotton gown, brushed her hair and braided it, and then, blowing out the candle, she lay down upon the low old maple bed that had once been her grandmother's. She had closed her eyes, expecting the instant sleep that was always hers. But it did not come. She waited, neither restless nor impatient, only wondering. And against the dark curtain of her eyelids while she waited she saw his face, at which for hours this day she had gazed so steadily. "I never saw a face so clear before as his'n," she thought.

. . . When she saw him come down the lane, the next day, it was already late afternoon. She had waited for him all day and then had given him up, and in anger at her own waiting, in midafternoon she had begun to stir up the fat for soap.

"It's late, her mother objected. "Supper'll be soon."

"I'll work quick," she said, and then because it burst out of her she said, "Truth is, Mom, that painter feller—he said he was comin' back for sure today. So I thought 'twan't any use to begin the soap. Now he ain't comin', and I won't have the day gone and nothin' done."

Her mother did not look up from her mending. "Well, I'll be along, too, as soon as I get this heel in."

"No, don't. I can do with myself," Ruth said.

But at the door her mother's voice stayed her. "He's not our kind, I reckon, Ruth."

She flung back her denial of anything hidden in her mother's words.

" 'Tisn't him I care about—it's only that I hate folks that don't do what they say they goin' to do."

"That's what I mean." Her mother's eyes did not lift from the long needle, weaving in and out of the crossed threads.

And then nearly at twilight she saw him coming, hatless, his hands in his pockets, down the lane toward the door.

"I'm here," she called.

At the sound of her voice his head turned and he saw her and came over to her.

"I'd given you up," she said. The fat was hot above the fire over which the great iron pot was hung. She had measured in the lye and was stirring the mixture with a spoon-shaped stick. He stood watching her.

"What are you doing now?"

"Makin' soap." She stirred slowly, feeling the mixture begin to thicken. "I thought you'd come earlier," she said, glancing up at him. He did not have his paints! "And where's your paintin' things?"

"I didn't bring them."

"Why—ain't you—you're not goin' to finish?"

"I didn't feel like work today."

She was angry with him, an anger she did not try to understand. "You call it work, maybe, to paint pictures?"

"On the whole, yes," he answered. "At least, it's my work."

She could not stop stirring for an instant now, for the stuff was nearly ready to pour. "I'm used to real work," she said shortly.

"Like what?" he inquired, half sullenly.

"Ploughin' and milkin'—paintin' the barn."

"Call my work on a level with painting the barn," he said bitterly.

"Help me to lift this off," she said. "It's ready to pour."

He came to her side and helped her to lift the three-legged pot from its crane and set it on the ground. Jars stood ready in rows and she began to ladle the clean-smelling stuff into them. He watched her, thinking, she could see, of something else.

"Will it harden?" he asked.

"When it's cold," she replied.

"It smells good," he said.

"Only like soap," she retorted. She was half through before he spoke again.

"Of course I'm going to finish the picture, Ruth."

She lifted her eyes at that. "I'll thank you not to call me by my given name afore I even know yours."

He smiled slightly. "William."

"William what?"

"William Barton."

She was dipping again. "I never heard the name."

He felt a secret joy. If his mother could hear that! "Why should you have heard it?" he asked.

"No reason, I reckon," she admitted.

They did not speak again until the jars were full. The sun was balancing on the horizon in a ruddy mist of thin, low clouds.

"What'd you come for if you wa'n't goin' to paint?"

"I don't know,' he said. "Perhaps to see if you were as pretty as I thought you were yesterday."

Her eyelashes quivered and she blushed. "I wish you wouldn't—" she murmured.

"Wouldn't what?"

"Just—talk."

He groaned a little in his heart. Why had he come when he knew it was not for work? This was not what he wanted to begin!

"Let's have a look at the picture," he said abruptly.

He led the way. It was milking time and he could see the girl's parents under the overshoot of the barn, milking. The house was empty and he strode into the parlor, angry that he was conscious of her firm light footstep behind him. He lifted a drawn shade and the setting sunlight fell across the picture. Pure pleasure rushed into him and filled him full. He forgot the whole tiresome day he had spent before he had made up his mind to come back to this place. Yes, the day had been ruined by Louise, stealing into his room before he was up. He was waked by her cool, narrow hand on his cheek and he opened his eyes to see her standing there in her dressing gown of frosty blue satin, her fair hair wrapped in curlers under her lace cap.

"William, do you mind?"

"What's the matter?"

"William, I wanted to talk to you last night, but Mother was so—William, will you help Monty and me?"

"How—what—wait a minute!" He had rubbed the sleep out of his eyes. "Now, what's up?"

"Darling, Monty's fearfully poor!"

"Poor!" He sat up yawning. "Why, I thought Father had him investigated and all that."

"Darling, it's happened since! Some mines or something turned out to be empty or something. They were supposed to be full of diamonds and they weren't. Do you suppose you could speak to Father—alone, I mean?"

"What can he do about diamonds, Louise?"

"No, dear, not diamonds, but invest something with poor Monty just to encourage him. He's so low."

"I didn't notice he was low."

"Oh, but he is! He hides his feelings so wonderfully, but *I* know."

He had struggled out of bed and she had stood talking at the half-closed dressing-room door while he shaved and bathed and dressed. Almost the whole day had gone into the absurd scheming with Louise and the talk with his father. He had been troubled between his loyalty to Louise and to his father, and his unacknowledged doubts that Monty was perhaps not to be trusted. He had been relieved when his father had with his usual shrewdness directed that he must have Monty talk with his lawyers. But so the morning had gone, and Louise had wept a good deal privately to him, and because he was fond of her he had stayed with her until even his impatience to work had died as the day drew on.

"You'll understand when you're *married*, William. Marriage is so *strange*—it just mixes you up with another person. When Monty suffers, *I* suffer!"

He had transferred his impatience entirely to Louise.

"Stop fretting," he had commanded her. She was the sort of woman it was almost impossible not to command. "After all, we're not going to let you suffer, Louise."

"It's not me—it's Monty I think of," she had sobbed.

"It's so hard on him to have this disappointment at the very beginning of our married life."

"Oh, Monty," he had said. "He'll manage."

And then she had cried at him that he did not understand marriage.

"I'll agree with you that I don't understand that," he had said with conscious irony.

"You'll understand some day," she had said, wiping her eyes and trying to smile at him. "Tell me, dear, don't you care about anybody, yet? What about that pretty Elise Vanderwort?"

He had not thought of Elise in months and said so. And then he had decided suddenly that he must have air and sunshine.

"You'd better go and wash your face or Mother will see through you," he said. The worst part of the day had been to show nothing to his mother.

And then he had walked to the station and he swung on the first train and rode to the village, and an hour's walk had brought him here before his picture.

"I'll be back tomorrow for sure," he cried. "Ruth— why shouldn't I call you Ruth? I'm William, you know— just William."

"All right—" she said. "All right—William."

June, July, and August. Ruth had stood still like this hour after hour, she who was strong and full of energy, and summer had passed her by in these hours and in the dragging days between. She had never known time could be slow in all the endless work of house and land. But now she knew. When William did not come, though her body moved with its usual calm haste the hours stayed at twice their length, and by night she was exhausted with inner waiting.

Her agony was that she could never be sure when he was coming. For several days at a time he did not come, and then suddenly he was there, all impatience as though it were her fault that she was not ready and waiting for him by the window. Ready and waiting she was, too, because there was no pretending she did not love him. She knew that she had loved him from the first day—no, from the very first hour. She loved him now until her heart felt sore. The picture was nearly done, and then what would she do? He would go away and she would never see him again. The long afternoons in the kitchen when he sat painting and she stood looking at him would be over. She could not any more watch him as he worked, his dark eyes seeing her and not seeing her. Sometimes she felt that all he saw was the girl in the picture, and then she grew jealous.

"She's prettier'n me," she would say to hear him deny it.

"No, she's not," he would reply. "It's a very good likeness, as it happens."

"My eyes aren't so blue," she insisted.

"They're the bluest eyes in the world. I can't make them half blue enough," he retorted.

Then she was comforted somewhat and returned to her silence, and he worked on.

By mid-August the picture was almost finished. He kept doing something to it, but they both knew it was finished.

"Another week," he said suddenly one day, "and it will really be done."

"Then I won't see you no more, I guess," she said in a low voice but plainly.

"Why not?" he said cheerfully.

His heart turned over when she spoke, but he did not want her to know it. He knew himself too warm, too weak before beauty, too easily ready to please and to love. And Ruth was sweet. It was delight that she had been exactly what he thought her, so exactly what she looked.

The strange summer was nearly over. He had simply come here day after day, or he had not come. For two weeks, even, he had gone to Bar Harbor and had renewed his half-playful friendship with Elise. What his father had done to help Monty he did not know, preferring if he could to avoid family difficulties. But something had been done. That his mother had directed it, he guessed from her increase of authority over Monty. He had rather admired Monty's urbane acceptance of this, while preferring not to know more about it.

Elise had been beautiful enough, but he had not wanted

to paint her. He had even kissed her once or twice. The first time, at a dance, he had taken her out on the terrace of her home that overlooked the sea. Most of the terraces did. His father's home had a terrace even finer than the one upon which he stood with Elise when the mixture of moon and ocean and soft night air had made him put his arm about her and turn her lips to his. The kiss was sweet enough, perfumed and warm. She waited an instant, and he knew it was to hear him speak. If he offered her marriage, she would accept it.

"Forgive me," he whispered instead.

She waited an instant more and then withdrew herself gently.

"There is nothing to forgive," she said lightly.

He had never been so near liking her as he had been then.

"Look, is that a little boat there, so late on the sea?" She had turned away from him.

He had kissed her once more another night, and that time she had asked him nothing. She had simply yielded herself to him and, to his surprise, she returned his kiss. This time it was he who drew away. If she had not kissed him, he had sometimes wondered, would he have gone on to marriage? She was very beautiful and her beauty was deepened and illumined by the proud poise in which she enveloped all she said and did. To feel this pride and poise break and melt beneath his lips should, he thought, have swept his reason away. Instead it had repelled him. There was demand in the kiss, and he shrank from all demand. He knew he did not want to marry Elise, now or ever. The next morning he had started back for the farmhouse.

When he was with Ruth she left him alone. His mind could pursue its thought undisturbed. And yet when he looked at her, there she was, waiting.

"You'll be busy in the city," she said; "you won't bother about comin' out here."

He did not promise anything. Aware of his own warmth, he was sensible enough to know that warmth in a nature like his could grow cold in an instant's distaste, as it had, indeed, with Elise. He saw this house, this kitchen, Ruth herself, with all the appreciation of his eye. But he could remember also, too sharply, things not beautiful—her father and mother, whose kind goodness was enough for them but not enough, perhaps, for him. Mr. Harnsbarger could talk and spit and cough with repulsive freedom, and Mrs. Harnsbarger was stupid. He wondered sometimes how Ruth could have come from those two. She had a brother who worked in the livery stable in the village. He had met Tom Harnsbarger one day when a windstorm had ended in steady rain.

"Stop in the town and Tom'll drive you to the railroad in one of his rigs," Mrs. Harnsbarger had said.

In a two-seated buggy he had had time in an hour to plumb Tom's depths. They were not deep. He was a talkative, good-hearted fellow, at his best with horses.

"Thought some of bein' a vet," Tom had said. "But Pop didn't think much of payin' out money to learn me about hosses. So I took me a job to the livery stable. I reckon it was for the best. I'm figurin' on marryin' a girl as has got somethin'. Linda Hofsammer she is, and we'll set up a business of our own maybe."

"The automobile will hurt your business some day," William had said.

"Reckon or'nary folks'll never do without hosses," Tom had said cheerfully.

That night he remembered clearly, because he had been so late that he had to tell his mother what he had been doing. She had invited guests for a dinner party and his lateness had annoyed her. And so out of an old childish fear which he despised and yet could not overcome, he had broken his resolve not to tell her of Ruth.

"I was painting, Mother, and the storm delayed me."

"Where is this wonderful painting, pray?"

At the head of the long mahogany table her head rose, taller than ever because she wore a small diamond tiara. At the sight of her his heart shivered beyond his control, as it used to do when he was a little boy and she swept into the nursery at night dressed to go out and scolded him for some fault he had committed in the day.

"It's in a stone farmhouse miles from here," he said too

brightly. "It's marvelous—an old, smoke-darkened kitchen and a pretty farm girl. I'm painting her in the kitchen."

"Bring it here and let me see it," his mother had commanded.

He had brought the picture home that night, thinking that if it rained the next day he would work on it. So he had had to fetch it down from his studio and he had had to endure what they said. Whether his mother liked it or not he did not know. She had lifted her gold-framed pince-nez and stared at it—stared, he felt, only at Ruth. And his father had only murmured something about the shadows under the beams. They had said nothing at all, then or afterward to him. But he had heard his mother say again and again since then to others, "Do come and see what William is going to offer to the Academy this winter —a little peasant girl! She could have been painted abroad, but the fascinating thing is she wasn't. She's a girl on a Pennsylvania farm."

"It's quite nice," his father agreed, antiphonally.

He had stood by many times, compelled to show his picture, and always vaguely angry at the handsome, well-dressed women who were his mother's friends, and ashamed before his father's silence.

"Sweet!" the women murmured. "A pretty child—" "How quaint the kitchen is!" "It could be Belgium." "Or Brittany." "No, it's Holland."

And yet not one of them but would be horrified if he had said, "That's the girl I'm in love with."

Lucky he was not in love with her—quite!

"I'm going to send you a pass on my father's railroad," he said to Ruth, "and you shall go and see yourself in a New York gallery."

"Will you be there?" she asked.

"Of course," he replied, and gave her the smile for which she had learned so painfully to wait because it made her sad and happy. If she was not to see him again she wanted to die. If he went away, then no one would be alive to her any more because whether she drew her breath or not she would be dead if she saw him no more.

One day in early September the picture was finally finished. He could no longer pretend to himself that it was not, nor pretend, either, that he came now for any other reason than to see Ruth. He could not come again without acknowledging to himself what this morning he had denied to his mother. For his mother had spoken at last. She had said in her imperious, direct fashion, calling to him as he passed by her door on the way downstairs to his breakfast, "William! Come here, please!"

He went in and found her breakfasting in bed, her greying hair smoothly curled and a lace jacket over her shoulders.

"Good morning, Mother," he said.

"Sit down," she replied. "William, I'm worried about your not finishing that picture—you've never spent so long on one. You're not becoming entangled with that girl, are you?"

"Certainly not," he had replied indignantly.

"Because it would never do," she said, breaking off a bit of toast and buttering it quickly. "You'd be very unhappy. Marriage is only tolerable when it takes place between equals. Even then it's not always tolerable."

He did not answer this. Silence, he had found years ago, was the swiftest way to release him from his mother.

"Well, go to your breakfast," she said, "though you might kiss me first."

He came to her, and suddenly she seized his hand and held it in her thin, strong hand. "Sure?" she urged him.

"Don't be silly, Mother," he had said impatiently, and leaned to kiss her; "as if I could!" And he had gone away determined that indeed he could not.

He put the final touch upon the picture late in the afternoon. It was to deepen the blue in Ruth's eyes. Then he laid down his brushes.

"It is done, Ruth," he said. "Come and see yourself."

She came to his side and stood for a thoughtful moment.

"Is that how I look to you?" she asked.

"Yes," he replied.

What she saw was a rosy, strong girl, full of health, in a blue dress and a white apron. She recognized her hands, always a little rough so that she was ashamed of them. He had not spared them.

"They'll laugh at me maybe in New York," she said.

"They'll think you are beautiful," he said.

"I could have put on my Sunday dress, though," she objected.

"You ought to wear nothing but blue, for the sake of your eyes," he said, and then he added playfully, "—make me a promise?"

"What?" she said quickly and felt her heart smother. What could he want of her but to tell her he loved her?

"Wear nothing but blue," he said.

She felt cast down enough to weep. It was nothing. "I couldn't promise that," she said. "My best dress is pink."

"I was joking," he said hastily.

"Besides, what would you care when you won't be seeing me no more?" she said.

"Don't forget you're coming to New York," he said gaily. And all the time he was putting away his brushes and his paints, and now he folded his easel and took up the picture. It was not very large and he carried it in a frame he had devised for his wet paintings. Now he was ready to go.

"I shan't say good-by," he said, "because we will see each other again."

She did not answer except to put out her hand and to try to keep from crying. He saw her tears and refused himself the luxury of comforting her. He took her hand, but he did not hold it beyond the instant.

"I'll write you when my pictures are hung," he said, maintaining his gaiety.

She understood so little of the hanging of pictures that she scarcely heard him. He was going away, that was all, and she loved him. And he, seeing in her eyes everything she felt, trembled and wavered and wished that he were gone, or that someone would come in, or at least that she were not so pretty, or her breath not so sweet or that she were less to him—or more. He stood a quivering second and then, hating himself, he seized her with his free left arm and kissed her, and then he rushed out of the house and down the lane. "Damn!" he said with fury to his shaken heart.

He came into the formal, handsome hall of his home and saw the light of a blazing fire between the dark velvet curtains of the drawing room. He went toward it and found his parents waiting for dinner. He stood there in his walking clothes, his picture under his arm.

"I've finished it," he said.

"Quite finished?" his mother asked.

"Completely," he replied, aware of deeper meanings between them.

"Then let us see it," his father said.

William opened the press which held his canvas and set the picture upon the mantel between the lighted silver candlesticks. It was a proper light for it. Shadows deepened and the highlights came forward. His tridimensional technique had never been more successful. His father rose to examine the picture.

"It's the best thing you've ever done," he said.

"I know it is," William replied. It was the only picture with which he had ever been completely satisfied when he finished it. He could see his father asking himself if this painting were good enough for his gallery.

"It is really quite fine," his father said, hesitating. "A slight immaturity is, perhaps, its only fault—a fault time will correct."

"Oh, it's immature, of course," William said, laughing. "It's not good enough to put among your immortals, I know. But I'll reach that some day."

His father was relieved at his gaiety. "I am sure you will, my son," he said.

"Now that your pictures are ready to exhibit," his mother said, "I wonder if you wouldn't like a winter in New York? Your father and I have been talking about it for you—a bachelor apartment somewhere, perhaps, where you could have your friends and your work, too."

He perfectly saw through her plan and was about to tell her so, laughing again, when it came to him that it might be useful to him to have rooms of his own in New York.

"Thanks—it's good of you and I'd like it," he said equably. "Now I'll go and dress for dinner. I shan't be a minute."

He left the picture on the mantelpiece, amused at his instinctive reluctance to leave it alone with them. They would both, he knew, look at Ruth anxiously the moment he was gone. But she could bear their gazing eyes, he told himself. They could not disturb her serenity. He thought with some shame of his kiss. But could she not bear that, too? How sweet her lips had been, how shy and soft! He remembered Elise's clinging kiss with fresh disgust. Ruth's lips were like a child's. At this distance, in this warm familiar room, the kiss seemed nothing. He had done a young girl no damage, and of this he was even a little proud. Not every man could have been so strict with himself toward a pretty and childlike creature. He had even gone away without definite promise of meeting her again. He would put off that meeting day by day until at last all desire for it had dulled. When that time came, it would be easy to forget he had said that she was to come to New York. Thus his heart assured itself. On the other hand, he thought, if he found it too hard never to see her, if desire were not so easy to dispel, he could summon her to New York. Anything was possible. No door was locked. Everything depended on how he felt, and with possibilities of any sort to fit his need he was now comforted.

He ran downstairs happily aware that he felt well and was looking unusually handsome. There was the picture of her upon the mantel, her steady dark blue eyes lifted as she paused in the cutting of the loaf she held in her hand upon the kitchen table. When he entered the drawing room it seemed as though her eyes lifted to his coming.

"What shall you call the picture?" his father asked him.

He paused, meeting Ruth's steadfast eyes. He had never thought of it before. "Give us this day our daily bread," he said, and knew it right.

Ruth, moving about the kitchen after supper, forced her mind to imagine what his home could be. She was sifting flour and mixing lard and milk and measuring yeast for the making of bread. At the same table at which she had stood so many hours while he painted her she now stood to do this, stirring the dough in the brown crockery bowl and turning it out upon the board for the first kneading. And all the time her thoughts were painfully trying to see what she had never seen, the sort of house he lived in, the clothes he wore. Dinner was at night. She knew that because he had often said, "I must hurry, I'll be late for dinner and my parents don't like that."

"Why, you mean supper," she had said the first time, and then he had explained.

Every night they put on their good clothes and then ate—she could never understand that.

"Don't you go somewheres when you're all dressed up?" she had asked, wondering.

He had laughed. "Only sometimes," he had replied.

She thought of them sitting at home dressed up. And what did they do? People who lived in the same house hadn't much to say to one another. She and her parents scarcely spoke for hours together except about the work.

She sighed and went on kneading with her strong hands, her thumbs turning the soft dough inward. Soon the yeast began to do its work and bubbles cracked as she kneaded and she knew the bread was ready for its first rising. She rolled it into a round mass and put it into the bowl again and covered it with a clean towel. Then she went about the room, settling the fire for the night and putting out dishes for their early breakfast. The small tasks left her mind empty and she filled it with thinking of William. But try as she did, she could not see him where he was. She could only see him here in this kitchen, as he had been hour after hour, looking at her. She went and stood by the table in the pose he had given her and looked where he had always stood so that the light from the open door could fall upon his canvas.

But he was not there. The door was shut and beyond it was the night. "He won't be here no more," she thought and forced herself to believe it. "It's all finished," she thought and turned toward the stairs and climbed them. "And better so," she told herself, undressing and climbing into the little low bed under the eaves, "for I'm not his kind."

And then she lay awake, not weeping, but in a humble literal sadness, to realize the truth.

The devil of it was, he told himself angrily, that he could not paint in New York. Here in his own apartment, with the good north light in the room he had made into a studio, he could not paint. The city was full of pictures. He saw them everywhere. But when he put his hand to his brushes, its cunning was gone. He had no heart for his work.

At first he had thought merely that it was the strangeness of the new place and the excitement of his success that made him restless. His success Louise had made the most of, grateful for the excuse it gave her to invite guests to her home who might otherwise have wondered why they must dine with her and Monty. She had found New York society cold and self-contained. Philadelphia might have been a continent away. And Monty, she discovered, had enemies. Whenever he lost money for people, they hated him.

"Though *why*," she told William plaintively, "when he has done his best to make them rich! He loses his *own* money, too, but they never seem to think of that."

William had enjoyed being something of a young lion, a handsome one, too, he was told. Elise told him herself in the half-reckless fashion she made part of her smoldering charm.

"You've grown too handsome," she had said at Louise's first dinner when she found him at her right. "The country air agrees with you."

He had examined this for a moment. Then he replied equably, "Let us see what the air of New York will do," and had accepted with a smile the swift look she flung him from her amber eyes.

When she turned her head without reply to this, he accepted that, too, and found upon his own right another pretty girl, a very pretty girl, he thought carelessly. Indeed, New York was full of pretty girls. In his first success he saw them around him as thick as bees and noticed them scarcely more.

For he wanted to be serious about his work. His exhibition had been greatly praised. He had sold nearly a dozen of his paintings. He could twenty times have sold the picture of Ruth, but each time he had answered it was not for sale. Yet he knew that he ought to sell it as soon as he could. As long as he had it he could not forget Ruth, and he had made up his mind now that he wanted to forget her. The picture hung opposite the entrance to the gallery, and he went there again and again alone, to meet her blue eyes looking at him. Sometimes he stood before the picture to test the quality of his art—or so he told himself. But whenever he did this he seemed to step again into her presence, to feel again her warm, robust health that clarified by its simplicity all who came near her. Each time he broke away from her. "I must sell it," he told himself. For he knew that she could never belong here. And here in New York, he was beginning to believe, was where he wanted to live.

But as the exhibition went on he was further than ever from being able to sell the picture. At last in a fit of sharp jealousy he took it out of the gallery. Too many men stood gazing at it. The director had protested.

"That picture has been praised by every critic. Why, people come especially to see it."

"That's why I am taking it away," William replied.

"You're crazier even than most artists," the director retorted.

But William had not listened to him. The picture was now in his own room safe from the eyes of other men. For the last and immediate reason he had taken it out of the gallery was that he had seen two of his own friends, staring at it. "Is the model a friend of yours, Bill?" one of them had asked him.

He had replied coldly, "She is a farmer's daughter I chanced to see last summer when I was on a painting trip and I painted her in her own kitchen."

"Give us the address, will you, old boy?" the other man said jeeringly. "We might be walking that way ourselves."

It was the idlest of talk, and yet he had been instantly angry and foolishly serious.

"It would be a liberty," he said, and had removed the picture that very day.

Now when he woke in the morning his eyes fell first upon Ruth, her eyes lifted to him, and she was what he looked upon last when he put out the light beside his bed when he slept. He enjoyed the variety of his daily life, and yet he had a sense of homecoming to her at night.

One night when for some reason he was sleepless he rose resolved to write to her, that he might perhaps ease himself by communication. Sitting at his desk he poured out a warm, swiftly written letter. He wanted her to know that he was keeping her picture. It hung in his room and he could not part with it. Some day he would have to come and see her, just to make sure she was flesh and blood.

He posted the letter without reading it again lest by day it seem too ardent, and he waited for her answer, wondering what sort of letter she would write, imagining its child-like quality and the longings she would be too innocent to hide. But she did not answer, and as week passed into week and he realized that he was to have no answer, this hurt him. He wondered why she did not write and whether she had forgotten him.

The real reason did not occur to him. When she received this letter Ruth was so sorrowful that nothing could have moved her to answer it. She could not read half of his handwriting. It was fine, beautiful writing, but to her, accustomed to the plain childlike script of the scarcely literate, it was almost entirely illegible. With the instinctive secretiveness of the partly ignorant that made her determine to keep everything in her life to herself, she showed it to no one. She sat hours in her attic room puzzling over the letter, writing down each precious word she deciphered. When she had read all she could, she decided sadly that she must never answer it. Her handwriting could only make him look down on her and her spelling was miserable. She had gone no further than the fifth grade in the one-room country school, and then her father had said she could not be spared, because that was the winter her mother fell down the stone steps of the cellar and broke her hip.

"I'm too far beneath William in every way," she told herself. So she took his letter and folded it very small and sewed it into a scrap of red silk ribbon and hung it by a cord around her neck for a good luck piece.

If she had written to him, her letter might indeed have cooled him, but when she did not, it seemed to him that he must see her again if only to make sure that he did not love her. He deliberately compared her sometimes with Elise. Elise after waiting the winter through had in March suddenly announced her engagement to an Englishman whom nobody knew. She told William abruptly one day when she met him upon the avenue. She had just been, she said, to see his pictures again.

"But you have painted nothing new," she said. "I go every now and then to see if you have."

"I know," he said abashed, "and I cannot tell you why. I have the impulse to paint, but when I take up my palette, the impulse is dead."

"You find nothing to inspire you here." She made the statement as final as though it were something she had discovered. And then with scarcely a pause she went on, "I wondered if I should meet you today. If I did, I had made up my mind to tell you before I told anyone else of my engagement. I am going to marry Ronnie Bartram— You don't know him. He's an Englishman—a younger son of Sir Roger Bartram. We'll live in London after we're married."

She said this quite calmly, standing there before him, the wind blowing her red skirts and whipping the fur on the big collar of her black jacket. She put up her hand to hold her small red hat, and at that moment he saw how incomparably beautiful she was, her hair so dark, her eyes amber, and in the pale gold of her skin, her red mouth. He noticed too, that she stood in front of a florist's window, so that behind here were massed flowers. Whether this was intentional he could not say. He could never be sure that anything Elise did was not intentional, and he was repelled again.

Some faint fear of his childhood crept up in him again, his mother's all-seeing watchful eyes had made him feel a prisoner. Spontaneity drained out of him now with Elise as it used to do in his mother's presence. Then he was impatient. Really there was no reason why Elise should be so willfully intentional in all she said and did. They had known each other too long to be evasive. He did not want to complain against her, because it would only begin one of her long argumentative conversations.

There seemed nothing for him to say, in spite of his irritation, and yet he felt stupidly sad to think that whatever he had to do with her was over. They had been children together in the close circle of their class.

"I hope with all my heart that you will be happy, Elise."

"You can scarcely hope it as much as I do," she said.

He was surprised into awkwardness. "Don't you know —aren't you—you wouldn't be foolish, Elise?"

"I don't know what you mean by foolish," she said. She leaned against the window and put her hands in her black muff and looked at him. "Women must marry, you know. None of us ever knows whether we'll be happy. We wait and find out."

He had so seldom seen her wholly serious that it embarrassed him. "Then—let me hope more than ever," he said.

"Thank you." She put out a small, black-gloved hand and he took it for a moment and pressed it, wanting to say more and yet knowing there was nothing to be said. She drew her hand away quickly, nodded and went on. He gave one glance at her graceful figure. She held her shoulders flying like wings and her head was high. He felt his irritation melt away and he was suddenly nearer to loving her than he had ever been. She was of his breed and his world. There was much in them that was alike. He restrained his feet from running after her. For if he should pursue her, to what would he persuade her? He wanted to persuade no one to anything.

So he went back to his rooms and when he was there he sat a long time before the picture of Ruth, comparing her with Elise, eyes to eyes, lips to lips, and all the difference there was between the two, and of the two, he chose Ruth. He chose her for her frankness and for her simplicity. Her silences hid no provocations, and when she spoke he could accept her words for what they said, and not for what they left unsaid. He wanted to be forever free.

"She shall be kept herself," he thought tenderly. And he came to think of her as a sweet and private possession, a loveliness that no one knew about except himself.

In the spring it became impossible to refuse his longing. The painting was only an invitation. Ruth was alive and he could go to her.

He went in May, without going home or telling anyone that he had left the city. He prayed the gods he did not believe in that she would be alone when he found her, even perhaps in the kitchen so that he could see his picture come alive. The prayer took on the aspects of passion as he approached the house, but without his painting knapsack. This time he had not come to paint. He had come to find her.

He had planned his coming for midafternoon, remembering that it was at this hour she was most likely to be idle. He came to the kitchen door, his heart beating. The door was open and he looked in. She was not there, no one was there. His heart subsided so quickly that he felt faint. He went in. The room was clean and quiet, and he felt somehow that she had left it only a few minutes before. His senses, always too quivering, felt her still near. He sat down to wait, hoping that it would be she who would enter and not her mother or father. Yet he was aware, too, of his own danger and he knew that it would be better if one of them came first to remind him of their being. For he was frightened now by the strength and steadfastness of his longing, and he still would not acknowledge any purpose to his coming except simply to see her. How would she seem to him after a winter away, after a winter among very different people?

He looked about the simple room. Everything was exactly as it used to be, except that the table at which he had painted Ruth, and which had used to stand by the fireplace, was now by the window where he had placed it. It stood there empty, its surface polished and old with use. As he looked about the room he had a strange feeling of homecoming, as though here in this house he had been born and had lived as a child. The full, rich silence, the faint ticking of the tall clock in the corner, sunlight falling through the door, the shining kettle on the stove, the worn chairs, and the small hooked rag rugs, he felt he remembered from childhood. He could scarcely have imagined a place more different from the house where actually he had been born and lived as a child. He could not comprehend this feeling of homecoming to what he had never had.

And then through the open door he saw Ruth coming down the path which led to the kitchen from the orchard. She had a trowel in one hand and a basket in the other. She came straight toward him, her brown head bent a little in the bright sun, her face grave. She was thinner, he saw, but lovelier than ever. He rose and stood waiting and all his heart rushed to meet her. As though she felt a warm force drawing her she lifted her head and then she saw him. She dropped the basket and trowel and came straight to him, not pausing or faltering. They said not a word. Their eyes held each other's eyes, and he drew her to him and she was drawn until they were face to face, and then he put out his arms and she came into them and he bowed his head and laid his cheek upon her hair.

Thus they stood. He knew it was not what he had planned but it was what he wanted. And she knew only that what was, must be.

And then, after this moment, long and close, he lifted her face with his hand under her chin and he kissed her. Thus without a word, he discovered and declared his love.

. . . Mrs. Harnsbarger, coming through the narrow hall in her soft grey felt slippers, paused at the kitchen door. She had forgotten to put potatoes to soak for the making of yeast. What she saw put everything from her mind. There was Ruth, and William had her in his arms.

"Well, well," she said heavily.

They sprang apart, only their hands clinging. William began to stammer.

"I—I don't blame you for being surprised, Mrs. Harns-barger."

"Surprised ain't enough yet," she replied slowly. "I'm all in a heap." This, to her, could mean only one thing.

"I found I couldn't do without Ruth," William said. He looked at Ruth. He was smiling but she was grave and silent.

Mrs. Harnsbarger sat down. "Well, young man," she said. She seemed unable to go beyond this.

Still Ruth said nothing. Clinging to his hand, she looked at him with her large clear gaze. In her silence he felt compelled to speak. He tried to do so with as much dignity as he could, yet feeling himself somehow in a foolish place.

"Of course I was going to ask you, Mrs. Harnsbarger—and Ruth's father," he said. "But this has only just happened to us."

"I don't know what'll *he* say," Mrs. Harnsbarger said.

William felt an uprising annoyance. "I hope he has no objection to me," he said. It would be amusing, he thought haughtily, if this farmer and his stupid wife objected to him!

"We was countin' on Ruth marryin' somebuddy that would help on the farm," Mrs. Harnsbarger said doubtfully. "Somebuddy like Henry Fasthauser, Ruthie," she explained to her daughter.

"I'll marry William, Mother," she replied.

William drew her to him. "Ah, that's right," he exclaimed. "We stand by each other." He was absurdly grateful to her. It was sweet to have her choose him even if his rival was only someone named Henry Fasthauser. He wondered who the man was and if Ruth had even thought of him. He held her hand tightly in his, a firm hand, not too small in his clasp.

"Well, it won't be so easy for your father, yet," Mrs. Harnsbarger said. And after a moment of long silence she rose, sighing, "I guess I might as well set my yeast, any-how."

She began her work, and Ruth and William moved toward the door together. William paused and she turned her head to him.

"Speak for me, though, Mrs. Harnsbarger," he said with his most charming smile.

"I reckon Ruth'll have her way," she said without turning from her potatoes. "She always has."

William laughed, but Mrs. Harnsbarger was serious. She was already peeling potatoes, her lips pursed.

"Come, William," Ruth said with decision. She led him into the garden and they walked on together shyly between rows of vegetables, past the chicken yard to the orchard. Now that all had been declared, they felt weighed down with what must be said and planned. And each had a secret weight besides. He was thinking, "How shall I tell my parents?" And she was thinking, "How can I learn enough, quick, to be his wife?"

Neither could answer these questions, and because they could not they turned the more eagerly to the simplicity of love. Because they were afraid secretly of what they had allowed themselves, they longed to be bound together more securely, so that they could not be separated by anyone. They went into the orchard and sat down in the long grass and thus hidden they put all else aside except the freedom they now had for love. It was easier to love than to think. She gave her lips to him with eager delight, now that he was to be her husband. And he fondled the sweet fullness of her throat and her smooth arms and took her hands and kissed the palms. They smelled of soap, clean and unscented. She pulled them away.

"I'm ashamed how my hands are," she said. "They're not fit for you to kiss."

"I love them," he said passionately. "They're strong, good hands, beautiful hands. When I hold them I feel I am holding to something." He kissed them again and put them to his cheeks. "My dear," he murmured, "my very dear!"

She had no words to match this. She could only listen, quivering. His words were music and singing.

"I love every look of yours," he said, "the curl of your eyelashes, your hair, the turn of your chin to your throat. When you walk I think of wind blowing over wheat. You're earth and water and bread and light."

She had no idea of what he meant, but she saw the

tremor of his lips and the blaze of his dark eyes. And when he took her in his arms she gave herself up to him. Why not, when they were to be married? She had longed for him. In this rich countryside it was no sin for man and woman to join themselves when love was declared for marriage. Many a first-born followed soon after a wedding. And he put aside ruthlessly all caution, all possibility of regret to come. This was return, the return of all his being to its self.

"I don't want to hurt you," he said thickly. "Tell me if I hurt you."

But she would have borne any pain when it was inter-mingled with this joy that rushed upon her and made her weak and strong, in which she was lost and found herself.

No words were needed now. Words encumber and delay. She had no words, and he did not want them from her. Her strong, fresh body was enough. It was enough and enough, and through her he satisfied himself. His deepest hunger was being fed by her, and then he was fed. And then he lay in such peace as he had never known. Under him the earth, above him the sky, and between was he.

He lay and slept, his head in her lap, and she sat motion-less, awake as she had not been awake since she was born. This was her husband. She bent over him in such tender-ness that in her breasts she felt physical pain. How far above her he was! But this which had been frightening to think about now no longer made her afraid. She knew now how to comfort him and stay him. She could not use words for love, but she had other ways.

"I'll be good for him—better than anyone else could be. I won't ever let him want," she thought.

He went that evening to his own home, meeting his parents' surprise with careful casualness.

"You should have telegraphed your train, William," his mother said. "We could have met you."

"I wasn't sure when I could get away," he said.

He felt dazed with the afternoon's supreme act of love. Everything was still misted by it. He and Ruth had gone back to the farmhouse at twilight and then he had found

Ruth's father, already knowing but waiting to be asked.

"I hope you don't object to our marriage," William said.

"No use if Ruth don't," he had replied, "though I'd looked for help on the farm after my son turned against it. I've spoiled her, William," he went on. "She's stubborn. Don't hold it against her."

Then they made a few plans for the wedding. He could see that her parents, yes, and Ruth herself, were halting in these plans. He was no ordinary bridegroom. How would they fit a man like him into a country wedding? But when he put forth a tentative hope for no ceremony, he quickly withdrew it. There must be a ceremony, he saw, or they would not think it decent. So it was arranged, that day week. There was no use in delay. Ruth had her hope chest long ready, as every girl had in the country-side. She would make a new dress, one serviceable for the wedding and yet to wear afterward.

"Blue, though," William interposed.

"Blue," she had agreed.

But when she had followed him outside the kitchen door to say good night, he whispered, "We're already married, you know, Ruth."

She had nodded, her eyes full of secret joy.

. . . "How is New York?" his mother asked. The drawing room was fragrant with early roses. A wood fire burned, though the windows were open.

"Well enough," he replied, wondering how he would begin.

"What are you painting?" his father asked.

William put down the cigarette he had lighted. "Nothing," he said. "I've—the truth is, I haven't worked well in New York."

"That's odd," his father said, and lifted his grey eyebrows. "I should have thought the intellectual stimulus—"

"I find I can't paint out of intellectual stimulus," William said bluntly. "I paint out of earth and bread and water—and light—" He repeated the words with all the reverence of love. "I'm going to paint again now, though," he said.

"I am glad to hear that," his father said cautiously. He

felt a little afraid of his son tonight. Had he perhaps been drinking?

William, sitting in a great black oak chair, glanced from one to the other of the two elderly, handsome faces. He would plunge into the truth, now and forever.

"I am in love," he said. "I am going to be married to Ruth Harnsbarger."

They had forgotten her very name, and they looked at him bewildered.

"She is the girl I painted last summer," he said.

"Not that peasant girl!" his mother cried.

"She is not a peasant," he said. "She is a farmer's daughter—a very different thing, Mother, in our country."

"Nonsense," she said sharply. "Harold, why don't you speak? Why do you sit there merely looking stupid? Why, it's absurd!"

"I don't know what to say," his father stammered. "Your mother is right, of course, William. I don't know that it's absurd so much as dangerous. Yes, that's it—dangerous."

"It's absurd," his mother interrupted. "A girl I would not have in my kitchen, ignorant—"

"Be quiet," William said sharply. "It is for me to say what she is. She is the sort of woman who is a man's daily bread. I want no more." He rose as he spoke and went out of the room and up to his own bedroom. He refused the possibility of their prudence. "The snobbery of the old," he thought bitterly. "Their cruelty! Their falseness!"

He took off his dinner clothes and put on again his worn brown walking suit. He wanted to be plain and poor-looking and blunt and harsh. He wanted to get away from the softness of carpets and velvet curtains and old paintings and the two rich elderly people who were his parents. Strong work could never come out of this house!

"I'll go back to Ruth," he thought. "They'll give me a bed." He let himself out of the house and turned westward out of the city.

. . . The nearer he drew to the farmhouse, the more he wanted to tell them, too, the truth. When he reached the house he went around it to the kitchen. They sat in the kitchen and the door was open. Though at his home it was scarcely past the dinner hour, here they were preparing for bed. Mr. Harnsbarger was winding the clock and Ruth was putting the bread to rise. Mrs. Harnsbarger was sitting by the stove nodding.

"Can you give me a bed?" he asked brusquely. "I've quarreled with my parents."

"About me!" Ruth whispered.

He nodded. "They don't know you," he said.

The old man looked angry. "Who do they think they are?" he demanded. "My folks are good stock. We've owned this farm for four generations and never asked nothing of nobody. You needn't marry Ruth. There's plenty wants her."

"I certainly will marry Ruth," William replied. "Where can I sleep?"

Mrs. Harnsbarger had waked up. She looked frightened. "Will your folks send the police after you?" she asked.

William laughed loudly. "Scarcely," he said.

Mr. Harnsbarger finished winding the clock and closed the face carefully. He was pleased at the young man's guts and somewhat surprised, not having expected so much from a painter. Besides it put him in a good humor to think of the son of two rich proud city folks having left them to ask shelter in his house.

"You can have Tom's room," he said. "Ruth, you show him."

Ruth had not spoken since she had cried out. She led the way now without speaking. When in the dimness of the stair he put his arms about her, she held herself away from him.

"What's the matter?" he demanded of her.

"I don't like it that your parents don't want me," she said.

"The only thing that matters is that I want you," he said, and forced her lips to his.

She gave up to him after a little struggle, and then he would not let her go until she kissed him. But at the door of the room she stopped.

"I won't come in," she said.

"Why not?" he asked.

"I don't feel to," she said indistinctly.

"Look here," he said, "you're not blaming me for my parents?"

She shook her head. "I think you're—good," she said, "to love me, I mean," she said, hanging her head.

He flew at her and shook her and lifted her from the floor against his breast.

"Never say that again!" he commanded. "Never, never! There's no goodness in me toward you—only love—" He held her a long moment and then let her go.

And she, stealing along the hall to her own room, undressed herself and put on her plain white cotton nightgown and crept into her bed and lay awake hour after hour. Her mind went plodding on, feeling its way, always to the same blind end.

"I ought to have said I wouldn't marry him if they didn't want me to. Then I'd ha' known what he'd say. I don't want him to think he has to marry me. But he does have to marry me. Not because maybe now I'll have a baby. Anyway, they say you don't often have a baby the first time. He has to marry me because I love him so. I'll make everything up to him. I'll promise that to God." She climbed out of her bed and knelt beside it.

"God, I promise I'll make up everything to him."

They were married a week from that day. He did not go near his home or write or let his parents know where he was. There was no way for them to find him because they had never asked him where the farm was. So he was lost to them. When he was ready he would write them, but not until he was married to Ruth and back in New York. For that was their plan, that they would live together in his apartment. She had agreed to all he wished. He had only to speak a wish and she agreed to it.

And he out of bottomless content spent the week painting. He was compelled to work, famished to work, after long idleness. He painted a great sycamore that leaned against the west end of the house, a spotted, grotesque old tree that had heaved itself out of the ground until its roots were like clutching arms. He worked so hard that the week was gone before he had time to see it go. And then he had to hurry to finish his picture before his wedding. He wanted it done because he knew himself well enough to know that if it were not done he would be hankering after it, even in the midst of love.

It was done, and the day came and he stood up in the parlor beside Ruth. The Lutheran minister read the service, and the roomful of farm folk listened, awed by this marriage. They were friendly enough, but they were sorry to see Ruth marry a stranger who would take her away. After the ceremony they shook hands with him formally and stood about awkward and in silence to eat cake and drink wine, with none of the jokes there would have been if Ruth had been marrying one of them. Their few polite remarks to him were doubtfully made, as though they were not sure what he would say to them, or what he would expect them to say.

And William, chafing, tried to break through their shyness by his own laughter and joking. It was not easy, and he gave it up at last. After all, it would soon be over. He and Ruth would go away together. As soon as they reached New York he would begin to work. He would do a picture of her in the nude. He had never been satisfied with his nudes. Commercial models had no bodies—nothing but figures. But her body would be instinct with love and young passion and all her silver white flesh full of light. He fell silent thinking of this and forgot all else. And one by one the wedding guests went away.

"A queer fellow," they said, "not typical, anyways," they added doubtfully, and spoke kindly to Ruth because they were so sorry for her.

>>>>>>>>>>>>>>>>>>> PART II

RUTH paused in her sweeping to look out of the window of the kitchen. Her blue eyes, bright with watchfulness, were upon her fourteen-year-old son, who was mowing the grass with crawling slowness.

"Hal!" she called through the open window.

"What, Mom?" he called back. His round face, turned toward her, was full of aggrievement.

"If you don't go faster'n that, you'll never get off this afternoon."

He did not answer. His face took on a stubborn pain, and he increased his pace by a little. Ruth, pressing her full lips together, began to sweep with energy. Mary and Jill had never been the trouble that Hal had always been, though she had tried to take the brunt of them all so that nothing would trouble William. But she did not know what to do with Hal. He had been restless even in his babyhood, and now it was almost impossible to make him finish his work. When he was small she had thought this restlessness must be the sign of some unusual intelligence in her only son. She still hoped it was, but could not be sure. He was lazy in school and his teachers had no good report to make of him.

"Harold does not seem interested in any of his work." This in one form or another was their summary, year after year, of what Hal did. Sometimes she herself undertook to try to discover what was behind that round-cheeked, boy-

43

ish face. Sometimes when she had him fast by sewing on a button he had dropped or bandaging a cut finger, she would say, "Hal, it's time you was thinking more about what you do and how you behave, son. Do you ever think about what you're goin' to be when you grow up?"

"No, Mom." The voice, the words were careless.

"Now, Hal, why not? Your father's not a rich man."

To this he usually made no answer. But once he had said, "Grandpop's rich, though."

"That's got nothin' to do with you nor me, Hal," she said severely.

But Harold was stubborn. "Anyways, stands to reason, since we're his only grandchildren—"

"Where'd you hear talk of such things, anyways, yet?" she broke in. "Never at home, that I know."

"Over to the store," he said. "They was talking. They was sayin' now when Pop's ole man died they reckoned we'd all be rich."

"They would talk," she said bitterly. "They'd talk till their teeth rot."

"Ain't it true?" Hal asked.

"If it is, I never hear tell of it," she said shortly, and pushed him away. Long ago she had made up her mind she would never, as long as she lived, ask William anything about his parents or his home or his life before he knew her. Letters came in his mail sometimes, though not now so often as they used, but she gave them to him unopened, and he put them in his pocket. She never saw him read them. But then he spent most of his day alone, painting. No one saw much of him, not even the children. William was so queer about the children. Sometimes she grew so upset with them that she begged him to help her with their discipline. But he never would.

"Why should I press my will upon another?" he always said.

"But we have to bring 'em up to be good," she insisted one day.

"You will do that," he replied, his smile upon her.

The girls were good enough, especially Mary, the elder one, but Hal she could never be sure about. She watched him now, her broom in her hand. He had stopped altogether, and suddenly at the end of the lawn he disappeared behind the crabapple tree. She set her broom against the door and walked quickly down the path. But he was gone.

"I can't run after him in this August heat," she muttered with anger. She was about to turn back to the kitchen when she saw William on the hill in the shade of the big old ash tree, painting. He was standing before his easel, a tall, cool figure, his blue shirt vivid against the green trees. How easy his life was! He never asked how she did anything. She bore the children, she took care of them, tended the house, looked after everything, even the land she rented on shares, while William painted his pictures. The sight of him in the green shadows sharpened the thought of her own Saturday cleaning still only half finished, the dinner waiting to be made ready. He would come in expecting everything to be just as he liked it, too.

"This time he'll have to help me with Hal," she thought.

Her anger gave her more vigor even than usual and she walked quickly up the low hill to the orchard. William did not see her. He saw nothing when he worked. Maybe he never saw anything. He lived in a dream, she often thought.

But he, putting down upon his canvas the strong white silver of the river, did see her, as he saw every change and accent in the landscape before him. He watched her with full appreciation of her value in the picture, as full as on that day when he had seen her for the first time in the landscape. She was heavier than she had been as a girl, but only pleasantly so. She would never grow into the repulsive lump of flesh her mother had become before she died. Ruth had too much of her father's wire in her, and an energy besides that kept her still graceful. She was very beautiful, he thought with quick passion as he watched her approach. Now he could see her face, firm-cheeked, rosy, untouched by powder or paint or indeed pretense of any kind. Her hair was still brown and her lips red, and her eyes bluer than ever in her browned face. She came near him, holding up her skirt as she climbed.

"Hello, dear," he said amiably. He had not ceased

painting and he went on brushing in the soft green cliffs above the river.

"William!" she cried. "What shall we do with that boy? He's disobeyed me flat and gone off!"

William laughed. Secretly he could never believe that the three sturdy young creatures who were in this house had anything to do with him. Practically, of course, he was their father. That is, something he bestowed upon Ruth had enabled her to produce, entirely, he felt, out of her own ancestry, her three robust, stupid children. She grew very angry when he called them stupid, but of course they were, on the whole, in spite of being well-meaning and always pleasant to him. Jill, the youngest, might perhaps be only a little less stupid than the others.

"You shouldn't make a boy work on Saturday morning, my dearest," he said gently. She was so beautiful he wanted to kiss her lips. There was never a woman in the world, he thought fondly, who could make a man forget as Ruth did that he had been married to her for these years, so that when she appeared beside him suddenly in the sunshine of a summer's morning, he longed as eagerly to kiss her lips as he had the first time. He knew intimately every curve and line of her body, and yet she seemed always new to him. He pondered this often. What was the gift she had of eternal freshness? It was not in her mind. He knew every thought she had ever had or ever would have. She could not surprise him in any word she might say. But in the freshness of her presence she astonished him continually. Perhaps it was no more than that he habitually forgot her when he was not with her and when he saw her again it was always a return. Perhaps it was that she herself was continually changing, at the mercy of every small happening in her day. Thus now her fury edged her beauty with electricity. Her hair sprang back from her forehead, her eyes were wide and matched the sky she stood against, her angry lips were scarlet and parted to show her sound white teeth.

He laughed. "Come here and let me kiss you," he summoned her. But at that same instant a butterfly darting at the fresh green on his canvas was caught in the paint. He forgot everything.

"Oh, this poor fool!" he cried in quick distress. "Ruth, see it! What's to be done? Its wings are broken!"

She came at once and taking a hairpin from her long hair she lifted the butterfly carefully out of the paint.

"Has it damaged the picture?" she asked anxiously.

"Oh, never mind that," he replied. "What'll we do to clean its wings?"

"We can't do anything," she said practically. She put it down upon the grass. William stooped to it.

"Oh, dear, it's simply quivering," he said in agitation.

"Never mind," she said. "I'll take it to the house. Maybe I can think of something." She would quietly destroy it, she thought, where he could not see her do it.

Many things she had had to destroy quietly without his knowing it—mice in the house, rats in the barn, a sick dog, an injured bird, kittens they could not keep. She had learned on that day years ago when without thinking she had put four blind kittens into a bag and tied it to a rock. He had happened to look out of the window of the spare room which he had made into a room for himself, and had come rushing down the stairs, shouting to her, "Ruth, what are you doing?"

She had looked back at him, astonished at his agitation. "I'm just going to drown these cats, that's all."

"*Drown* them?" His face went stone color.

"Why not?" she asked. To her fright, he turned away from her and leaned against a tree, his head on his arms. She dropped the bag of mewling kittens.

"Why, William, what's wrong? Did you want I shouldn't? But we've more cats in the barn now than we'd ought to have. Six cats have too many kittens to keep. We'd be all cats soon if we'd do that."

"Of course," he said. He dropped his arm and stood staring at the squirming mass. She saw he was sick.

"Look, William, I'll let 'em out."

"Will you?" His face cleared. "That's right, let them out. Here, I'll help." He stooped and loosened the string while she held the bag, and the small creatures crept out and the frantic cat-mother, hearing them, came hurrying across from the garden, howling as she came. He watched while she licked them and lay down and offered them her tits. And in a moment they were sucking and pacified and the cat was purring and looking at them with arrogant mother eyes.

"See how proud she is," he said laughing.

Ruth did not answer. Someone still had to kill the kittens, she was thinking. It had to be done. They could not have hundreds of cats. She must do it later when he was gone.

When she had it done, she wondered if he would miss the kittens or notice the mother cat, searching and crying. But no, he noticed nothing, and this surprised her again. It was not that he cared anything for the cats. He never fed them or indeed paid any heed to their existence. She concluded that he simply did not like to see things killed, and after that she managed to have everything killed when he was away, even the fowls she cooked for dinner. For this, too, he did not like to see. She could twist a chicken's neck so swiftly and cleanly that there was no pain, and at first she did it before him without thinking. Then one day she saw the look in his eyes and stopped, though she defended herself, "How'd we ever eat meat otherwise, William?"

He was ashamed. "I know, but somehow I don't like you doing it, Ruth. You ought not to—you're life-giving!"

She did not know what to say, so she said nothing. But from that day on she managed that he never saw her kill a fowl again.

Now she said of the butterfly, "Maybe I can brush its wings with turpentine."

"Do," he said gratefully. "I never had such a thing happen before."

He was so perturbed that she saw it was useless to talk to him now, and she lifted the butterfly into her apron and went down the hill.

When Hal came home at night she would whip him, she thought. Someone must manage him.

Up on the hill William could work no more. He had

caught upon Ruth's face that look he could never wholly comprehend. It was a patient and accepting look, tinged only a little with rebellion now, when something he did or said was beyond her comprehension. He wondered if she despised him. Thus wondering, he approached her sometimes with diffidence. But never, never did her warm response fail. That was her greatness, that whatever he was, whenever he went away from her, he could return, sure that she never changed. He returned to her and lost himself in her, the self which he so often found a burden, its moods, its melancholy, its aimlessness, its strange, endless energy. She did not understand him, but he did not want understanding, nor indeed expect it. The last time he had seen Elise at his father's house in February she had asked him in that half-direct fashion in which they found they had been able to speak to each other after marriage, "Do you find in your life any understanding?"

He had pondered her question carefully. "Let us say, rather, that I find—what I want."

For he did not want understanding, necessarily, nor companionship. Long ago he knew he was happiest when lonely, happiest because then he was most free. He did not want a mind pursuing his mind, nor an imagination keeping pace with his. Had he been married to Elise, in spite of himself he would have found ways of evading her. But Ruth he need never evade, for he could leave her whenever he liked, his mind far from hers, his body, too, if he liked, though less and less often now did he leave this house. He needed to leave it less, physically, because mentally he left it when he liked. He had only to go into his own room or climb this hill, he had only to lift his brush and he was miles away. But Elise, had he married her, would have been at his side, and most of the time he could endure no one there.

But then when there came that inevitable moment when he was weary of loneliness, frightened at loneliness because the universe is vast to the lonely soul, he had only to leave his room, come down from the hill, put aside his brush, and return to Ruth. And with that return he returned to the busy home, to the smell of baking bread and to the sound of churning milk and to the laughter and noise of children and food set upon the table hot and ready to eat, and to Ruth, always ready for him. Oh, the sweetness of night and the comfort of her strong, warm body! He looked out over the rolling hills, the rich fields, the lifting spires of small, comfortable towns.

"God, what a good life I have!" he thought.

. . . In her kitchen Ruth lifted the lid of the garbage pail and threw the butterfly into the refuse. Then she went back to her work, her strong face closed over her thoughts. The girls came in from blackberrying and she directed them quietly, with no spare words.

"Put the pails down cellar. You can help me this afternoon to make jam. Now get yourselves washed. Your father'll want everything ready when he comes in."

She had brought them up so that the two words "your father" were the sign of last compulsion. William, who never commanded them, was through her in command of them all. They loved him and yearned to be close to him, but their mother had kept him far from them with her threats of him. "Your father won't like so much noise," she said. "Your father don't want you girls should go barefoot so big," she said. "Your father wants you to grow up a hard-workin' good man," she told Hal. None of them had heard such things from their father, but they believed her and their love for their father was shadowed by fear. For they, each child felt, belonged to their mother. They were made of her. Their speech was like hers and they took their manners from her and never from their father. This they did without knowing it, and if they had been pressed for a reason they would have said in wonder, "But nobody talks like Pop does. He talks like out of a book. Real talk is what Mom talks."

So also did her hearty ways of eating seem to them the real way. She lifted a chicken bone in her fingers and bit the meat from it and so did they. Not one of them cut the meat away in bits as their father did. Like her they drank milk and not the foreign wines William kept in the cool earth-floored cellar. Not even Hal had ever tasted his father's wine in secret, nor had it occurred to William to offer it. He did not so much share their life, the children felt without being able to say this, as come into their life that went on so heartily about their mother. They loved him delicately, in a restrained fashion, as something precious and fine, but which they did not know how to use. And without knowing it, William by his difference from them deepened the distance between himself and his children. Though they learned to do as their mother did, they saw William's difference in his fastidiousness at table, in his scrupulous cleanliness of person, in his speech. And a fastidiousness of his spirit which they could not perceive forbade him to judge them, lest in so doing he seem to judge Ruth. For he had said to himself until it was now the habit of his being, "I will not have Ruth changed. What she is, is what I want."

Once Mary asked her mother, "What is Pop's job?"

"He's an artist, and you know that," she said, "and don't call him Pop, even to me. He doesn't like it."

"Is being an artist a job?"

"Of course it is," Ruth said.

But in her own heart Ruth often wished that William had what she called a real job, that he was a farmer like Henry Fasthauser, or that he had a garage like Tom's. Tom had been smart enough to buy out the livery stable and then sell off the horses and set up one of the first garages. Everybody was going to have automobiles pretty soon, he said. Tom was making good money. But picture-making was never sure money. Even if William did sell four or five pictures a year, she hated the uncertainty of money coming in.

"I'd rather have fifteen dollars a week steady, year in and year out," she often thought, "than a couple of hundred all of a sudden."

She watched her children narrowly for signs of interest in painting, ready to work passionately against a thing in them which she accepted as inevitable in William. But there were no signs.

. . . William, coming home to his midday dinner, entered the door with his invariable pleasure. Ruth kept the house always clean, warm in winter, cool in summer. He had made changes enough in the farmhouse until now it seemed his as well as Ruth's. Nothing, of course, could be changed while the old pair had lived. He had spent many an hour planning, while he listened to Mr. Harnsbarger telling over and over again the same stories of his boyhood on this very farm, how one day he would rip the ceilings from the old hewn beams, how he would take out partitions and enlarge the rooms, how he would put back the old bricks into the dining-room floor. For years it had looked as though Mr. Harnsbarger would live forever after his wife died of dropsy. But a new highway had been made out of the road beyond the lawn, and he had stepped in front of a truck one day and had been killed. He was then eighty-one. That morning he had eaten his breakfast with all his usual zest, and, putting on his old straw hat, he had said to Ruth as he always did, "Guess I'll walk around a little."

"All right, Pop," she had said.

William, coming down late as usual, that he might breakfast after the garrulous old man was finished, was in time to see a strong young man, a stranger, carrying a crumpled heap in his arms which he laid on the parlor sofa. It was old Mr. Harnsbarger, his face untouched, but his thin body crushed across the loins.

And William had been ashamed because his first involuntary thought at that moment, though driven away at once, had been that now he could make the house what he wanted it.

But he had had to make what he wanted out of what he had, ever since he knew that because Ruth could not become part of his world, he must become part of hers. Would not or could not, he would never know, because he would not inquire. If she should be unhappy, it would not matter which it was. To keep her happy had been essential to his own happiness. And because she never complained, he had made himself sensitive to every change in her look and voice. When he returned to her, he must find her content. Her content was the atmosphere of his soul.

"Dinner ready?" he called gaily from the hall.

Ruth came out of the kitchen. Her hands were white with flour and her look was anxious.

"Aren't you a little early, William?" she asked. "I'm just makin' the biscuits."

"No hurry," he said quickly, "I have to clean up. Did the butterfly recover?"

"The butterfly?" she repeated. Then she remembered. "I fixed it up all right," she said calmly. "It flew away as good as new." Long ago she had arranged her conscience to cover anything that was necessary for William's comfort.

"That's good," he said gratefully. He saw his daughters coming up from the cellar and waited for them. "Hello," he said.

"Hello, Father," Mary replied. Jill did not speak.

"Come and kiss me," he said. They came to him warmly and laid their cheeks against his shoulders. He kissed one forehead and the other. They enjoyed his caress. Their mother never kissed them. They would have been shy, because she would have been shy had she done so. Why this was, they had never thought to wonder. She was as close to them as their own bodies, and perhaps that was why. But William kissed his children often. Even Hal he had only recently ceased to kiss good night, and then because he saw the boy himself was ill at ease. When he saw this, he never kissed him again. Without saying anything he had the next night clasped his shoulders for a quick instant in his arm.

"Good night, son," he had said.

Hal was too young to hide his relief. And William, catching that quick lighting, had thought half morbidly, "I mustn't be a burden on them with my difference."

But the girls liked to have his affection and offered him their fresh cheeks and smooth foreheads.

"You smell of sunshine and earth," he said. "You smell the way your mother smells, and that's the best perfume for a woman. Want to clean my brushes?"

"Yes," Jill said eagerly.

"Fine—then I'll only have to clean myself," he said. He put the dirty brushes into her hand and went upstairs. The bathroom he had made almost at once after he married Ruth. The old man had not objected to that, though he himself had still bathed in the tin tub on Saturday nights, in the woodshed in summer and the kitchen in winter. He became curiously shameless in his old age. When Saturday night came, he bustled about his bath caring nothing for anyone. Ruth remonstrated with him sometimes.

"Pop, you'd ought to draw the bar across the kitchen door or give a yell to a body when you're washin' yourself."

"I don't care a mite," he said gaily. "Them as comes around can see what they can see, far's I care."

William, to whom Saturday night was no different from another, grew used to coming upon the sinewy old man, standing naked in his tub, laving himself. Once he paused, struck by a certain beauty in the sight, an old man making himself clean.

"You would make a picture as you are now," he suggested.

But the old man threw the bar of homemade soap at him. All his old decencies sprang to life.

"You git out of here with that talk!" he bellowed. "I ain't goin' to have my picture hangin' up nekked for folks to see, yet!"

William had gone away laughing, but still regretful. He was always regretful if a picture escaped his brush. He painted old Mr. Harnsbarger half a dozen times, but never without thinking of that one pose refused and remembering how beautiful the water and the firelight had been upon an old man's body.

Now he whistled softly while he scrubbed his hands. He was pleasantly tired, very hungry, and almost content with his morning's work. He was accustomed, or nearly accustomed, to this feeling of almost content with his work. Why he could never quite bring it up to the measure of fullness he was not sure. He went into his own room when he had washed, and sat down in the big chair by the window and pulled out his pipe. It was not that he had evaded the investigation of his own state of mind. He had dug deep into himself again and again. Was he or was he not sure of the quality of his work? He had thought sometimes of talking with his father about it. There had never been a further mention of a picture of his going into the gallery of the great house which was no longer his home.

But this fact gave him no light upon himself. Even when he and his father were alone, there lay like a mountain between them the disapprobation of his mother, and indeed, of his father too, a disapproval the more intense and the more difficult because his mother chose to ignore it altogether, and by this ignoring magnified it infinitely. If he could have gained greater awards, found high commissions, made his pictures valuable, he could have won his own assurance. But he had chosen to live here with Ruth, far from the places where prizes were given and commissions won. And he was too cynical not to know that no more in painting than in other art were awards and commissions given for pure merit. No, merit had to join with influence and flattery. Well, he thought abruptly, he had avoided all that. What he longed for was not such reward for such work, but merely to know absolutely the quality of his own work. Was it good? Could it have been better?

He never put it to himself—could his work have been better had he not married Ruth?—for he could conceive of no life without Ruth. And if he had stayed in New York, what would he have painted? Not landscape, certainly! He had been working on a nude when he left. He had never finished it because he had found out suddenly how Ruth felt, while she stood for his model.

"Stand in the sun," he had told her that morning. "Let me see the sun shine through your flesh."

She moved into the long block of sunshine that fell through an eastern window, and tried not to mind. She was married to him. Nothing could be wicked between her and William, could it? It was not wicked for her to take off all her clothes in the daylight before him so long as the doors were locked, was it?

"That's right," he said eagerly. "That's what I want. Now pretend the sunshine is a mantle. Pretend you are wrapping it about you."

She obeyed again, putting out her arms as though they

drew to her fold and fold of glittering, silver cobweb stuff.

"The silver mantle!" he murmured. "The mantle of light—" He began to paint furiously and she stood motionless. The sunshine would last less than an hour. Then a high building would cut it off. She would put on her clothes and do her housekeeping—that is, if he would let her. He did not let her. When the sunshine disappeared as though a touch had put it out, he threw down his brush. She had already turned, and was reaching for her garments.

"Wait!" he commanded. He went to her. "Don't put your things on just yet!" he whispered.

"But there's the room to do," she said unwillingly.

"Ah, no, there's no haste about it."

"I like to get my work done in the morning," she said.

"Your work!" he said with fond teasing. He had taken her lovely bare body in his arms. This beautiful flesh which in the sunshine had been light and substance for painting was now only material for love. But she would not yield and it was not in him to force her.

"What is it, sweetheart?" he inquired. "What's wrong?"

She hung her head until her long brown hair covered her face. "I don't like to—in the daytime," she said. "It seems —wrong."

"Wrong!" he repeated. "But darling, how can anything between us be wrong?"

It could be, he discovered. He listened to her little argument and felt the magic steal from her flesh, a perfume dispelled.

"Nice people don't—" she said, "in the daytime."

"How do you know?" he asked. "Anyway, what *is* nice?"

"I don't—feel right—when we do," she said.

"Ah, that!" he said. "That's different, that's important." He had held her only a moment longer. Then she had put on her clothes and he had taken his brush and worked a long time in silence upon the dark background behind the silvery figure. All the time he worked he was aware of her as she busied herself about sweeping and dusting and preparing the lunch. But the room which could be at times the vessel of all his dreams was only an ordinary room. He spoke to her once or twice cheerfully.

"Shall we dine out tonight, Ruth?"

"Whatever you say," she replied.

"No, Ruth, what do you want to do?"

"I want whatever you want," she replied, and when he did not answer, she paused to say anxiously, "Honest, William—I mean it."

She did mean it. He knew she did. She gave him all within her power. And was she to be blamed for anything? Her pretty face begged him for tenderness.

"Then we'll go," he said gently.

They came back from an evening of loitering over a sidewalk table within hearing of a park band. And in the night, when decent darkness covered her, she atoned. Was it a conscious atonement? He could never discover. But he thought it was not, because he believed she was never conscious of anything she did. She moved, she spoke, she kept silent, out of the moment's instinct. This, he often thought, was her endless charm for him, that whatever she did it was what she deeply felt.

Thus he perceived with exquisite acuteness the softness about her lips when they came back that night. She undressed slowly, almost languorously, stretching her pretty arms and flinging back her long hair. He watched her every movement, each naïve in its meaning, until she slipped off her last garment and was about to put on her long nightgown, her hair falling from one shoulder.

"Wait," he commanded her.

She looked up, lovely and shy and bold together.

"Come here," he said.

He watched her as she came, the lover in him heightened to ecstasy by the painter who saw the perfection of her. He held out his arms and she came into them, and he perceived, as he did each time, the freshness of her being. She was eternally new to him because she came to him newly out of each moment which was never quite like any other. Had she been reasoning, had she been less instinctive, she could not have been herself. How rich she was, how generous, how deeply abandoned to him! He forgot everything in her abandonment. Great as his need was, so great was she.

She could conceal nothing, and when she sickened of the city he knew it, too, though she said not a word, because her instincts sickened and it was through her instincts that she spoke to him. So as spring became early summer, she repulsed him when he came near her. This repulsion was not in what she said but in her silences. She withdrew from him. She sat for him hour upon hour, passively, as though she did not know where she was, and he felt, as he painted, that he was copying another painting, not as though he were working from a living model.

He cried at her one day, "Ruth, come back!"

She did not move from her pose, her hands crossed upon her lap, but into her vacant blue eyes something returned.

"Where have you been?" he demanded.

She did not answer, and he threw down his brushes and went over to her and took her in his arms.

"You aren't happy," he said.

"Yes, I am," she said. "At least I wouldn't be happy anywhere else if you weren't there."

"Where would you be happiest with me?" he asked gently.

"Oh, at home!" she cried.

And then he found out that she hated the city and these rooms and all her life here. She hated all the people he brought to her and the people she saw on the streets. Now he understood her remoteness when anyone else entered these rooms. He had thought her only shy, and at first he had pleaded with her.

"They're my friends, Ruth, and so they are yours."

"No, not mine," she had said, her eyes wide.

"You're afraid," he had accused her another time.

"They are strangers," she had said.

Now he knew that she hated them, simply and instinctively, because they were part of the city. All the time she had been living through the days and nights she had lived out of increasing hatred.

"I can't hardly draw my breath here," she whispered. "There's no air."

"Plenty of people do breathe here," he said.

"That's why," she said, and lifted her head restlessly. "All the air's been breathed over and over. I'm used to the air comin' clean over hills. Besides, it's the people I hate."

"But Ruth, nobody has hated you!"

It was one of the things he found lovable about New York, that for all its size and self-preoccupation, one could find friendly talk in any cab, at any counter, with common folk.

"I hate 'em all," she said stubbornly.

"Why?" he demanded of her.

"They're not my kind," she said.

He was wholly helpless in this large, soft stubbornness. It was instinct, unlit by reason, and against it he was like a man lost in the dark, silent night without a light to guide him anywhere.

"But Ruth, you told me nothing of this before," he reproached her.

"Because you—you like it here," she faltered. Her head was against his breast again, and he looked down on her drenched black lashes and he saw that she was helpless, too, against her instincts.

"I don't like any place where you aren't happy," he said.

"You do—you keep talkin' about how beautiful New York is," she said, and began to sob, "but I think it's terrible. It's—it's like livin' all crowded together at the bottom of a well. There's only a little strip of sky above. I'm used to the whole sky."

In silence he sat holding her against his shoulder. It was true that he had in these months come to an increasing perception of the beauty of this city, and because of it he had battled against her hatred of it. He was continually pointing out to her the beauty he saw, the upspringing lines of buildings, the river, the smooth, sleekly flowing traffic along the streets, the sidewalk markets and the polyglot peoples. He felt in himself every day now a trembling surge of creative energy. He was coming out of himself at last and out of the narrowness even of love.

But it was she who had first led him forth. Until he had found Ruth that day, he had been locked in himself. She had freed him, she had forced him to leave his father's house and to begin life for her and for himself. And having made that escape, he was now strong enough to escape again even from her. Not that he would ever leave her, or cease to love her. That he could not. But he knew that one of these days he would stop painting only her and he would go out and find his material in one after the other of those millions about him. People were what he now wanted to paint, not landscape. It became certainty in him at this moment while he held her in his arms and listened to her sobbing.

"Hush," he said, "hush—"

They spoke no more that night. They made ready for bed and she curled herself into his arms and gave herself up to him as she had not in months, until he was dazed with the sweetness and the wildness of her passion. He responded to it, wondering and full of delight. There was no coldness in her anywhere. She was all warm and soft and eager for him. Then he knew that whatever else he must give up, he could not give up this woman.

But as the summer came on, day by day he was appalled by what he discovered, and silenced by her helplessness before her own hatred. For she was the sort of creature, he was beginning to perceive, who is part of the soil which gave it birth. Her being shriveled and withered when she was away from that soil, and no work seemed really worth doing to her and yet work was essential to her health, body and soul. He saw to his alarm that she was actually less beautiful than she had been before she came, and he began to look about him and to consider whether or not he could leave New York. Why should he have to live here? His genius was strong enough to work anywhere—or ought to be, if it was worth anything.

One day in June, when he was thus reasoning, he entered the gallery of a dealer who had taken six of his paintings for sale. He had not heard from the man in some weeks and it was time, he thought, to inquire. The dealer was not in, the girl at the desk in the hall said, but he could go in and see his pictures. One, she said, had been sold to an old gentleman who had come in about an hour ago, and might still be there. At least, she had not seen him go away, although she had been out to luncheon in the meantime.

"Let me see his name," William said.

She flipped over the pages of a ledger and ran her finger down a column.

"There," she said.

He bent to look, and saw his father's name, Harold James Barton. He did not speak, being too moved to reveal to this common, gum-chewing office girl what the name meant to him. He looked at the title of the picture. It was, he thought, one of his lesser ones, not a picture of Ruth, but a quick thing he had done, one spring morning, of a wagonload of flowers that an Italian gardener had driven to the city to sell. For a dollar the man had been willing to draw his horse to the curb and sit slouching with crossed knees and slack reins while William worked. Afterward he had bought a pot of primulas for Ruth. The canvas was small, but he had caught sunshine in it, and the old Italian face, shrewd and gay.

"You say he may be in the gallery still?" he asked, looking down at his father's name.

"He usually stays quite some time when he comes in," the girl said and put back the ledger.

He hesitated. Did he want to see his father? He had not seen either of his parents since his marriage, nor heard from them nor from Louise. Some day, he knew, the silence must end. It was absurd for a son to be parted from his parents because of a creature as beautiful as Ruth. He had only to arrange a meeting and everything would be well again. He had been so sure of this that he had put it off, month by month. Now, he decided, was the time. If he could bring about a meeting between Ruth and his father now, his father could carry home the good report to his mother.

On this impulse he walked quickly into the gallery. There were a dozen or so people there and he had to search for his father. But he found him easily enough. He was sitting upon a small upright chair which he had drawn to a proper distance from the wall where William's paintings were hung, and there he sat, his back to the door, his gloved hands crossed upon the silver knob of his walking stick and his white head lifted.

William approached him softly. "Hello, sir—good morning!"

His father started and half rose, then sat down again before answering.

"Oh, there you are," he said.

"Yes, sir," William said gently. His father looked tired, he thought. Then he remembered that this was the time of year when he usually looked tired, just before they went to Bar Harbor. "Are you all right, sir?"

"I?" His father looked surprised. "Certainly."

"And Mother?"

"We're both about as usual," his father said mildly. He looked at his son carefully. "You seem in good health," he remarked.

William smiled. "I am—excellent."

"Seen Louise?"

"No, sir."

His father nodded at a picture. "That your wife?"

"Yes, sir." He moved to his father's side and stood there, and the two of them gazed at Ruth's fresh and pretty face. He had caught her in one of her shy moments. That was because though it was only a head, she had been sitting in the nude for him in the morning light.

"She looks very young," his father said.

"She is just twenty, sir." And then because he imagined a softening about his father's pale lips, he went on, "I wish you'd come home with me, sir."

"Home?" His father's look was vague.

"I mean, to our home."

"Oh!" His father understood. "Yes, well, I haven't much time."

"Please, Father! It's not far. It will mean a lot."

It ended by their getting into a cab and going back to the apartment. It was about noon, and Ruth was cooking their meal over the small gas range. She came out quickly at the sound of the door, then stood motionless like a child before a stranger.

"Ruth, this is my father."

He marveled at the change in her. Light went out of her face. She put out her hand awkwardly.

"Pleased to meet you," she muttered, her hand heavy in his father's delicate old one.

He hurried to make amends. "Come in and sit down—lunch with us, sir? I'm sure Ruth has something good. She's a fine cook."

He carried them along with him, ignoring Ruth's stricken look at the mention of lunch. His father saw it, too, and made haste to reply.

"I can't stay, William. Your mother and Louise are expecting me at Sherry's at one. I believe Monty is bringing somebody up from Wall Street about investments. Railroads aren't quite what they were, William."

"I'm sorry, sir," William said.

"It's these automobiles," his father said. Then he sat down, looking very precious and fragile, and spoke pleasantly to Ruth.

"William must bring you to see us sometime, my dear, when we get back to town in the autumn."

Ruth could not answer. She turned her beseeching eyes on William.

"You'd like to, wouldn't you, sweetheart?" he said to encourage her, and she nodded.

His father stayed only a few minutes. It had not meant much, after all. He was not sure what it had meant. His father had revealed nothing in his polished pleasantness, and Ruth had said nothing beyond her faint "Good-by."

"Why didn't you talk?" he demanded of her when the door was shut.

"Oh, William, I couldn't!" Life had come rushing back into her blue eyes and vivid cheeks.

"But why, goose?"

"I hadn't never seen anybody like him!"

"He's my father, Ruth. You might have tried."

She felt his irritation, and clear tears welled into her eyes.

"I couldn't think of anything, William. I tried to—I did!"

"Well, there, don't cry. What have we to eat?"

"Lamb stew."

"Lets have it."

They had eaten almost in silence, and it had taken a few days before he could put the incident into its place again. Then he did so because he saw her drooping in the sudden heat of a June Sunday. She sat beside the open window, not looking out, and his heart pitied her white face.

"Darling, we need some fun. I'm going to take you to Coney Island."

"Where's that?"

"Where the sea is. We'll get a breeze there, at least."

He hated to go because he was working exceptionally well that morning. But he threw down his brushes and they went, though it did not do her much good. She shrank from the people.

"Isn't there any place we can go to be by ourselves?" she asked him.

"Not on a public beach," he said shortly.

They sat the afternoon through, feeling the breeze cool indeed, but never for a moment did she relax her tense awareness of the people around them. And he was cast into alternating love and hate of what she only hated. Thereafter sometimes he saw the city as she saw it, a place of noise and quarreling confusion. Then every face he saw was hideous. "These people look at me out of a nightmare," he thought as he passed them on the streets or sat staring at them in the long row of a trolley car. But there were other days when the same faces spoke to him and then they were not ugly. But to her, ugly or not, they were the faces of eternal strangers.

They returned to the farmhouse without suddenness and without intention of permanence. Her mother was taken ill and her father wrote to know if she could come home for a little while until things were better. It was July and the city was hotter than ever.

"No reason why we shouldn't both go to the farm," he said cheerfully. "I can paint there, too," he added.

"Oh, William, can you?" she cried, and for the first time in many days she flung herself into his arms. She had not complained but it had not been necessary. Every nerve of his being was acute to her and he knew that she had been enduring her life, moment by moment.

They had left everything in their rooms exactly as it was. Neither of them spoke of return or of no return. They merely went away. And she, as the train drew out of the city, was like one reviving from an illness. He watched her and he could tell by the light in her eyes again, by the old vigorous movement of her head, when the city was left behind and when they were back in the rolling hills and the fields. She began to talk, she who in New York had found nothing worthy of talk or notice.

"Look, William, look at that stand of corn! I don't know as ever I see such a stand as that. They must of planted it good and early. I always tell Pop he plants too late every year. Oh, William, see the ducks! I hope they've got little ducks at home this year, though if Mom's sick I guess they haven't. It's too late to start maybe now. Look, William, at that barn—green! Now who'd paint a barn green instead of red? Must be city folks, sure!"

Her brown hair was curling about her face in the heat and her cheeks were pink. She sat clasping his hand, and he could feel life pouring into him through the union. She was alive again and she made him alive. He caught the smell of her and she was fragrant. He remembered a story that he had read somewhere of a Chinese emperor's concubine whom the emperor had loved for no other reason than that the woman, when she was hot, gave off a fragrance. Loving Ruth, he could understand loving a woman for no other reason than that she was fragrant.

When they reached the farmhouse she ran everywhere with exclamations of joy and relief. Nothing was changed. Nothing had been changed in a hundred years. But it was all new to her because she had never been away from it before. Now that she had come back to what she knew, he saw her in an hour return completely to herself. It was as though the whitefaced, drooping girl he had grown used to seeing had never existed. Here was the girl he had fallen in love with and married in this old house. In a few days he, too, began to feel they had never been away. He put aside the unfinished canvas he had brought with him and began a new one, the scene westward from the old ash tree under which he had lain that summer's day now a year ago. He had not been able, that day, to find a picture. He wondered at himself for that.

"Why didn't I simply paint what was before my eyes?" he thought. It seemed to him as he thought this that he had found a painter's secret.

He had kept paying the rent on the apartment through the summer, but they had not gone back. Nor had he, after long self-questioning during that autumn, gone back alone. If he went back alone he would not be able to work. He could only work when he was with her. It was necessary for him to be with her in order to forget her, as a man when he has eaten and slept forgets these necessities and goes on with joy out of the strength he has found to do what he likes. He found that he could leave her easily in this house. In New York he was always uneasy when he was away from her. At first he had even made her come with him to the parties and evenings to which he was invited. But that was before he knew her hatred of strangers. He had gone with her to buy frocks and hats suitable for these occasions.

"Now you must feel at ease," he had commanded her. "You can, you know. You need only to say to yourself, 'I am the prettiest woman here. William says so.'"

But it had been no help, neither frocks nor praise. She had not been at ease. And after a few times, seeing her misery, her clenched hands and scarlet face, he had let her stay at home and had gone alone. Then he was not at ease. He found himself impatient to be with her, not only because he was genuinely happiest when he was with her, but because he could not bear to think of her loneliness in those rooms of theirs.

But here in the farmhouse she was never lonely. Without any jealousy whatever, he knew that here she was no longer dependent upon him. The fowls she fed, the cows she milked with such pleasure, the work she did and loved, all these gave her companionship. He might have been jealous, perhaps, if she had not given him her love with such ardor and continuous intensity that he felt himself indispensable to her at least in love. Joy now overflowed in her and she let that abundance pour into love for him. With all she had to do, the incessant care of her sick mother and the care of the home besides, she was never too weary for him.

Out of his absolute physical satisfaction he found he could leave her easily, and so one day in early autumn he had gone on the impulse of a moment to see his parents.

"Do you mind if I go to see my father and mother?"

He went into the kitchen where she was making bread and asked the question abruptly. She answered him, he was sure, with whole honesty.

"Why, no, William, I don't believe I do." She paused, her hands in the floury dough, and considered him.

"If you do, I won't go."

"I can't see why I should mind—stands to reason you've got to go sometimes, and it's real nice today. You'll be home to supper?"

"Yes—that is, they might want me to stay for dinner, of course."

"Dinner?" The old confusion caught her for a moment. Then she laughed. "Oh, I'd forgot—your folks do call it that. Well, anyway, you'll be home tonight, William? I do think I'd kind of mind if we sleep apart when we never have."

"So would I." He bent to kiss her damp throat and smelled again her peculiar roselike fragrance.

"I'd say you fed on rose leaves if I didn't know you need more solid fare," he said.

She only smiled as she always did when he said a pretty thing. She was kneading dough again, the firm thrust of her rounded fists beating the dough into life. So he left her.

He had caught a local train and sauntered into his

father's house as though he had never been away. The old butler let him in.

"Mr. William!"

"Hello there, anybody home?"

"Mr. and Mrs. Barton have gone to the Academy, sir, but I expect them back at any moment. Tea is ready in the library, sir."

"Then I'll wait there."

But he did not. On the way he turned down the passage to his father's gallery and went from picture to picture. There were, he knew, two hundred of them, never more, never less. When his father found a finer picture than any he had, he took one down from these walls and hung it in the museum of art that he was building for the city. After his death, these would all go to that museum. He had made this plain to everyone, saying that he would have no sort of quibbling over his pictures.

William walked slowly along, seeing one familiar picture after another. There was nothing new. He wondered, acknowledging the folly of his wonder, whether perhaps his painting, which his father had bought, might be hung here. When he saw plainly that it was not, he was scarcely disappointed, because he had not expected to see it. Yet because it was not there, unreasonable though it was, he felt a foolish hurt and a determination that one day a painting of his would hang among that company.

He left the gallery, fortified by the hardness that his hurt pride gave him, and entered the library, his head held high, to find his parents waiting for him.

"There you are, William," his mother said. She put out her hand and turned her cheek to him. He bent and kissed her and smelled the dry, powdery scent which he remembered from childhood.

"How are you, Mother?"

"Very well, thank you, dear. We always are, after Bar Harbor. It's the air." She did not, he noticed, ask him how he was.

"Well, William," his father said. He was holding his cup of tea and stirring and he did not put out a hand to his son.

"You're looking better than when I last saw you, sir."

"I'm very well, thanks."

He sat down, took his cup from his mother's hand, helped himself to thin chicken sandwiches, and found that he had nothing to say to his parents. They were determined, he saw, to ask him nothing. Very well, then, he would say nothing.

Then in spite of himself he began to be softened. After all, this was their home. And this home began to influence him, with its mellow, meticulous beauty. He had not realized how much he had missed this sort of beauty, the careful cultivated beauty of old books and the fire burning under a carved mantel, and the great Corot over it for the keynote of the room. Its green, deep and mossy, was repeated in the carpet and the hangings. He caught a ruddy glint in a corner against a dark panel and saw his own little painting.

"That's where you hung it," he said impulsively.

Their eyes turned to it.

"A very charming thing," his mother said.

"I think so," his father agreed.

It was the first time his father had ever hung a painting of his anywhere in the house, and he felt pleased in spite of himself.

"I'm glad you think it's good enough to put in here," he said.

"We thought that corner needed a bit of brightening," his mother said.

He felt silence would be ungracious and he went on to ask of his sister. "How is Louise?"

"Quite well," his mother said. "That is, as well as could be expected in her condition."

"Oh, is she—" he hesitated.

"Yes, next April. I'm sorry she didn't wait a little. I always feel it's better taste to wait a few years."

His mother lifted her eyebrows and put the subject aside. His father delicately said nothing for a moment. He tasted his tea and put in more hot water. Then he said,

"Elise was married this summer in Bar Harbor."

"Was she?" William asked stupidly.

"Didn't you get an invitation?" his mother inquired.

"No," he said.

"That's odd, I think," she said. Her voice rose a little toward sharpness. "Everyone was invited."

"It was a handsome wedding," his father said.

"Too many people." His mother's lips were firm.

"Well, she has connections," his father agreed mildly.

What sort of man did Elise marry? William kept the question unspoken. Why should he ask it when he did not care? Then his father began to speak exactly as though he had asked it.

"She has married a very fine man—imposing looking, rather, eh, Henrietta?"

"Very handsome," his mother agreed.

"I suppose Elise will live in England?" He asked the question out of an incurious mind, but he must show an interest.

"Yes," his mother replied, "but they are not sailing for another month yet. She wants him to know something of her country before they leave it."

That sounded so exactly like Elise that he could hear her voice saying it. She loved her own country and he wondered if she would be happy away from it. But he did not put the wonder into words, either.

When he had gone away he felt that most of the conversation with his parents had been in what they did not say. And yet there had been a gain, too. His mother had said in a business sort of voice as he left, "By the bye, William, perhaps we should know your address—in case, that is, you are not returning at once to New York."

"I don't know when we are going back," he said. "Ruth didn't like it there. So for the present just address me at Hesser's Corners, care of Harnsbarger's Farm."

His mother's face had never been more inscrutable than it became when he mentioned Ruth. But her voice was kind.

"Very well, dear boy." She put out her hand to him and his father went with him as far as the library door. He let himself out.

But it was Elise who had made him finally determine that he would live where he was. On the morning after his visit to his mother he went out on the hillside to paint and he found himself confused by the landscape around the farmhouse as he had been confused when he first saw it. He was not able to eliminate its infinitely rich detail. The undulating folds of one hill upon another, the fat cattle, the great barns, the plethoric, sturdy houses, the thickly spotted woods and the lush fields, became monotonous in their plenteousness of color and fertility. He thought of painting Ruth again, in their house, but now she seemed no longer the accent, as she once had been. She had become part of all else.

"After all, Millet painted the same peasants over and over," he muttered. But those peasants of Millet's expressed something in themselves, he thought. They were combatants and they fought the earth they loved, they struggled with it and wrenched their bread from its reluctant grasp. There was no struggle here. This earth was so rich that it yielded instantly. And man did not fight it with bare hands and a hoe. He rode high above it, crushing it to dust under the harrowing teeth of a machine, and the earth was submissive. There was no sign of struggle in the smooth, fat faces he saw when he sauntered to the village. Even Mr. Harnsbarger's round face was then marked by little except years of plenty. He had considered painting that old face under its fringe of white hair and then had given up. "Who wants to see nothing in a face but too much scrapple and pie?" he thought. He closed his paintbox, folded his easel, and spent the morning in the woods on his back, staring into the dappled trees. At noon he found a letter in the mailbox by the road down at the end of the lane. It was from his father. His father's handwriting was growing old and it quivered upon the page.

Dear William:

Elise and her husband are spending the week end with us before they sail. It occurs to your mother and me that you might enjoy seeing her. Will you give us a week end, dear boy? It would be a pleasure to us. Your mother sends her love.

Yours,

Father

They wanted him to see Elise—that was his first thought, and his mother had been too clever to write him. She had told his father to write the letter, so gentle a letter and yet without mention of Ruth. He stood in the road, looking at the tremulous handwriting. No, in their way they missed him. In their way, too, they were shy. They dreaded new situations. His father doubtless had told his mother of meeting Ruth, and of how speechless she had been.

"It was like having to sit down with a housemaid." He could hear his father say that. Why? Because, he now realized in a sudden agony, he had, against all his will and inclination, thought that very thing himself.

"Oh, my dear wife!" he cried passionately to the blue and silent sky.

But still he could understand his parents so well. It was not that they were snobs. It was simply that they were uneasy when people were, as they thought, out of place. They were themselves easily abashed. His father had been as uncomfortable with Ruth as she with him.

He turned sharply and strode up the sunny lane, the open letter fluttering in his hand.

"Ruth!" he shouted.

She was behind the house, hanging up snow-white sheets upon a line, and the wind bellied them and she struggled with the clothespins, her arms high above her head.

"What a picture you make!" he shouted against the wind.

"Stop thinkin' of pictures a minit and help me!" she cried back.

But he was no good at it. His hands, so nimble and dexterous with brushes, fumbled with clothespins and shrank from the wet cotton cloth.

"Oh, well," she said good-humoredly, "go along."

Then he saw the letter flying over the grass. The wind had snatched it from his pocket. "I say!" He rushed after it, caught it, and brought it to her. "Ruth, tell me what you want me to do."

He read the letter to her, watching her puckering her

brows over the edge of the paper. She looked steadily at him.

"What ought you to do?" she asked.

"Only what you want me to do," he said.

She considered the letter again. "Who's this—" She hesitated.

"Elise? Oh, an old friend."

"Partikler?"

"Not very."

"Do you want to see her?"

"Not especially."

"What do you ask me for, then?"

"They are my parents, of course. They'd like to see me."

Upon the smooth rose and cream of her skin the sunshine fell piercingly, but there was not a flaw. The clear blue and white of her eyes were as faultless. He could see the separateness of her dark, upturned lashes rooted in the delicacy of her eyelids, and above them the soft brush of her full brows. Her lips were parted and the sunlight gleamed upon her white teeth. She breathed health as she stood before him, and there was wholesomeness in all her beauty. Her eyelids fell. She stooped for another curl of wet sheet.

" 'Tain't for me to say what you should do about them."

He looked down upon the nape of her neck, smooth and white beneath the knot of shining brown hair.

"It is for you to say about you and me, though."

" 'Twon't make a bit of difference about you and me, I reckon, whatever you do. Here, take a-holt of this with me and let's wring it dryer."

He took one end of the heavy sheet and held it fast while she twisted out a few drops of water.

"If you really feel that, dearest, then I will go," he said.

"I don't say one thing and feel another," she said.

Did she speak curtly or did he imagine it? "I know that, dear," he replied.

She was inaccessible as she hung up the fluttering wet sheet, and so he leaned and kissed the top of her head and went away.

Was it good to sleep in his childhood home? He weighed himself as he went through every old habit of movement. Did he like this better than he knew? He watched himself, taking the pulse of his emotions and measuring his enjoyment. Certainly there was much he enjoyed. It was more than the physical enjoyment of his old rooms, his books, and the furniture to which his hand went out in accustomed usage. It was something in the atmosphere of the whole house, he decided. The people who had lived in it, his grandparents and his parents, yes, and Louise, and he, too, and all their friends, had left their echoes here, their shapes, the habits of their thought and being, just as the farmhouse was full of Ruth's ancestors.

He enjoyed with conscious pleasure this atmosphere of his own kind, wondering if he were disloyal to Ruth. But in his mood of temporary detachment he wanted to find out if he could be disloyal to her. If he could be, that also had its significance. He was too much a man of the world not to weigh the depth of his love for Ruth.

He gave himself wholeheartedly therefore to this house. Since neither his father nor his mother mentioned Ruth, he did not mention her. It was exactly as though he had been away on a tour and was home again, except that no questions were asked him of where he had been or what he had seen. He went about the house, seeing everything freshly after his absence, playing the piano, studying the pictures, discussing with his mother the placing of a new rose garden for the spring. His father was excited over the possibility of a Titian being put on sale in Italy and he was cabling every few hours to his dealer in Rome. It was all exactly as it used to be.

"I shall telephone to see if Louise and Monty can come for Sunday," his mother said. "It will be quite a family party."

"That will be nice," he said quietly. Well, he would see what his family seemed to him now, after Ruth.

He went that afternoon to the station to meet Elise and her husband, still weighing, still reasoning. Did he mind, would he mind if he saw Elise step off the train with another man? His father had sent his own private railway car to New York for them, and so he walked to the end of the platform where he knew it would be. As a boy he had known that car very well. It had taken them back and forth to Florida in the winter, and once he had been brought home in it from Groton, very ill with influenza, so that his mother's doctor could tend him. She trusted no other. Well, he had not died and so her judgment was justified, though the school doctor had considered it folly.

He stood waiting while the train rushed to him, bore down upon him, and then rushed past him. The heavy private car paused almost in front of him, and in a moment the door opened and the old Negro porter, who had always taken care of it, put down the steps. In a moment Elise came out, looking, he saw instantly, more handsome than he had ever seen her. She was in dark fur from head to foot, and a scarlet camellia was pinned to her collar. Her pale, scarlet-lipped face was cool and pleasant until she saw him. Then the cool look broke. Her dark eyes laughed and she cried out,

"William, how perfectly delightful! But I didn't dream— Ronnie, this is William!"

A tall, thin Englishman with a belted coat appeared from behind her and put out a long, thin hand and shook hands with painful force.

"How do you do," he muttered under his short blond mustache.

He looked so exactly like many another Englishman that William had seen in various parts of the world that it was not possible to understand yet why Elise had chosen him from all the others. But there must be a reason.

"How do you do," William said, and withdrew his hand. He wondered a little if Ronnie minded Elise's joy. For as they walked along the platform she made no concealment of her joy. She was franker than she had ever been, as though she dared to be so now that she was safely married.

"William, if anybody had asked me what I wanted most in the world, I would have said to see you!"

He smiled, not knowing quite what to do with this and wondering, had Ronnie's thin profile not been on the other side of that glowing face, if he could have responded more suitably. But he found it easy to forget Ronnie. That tall, lounging figure, his hands always in his pockets, loomed amiably silent in the background, laughing suddenly when a joke was made, answering a question with the greatest possible economy of words, and never volunteering anything in the way of speech. And it was easier than it had ever been to be with Elise. They felt free with one another as neither had ever been free before.

He had not suspected her of so much gaiety. She had never been gay with him, being always weighted with something he did not want to understand. But now she danced with him, sang to his playing in a deep soft contralto, put her hand in his arm to saunter about the house, sat by him in the car, and one night to his quivering alarm slipped her hand into his under the fur robe. He held it hard for one second and then, conscious of Ronnie's shadow in the darkness just beyond her, he put her hand down. But he had time in that second to wonder at the narrow hand that could be crushed like a handful of petals. This hand he held, but Ruth's sturdy, warm hand held his as firmly as he held hers.

On Sunday, when Louise and Monty came, the home was complete; that is, nearly. For they sat seven at table, an awkward number, his mother said, but they must just do with it. He sat between Elise and Monty, and not caring greatly for his brother-in-law, he devoted himself to Elise easily. No one mentioned Ruth. He waited for Louise to ask him about her privately, and he made opportunity again and again, but Louise let all pass. He saw at last that she was determined not to speak of Ruth. His mother, perhaps, had commanded that.

He began to feel by Sunday night that someone must speak of Ruth. If no one did, then he himself would begin to tell of her, how lovely she was, how sweet. If he could speak of her he would prove his loyalty to her. But as though they felt the possibility of her name being spoken before them, they began to talk, his mother leading the conversation through her recall of an experience in England many years before. William heard her laugh.

"I am not at all psychic," she said, "but I was at Fairfax one year—the year I was to be presented. Do you know Fairfax, Ronnie?"

"Rather," Ronnie said, taking his pipe out of his mouth. He looked vaguely enthusiastic, as though he were about to speak, then he put his pipe back in his mouth and said nothing.

"I went up those long stairs to my room to go to bed." Mrs. Barton went on. "I remember it was quite late, we had been dancing. Just as I reached the top I heard a rustle of skirts, not silk, and there were two nuns. I was so surprised. But I bowed and they passed me, smiling. In the morning I asked the old Earl, 'Who are the charming nuns?'

" 'Nuns?' he said, without being in the least surprised. 'Did you see them?'

" 'Yes, two of them,' I told him.

" 'Oh,' he said, 'they lived here nine hundred years ago. Fairfax was a nunnery then.' "

Ronnie took his pipe out of his mouth again. "There's a window at Fairfax, nobody can find the room to it."

"What do you mean, Ronnie?" Elise asked. Her amused eyes sought William's.

"Went to a house party there once," Ronnie said, holding his pipe carefully poised. "We went into every room in the castle and hung towels out of all the windows. Then we went out and damned if there wasn't one window with no towel. They said any number of people had tried it and it's always the same."

Monty opened his sleepy, long-lashed eyes at his wife. "Isn't that where you said the bells ring in the ballroom at dawn?"

"Yes, I've heard them myself," Louise said. "The ballroom was once the chapel."

"Ah," old Mr. Barton said, "there's nothing strange in all that. People go on living where they belong."

"Let's dance," Elise said suddenly.

And a moment later William was dancing with her.

"I wonder if I dare to live in England," she said to him. "Will I grow to believe in ghosts, too?"

"I can't imagine it," he said, smiling down at her.

And then she of all people in this house spoke to him of Ruth.

"Are you quite happy, William?"

"Do you mean—now?"

"No, of course not. I mean with your wife. Isn't her name Ruth?"

"Yes, it is. And I am happy."

"Quite?"

"Perfectly."

"Would I like her?"

"I cannot imagine anyone not liking her."

"Shall I ever see her?"

"I don't know—that is for you to say."

"Not just now, William. Perhaps when I come back next year. I am coming home every year, you know. Ronnie has promised me."

"But England will grow to be home to you."

"How do you know?"

"Because—in a sense—I have gone very far away to live, too, though it's only a few miles."

"Is it altogether different from this?"

"Yes."

"But it is home?"

"Wherever Ruth is, that is home."

She sighed at that, and soon she stopped and said she was tired. She put out her hand to him.

"When are you going away, William?"

He had not known until this moment. But now he knew that all here was ended for him, this house, this company, this life.

"Tomorrow, after an early breakfast."

They all looked at him when he said this, but no one spoke except Elise.

"Good-by then, William."

"Good-by," he said.

He went upstairs very soon after that. No one else said good-by, and yet he knew and they all knew that he would not see them again—not like this. Then, looking about the room which had been the refuge for his boyhood, he made up his mind suddenly that he would sleep under this roof no more, no, not even tonight. He changed his clothes, and when the house was still he went down and opened a side door into the garden and climbed over a low wall and found himself in the quiet side street to the west of the house. Three blocks and he caught a late trolley that took him to the railroad station. He waited an hour and caught a milk train that dropped him within walking distance of the farm.

The farmhouse was never locked at night. "I haven't never turned a key in my house," old Mr. Harnsbarger often boasted. "Only city folks lock up." So the doors were open and William had only to walk in. But he paused a moment before he entered. Night had never been so beautiful upon the land. There was no wind and every tree and bush stood still and to its shape, and the moonlight poured down, white and clear, so clear that he felt all things growing in the quiet, bright night. These were his, these valleys and hills, the woods and the stream and the small lake at the bottom of the hill, and behind him was Ruth's home and Ruth.

He opened the door and went in and the house received him with its familiar odor of old wood and clean lime plaster and the spiceries of cooking. He went up the twisting stairs, his way lit by patches of moonlight upon the floor, and lifted the iron latch of the bedroom and went in. Perhaps Ruth was awake and waiting for him. He tip-toed over to the bed and looked down at her. She was asleep, her two long brown braids tossed over the pillow. Above the ruffle of her high-necked nightgown her face was lovely as a child's in its calm. But it was not a child's face, it was Ruth's face, the red lips full and firm, the brow a woman's brow, wise and wide.

"Oh, my beautiful," he whispered.

And every other face in the world, Elise's face, faded and left him. This was his wife.

He undressed and crept into bed beside her and curled against her. She woke, not to speech, not to exclaim at his return, but only to put her arms about him, to receive him and make him her own again.

When he woke in the morning he knew that here with her was his home and here alone.

He had not seen Ruth's mother for weeks before she died. Ruth would not let him go into the room. " 'Tisn't good to see her now," Ruth said shortly. But he knew from Ruth's grave, quiet face one late afternoon when he came in from a day's painting by the river that death was coming into the house. He wondered if he could help Ruth to bear the sorrow, and yet he wondered if it was a sorrow, so calm was Ruth's voice when she spoke. He brought death out into the open that night when they lay ready for sleep, so that he might know what its weight was upon her.

"Do you think your mother will die, darling?"

"I know she will—any day, any hour. The doctor told me last week."

"Dearest, why didn't you tell me?" He waited for her voice to answer through the darkness. When it came, her voice was full of honest surprise.

"Why, I don't know, William."

"I don't want you to keep sorrows to yourself, sweet."

She pondered this. "It's funny, but it don't hardly seem a sorrow for poor Mom to die," she said gently. " 'Course I wish it hadn't to be. But when I see her like she is now—it seems as if death was just the next thing for her. If she was young and struck down, I'd grieve turrible. When a thing's right and to be, I guess it isn't a sorrow. It's only natural."

She spoke out of profound harmony of her own being with all life upon the earth and he could say nothing. He drew near to her and breathed in her health and her repose, and felt himself made quiet and simple again. This was her secret, that in her presence all that was fretful and complex with his own complexity resolved itself into what was essential. All else fell away.

So on the day of her mother's death he felt scarcely a shadow upon the quiet house. The end came, the expected, foreordained end. Ruth had everything ready for it. It seemed almost that she knew the very hour. She came out of her mother's room one early evening when they had just finished their supper, and she spoke to her father.

"Dad, Mom's passed away."

Mr. Harnsbarger put down his farm journal and went at once to his wife's room. William rose and put out his arms and she came into them. Thus clasped he felt her body stiffen for a moment against tears and he said very gently,

"Don't mind crying, dear."

So she wept, but only for a moment. Then she shook the tears from her lashes.

"I'm cryin' for myself, I guess—not for her. She was all right, she just shut her eyes and sighed and slipped off. But it comes over me now that I won't see her no more."

In a few moments she was herself, and he did not see her weep again, no, not even in the little church where, it seemed to him in the least civilized of burial services, they listened to a sermon upon the dead woman, who lay in the open coffin beside the pulpit.

"Our neighbor was a woman of few words but many good deeds," the little preacher shouted. His round face and round belly were not necessarily signs of appetite so much as of the fact that his salary was partly paid to him in food and he had to eat what was given him, scrapple and sausage and pies and cakes and sides of pork and sacks of potatoes. He would miss Mrs. Harnsbarger's doughnuts. Twice a month she had brought him doughnuts, and double on Ash Wednesdays. "She lays here having earned her eternal rest," he said solemnly at the end of an hour.

Then they walked out into the clear, cold afternoon and stood about the grave. The sunlight shone into it joyously and marked the clear division of the soil. The dark, fertile topsoil was two feet thick. Beneath that was red clay, and beneath that the shale upon which every house in the region was founded. The bottom of the grave was shale, but a spring had seeped through, and that the coffin might not rest in water the old sexton had cut two red cedar logs and fitted them into the ends of the grave.

They stood about the grave and sang a hymn and heard the minister's voice reading and praying. He was bald, under a long lock of pale tan hair, and the wind lifted this lock and it fluttered on his shoulder and across his eyes until he fumbled in his pocket and found a small skull cap and put it on without stopping in his prayer. William, unable to bow his head, watched this and then looked away across the old, deeply set tombstones, across the rolling hills and valleys. Just beyond the churchyard was a quarry, now no longer worked. The township had waged a lawsuit against the owner of the quarry to prevent his blasting under the graves and had won it, and he had moved away in disgruntlement. William could just see the edge of the chasm a few feet from where he stood.

They walked back to the farmhouse after the funeral was over, and there the people ate and drank cake and wine, and talked in quiet tones of everyday affairs. There was even a little mild laughter. Among them Ruth moved competent and self-controlled, seeing that all went well. They went away soon and decently, shaking hands with the family.

" 'Twas a nice occasion," they said.

"Everything went off like she'd of had it," they said.

They went home each to take up his life as he had before, and in this house too all went as it had, except that Tom, Ruth's brother, stayed for a day or two. But then he grew restless for the village, especially because he was debating the question with everybody whether he would "cater" to the new automobile trade that was now beginning to cut into the livery business.

"A newfangled thing that won't last," old Mr. Harnsbarger snorted. "Horses has always been and always will be."

"Says you," Tom retorted with good humor. He looked, this brother of Ruth's, like any of the men anywhere in the valley. There was nothing to mark him as Ruth's brother and William felt no kinship with him. But for that matter, he felt none with anybody except Ruth. As long as he lived he would call her father Mr. Harnsbarger.

But Mr. Harnsbarger grew suddenly old. He wanted them now to promise him they would always live in the farmhouse.

" 'Tisn't as if you had reg'lar work, William," he said. "What you do can just as well be done here as anywhere." The change in this old man was astonishing, and William saw it with keenest perception. He would have said that old Mrs. Harnsbarger had for years meant nothing to her husband. They had interchanged not a dozen words a day, and his tone of voice toward her was a habitual grumble to which she gave no heed. And yet when she died he was maimed.

"I didn't think I'd ever be a widower," he said mournfully to Ruth.

"If 'twouldn't been you a widower 'twould 'a been Mom a widow yet, though, Pop," she said.

"So 'twould," he said, struck, "but I'd never thought it out thataway."

He muttered the thought over to himself occasionally in the days after the funeral and seemed to find comfort in its inevitability. "What you said was full of common sense," he told Ruth. It was after this that he spoke to William.

But in the night Ruth spoke to William herself with the delicate directness which was her particular manner of speaking with him. She spoke to no one else with just this mixture of timidity and frankness and sweetness.

"I put you first, William," she said to him. "If you want to go, we'll go, and Father can hire somebuddy, though I pray we don't have to live in a city."

"Let's stay for a while, anyway," he said reasonably. "Maybe I can work here as well as anywhere."

In a week the house went on as though death had not come into it. It was not so much that old Mrs. Harnsbarger seemed gone as that it seemed she was still there. Ruth, William thought, pondering it, became her mother, too, in some way of her own. There was nothing of her mother about her, and yet she moved more quietly. She ran less often, and now she did not leap up from her seat as a girl does but she rose gracefully slow as a woman does to do what must be done. Thus, perhaps, the dead live on.

But William loved this Ruth if anything more passionately than he had Ruth the girl. He began to be a little more helpless than he had been, waiting for her to do for him small things that he once had done for himself or even for her. Thus he sat at table and waited for her to refill his dish or to bring the coffee pot from the stove, or he waited in his room while she fetched his clean shirt in the morning, or his cap and coat when he went outside. He was not aware of this change in himself. He only knew that she did everything for him and that now he could not live without her.

She had never looked so beautiful nor been so content. Out of her content her body had blossomed until there were times when he could not bear its beauty calmly. He must woo her and possess her, then, even when he came upon her in the day. And here in the shelter of her home she allowed him and gave to him freely and with joy. Their marriage began again, as the house became their own. It seemed to him that he discovered for the first time how deeply passionate she was. And then she conceived her first child.

It was by now spring of their second year together. Without saying that they would stay he knew that for the sake of their love he would never take her away from this house and this land. She was nourished here to her fullest being. At the work she loved best she grew so beautiful, so rich, that he could not disturb that sacred growth.

"Selfishly," he thought, "it suits me to have her perfection. I ought to be able to work—out of perfection!"

He began to study the landscape and the people that he might discover pictures for himself. Twice he painted Mr. Harnsbarger, once in the old wooden armchair the old man's father had sat in and again outdoors, against the red barn, the summer wind blowing his white beard. He sent the pictures to New York and they were received as promise of some change to come in his work. "There is a mildness in these pictures new to William Barton's work"—this is what he read. It made him angry.

"I am too damned well fed," he thought. He pondered this a while, and, still angry, put it aside. It was tradition that art could not come out of plenitude and peace. But there was goodness in plenitude and peace, and why should he not prove them as rich a ground for creation as any other? The arts, if not art itself, flourished when men were free from fear and poverty.

He gave himself up therefore to this landscape, determined to possess it through full enjoyment of all its fertile beauty. But he decided that he would do no more portraits. The faces he saw in the small town and at the farms here did not make his hand reach for brush or pencil. They were too placid and cheeks were sleek and full. The smoothness of the landscape had bred them alike. He turned to sky and hill, to the anguished white sycamores that the winds had twisted and suddenly rising streams had torn and tried to drown, to birch trees shivering in the spring wood, to unexpected rocks upon a hill. There were not many rocks. Under the rich topsoil there lay the foundation of hidden shale and this was the bedrock of streams. But the thick dark topsoil hid every edge and harshness, except sometimes upon the crest of a hill, where the red rock broke through. His one painting that year which brought him notice was "Red Rock, Pennsylvania."

And yet he knew that only a few hundred miles away the bed of shale which spread underneath all this county to the north and the west of the farmhouse held iron and coal. If he had traveled only that short distance he might have seen faces again to paint. But he did not travel away from Ruth.

He waited for the birth of his first child, more curious about himself than about Ruth. For to have a child, he saw, was simply her own furthering. It was so natural to her to conceive, to grow toward motherhood, to look forward to the child's birth as she might toward a festival, that none of it was strange to her.

But he felt changed by the very contemplation of a new creature with him and Ruth in his house. He felt unwillingly drawn into these generations, as though for its own purposes the house had enticed him here and when he had taken Ruth away it had drawn her back again, and him through her, until it had what it wanted, yet another generation.

"Six generations," old Mr. Harnsbarger gloated. "It'll be a boy, too. We always have boys first."

It was a boy. William stared down into a small round face and tried to realize that this was his son. But he could only see the likeness in this face to all the generations that had been in the house.

Ruth lay back upon her pillows serene and triumphant. She had been right and William wrong. William had wanted her to go to a Philadelphia hospital to have the baby. But she had said she must and would stay at home as her mother had done, and old Mrs. Laubscher would take care of her.

"But if something goes wrong?" William said.

"I know a'ready it won't," she had said.

And nothing had. Old Mrs. Laubscher had done everything right, even to bringing in the axe under her apron so that William wouldn't see it. She cut the baby's cord with the axe so he would be a good woodchopper. And Ruth herself had listened to all the midwife had told her while she was pregnant. She had even walked under the washline so the cord wouldn't be wrapped around the baby's neck. From the beginning everything had been right. She was sure she knew what that beginning was, a Sunday when she had been plain happy all day, when everything had gone right from the moment she had got out of bed. The bread had baked beautifully on Saturday. She had gone to bed happy that night.

"This child was begot on a Sunday for sure," Mrs. Laubscher had said when she caught him. "He just jumps out, he's so strong."

"He was," Ruth said. "And I remember I laughed."

"That's why he's so handsome a'ready," Mrs. Laubscher affirmed. She had wrapped the baby in a blanket and held him up, a roundheaded fellow. "Now will I dip his hands and feet in spring water," the old woman said. She dipped the small, clenched fists, one then the other, into a bowl of water that stood on the table, and then his feet. "So he won't never get frostbite."

She washed him then and tidied the room, and when William came in, she hurried out with the child's placenta tied in a bit of rag. Out in the garden she buried it under a rose bush, so that Ruth's beauty would not fade.

"A sweet, pretty girl," she thought, and smoothed the earth over the roots. She sighed, for she was very fat, and then rose to her feet and dusted her hands. She would give the new father a few minutes to look at his son, and then she would carry the baby up to the attic herself to make sure he was upstairs before down. "People fergit so," she muttered, "and then they don't know how it is they gits bad luck."

In the bedroom William stood looking at his son. He knew in that instant that he would not be a good father. He felt no extension of himself in this small creature.

"Isn't it rather fat?" he inquired.

Ruth laughed. "He's a fine fat baby," she said with joy.

He looked at her instead of the baby. She was more beautiful than ever.

"I believe you've simply been having a good time," he said.

"I have," she retorted.

"I thought women were supposed to suffer or something," he grumbled in mock reproach, and she laughed again so that he had to restrain himself from taking her in his arms.

"Let's not have any more," he said jealously.

"What would I do with only one?" she asked him. "There's got to be somebody for him to play with."

"Why?" he said stubbornly.

"Oh, you're silly," she answered, smiling. "What'll we call him, William?"

"Harold," he said, "Harold, after my father."

Ruth considered the name. "There's never been a Harold here," she said.

"There'll be one now, then," William said.

She bore him two more children after that, both girls, one after the other, and then he declared it enough. He saw her enriched by them, her beauty new again in the midst of the three small creatures. He painted her thus once, and was surprised when the critics failed to see improvement in his work.

"It's the best thing I have ever done," he said to Ruth with anger.

"It is, too," she agreed warmly. "But those people think everything has to be done in New York or it's no good."

"Right," he said, secretly surprised by her shrewdness. He resolved then in his wrath that he would show them what he could do. He would never send pictures to New York again. He would give exhibitions himself. He would live in this quiet spot and paint such pictures that everybody would come to see them. He painted diligently, and each year he exhibited his pictures in the village Masonic hall. Country school children were brought to see them, and the village newspaper wrote loyally of them every year. Usually a few newspaper men came from Philadelphia. Once he read, as he might have read his own obituary, a column by a great critic in a New York newspaper, deploring his loss. "William Barton's promise, so strikingly begun, has not fulfilled itself," the article had said. He had read his own death, or so it seemed that day. He had burned the paper so that Ruth would never see it, but he could not burn his brain to ashes and his brain held the words, unforgotten.

They had their use. Whenever he felt himself growing lax and ceasing to find inspiration, he remembered them and began a fresh picture. Eight hours a day, he told people who asked him, were his minimum. "I work regularly," he said, "because it is the only way to accomplishment." For twelve years he had painted steadily and as steadily refused to believe that he was being each year more wholly forgotten.

. . . "Daddy!" Jill's voice upon the stair called him.

"Yes, dear?" he called from his room.

"Dinner's ready. I've done your brushes."

"All right, dear." He combed his hair and rubbed a bit of paint from his shirt with the stopper of a small bottle of turpentine which Ruth kept in his room. Jill was still on the stair.

"Can I come in?" she called.

"Of course," he said. She came into his room and stood

watching him, not quite at ease and yet longing for ease with him. But he could not give it to her. By some curious freak of mischievous nature, this child had exactly old Mr. Harnsbarger's small grey eyes in her fresh face and he saw every time he looked at his daughter the soul of the old man seated in her eyes. It was unreasonable, but there it was. Even though he saw her longing to love him, she looked through those eyes and he was repelled.

"Daddy, are you going to do anything special this afternoon?"

He had not planned it, but when she asked him he suddenly thought that it was time he went to see his parents. He did not go half often enough, now that they were so old.

"I'm thinking I ought to go to the city," he said.

"Oh," she replied, disappointed.

His heart reproached him. "Had you anything in mind?" he asked.

"I thought maybe you'd think of something nice we could do," she said.

If she had made a dear plan of her own, he might have yielded to it. As it was, he thought a little impatiently that she had no imagination. None of the three children had any imagination.

"I think I ought to go see my father," he said gently.

She did not answer, and he made amends by squeezing her shoulders in his arm as they went down stairs. He had taken the children one by one to see his parents, but it was not successful. The children, who looked only rosy and healthy at home, were bumpkins in his mother's drawing room. Their manners were Ruth's making. "Yes, ma'am," she had taught them to say, and "Pleased to meet you." He had not the heart to tell her that these phrases were not what he had been taught, nor that when his children uttered them out of their anxiety to behave well, his mother's sharp, handsome old face grew ironical, though she said nothing. He had taken none of them again since. Hal last year had upset his grandfather's wineglass over the lace tablecloth and his mother had said, "Never mind—the child doesn't know any better."

"Where's Hal?" he inquired at his own table, a few minutes later.

"He ran away," Ruth said. She pressed her beautiful, full lips together as she dished out chicken stew rapidly upon the plates before her. "And William, I shall whip him when he comes home, for I told him he wasn't to go till his work was done."

"Now, Ruth," he said, "I hate whipping."

She was about to speak and did not. "Somebuddy's got to do something," she had been about to cry out. But silence she had learned. She glanced about the table to see that all was right, and she did not answer him.

In his library old Mr. Barton examined carefully the painting William had finished this morning. Upon an impulse of doubt William had brought it with him. It was good, or perhaps it was not. His father stepped back from it without speaking.

"A very American sort of landscape," William said uneasily.

"Ah," said his father, "yes, it is."

"I had a curious thing happen to it," William said. "A butterfly flung itself against the paint. Its wing dust stuck and I had the feeling of painting it into the picture."

Mr. Barton looked at his son. He had put away his glasses and now he sat down to steady his legs. He was very old, and he had always dreaded speaking of anything unpleasant. But he and his wife had often talked about the question of speaking to William.

"It is no use not to speak the truth," she had said firmly only this morning at breakfast. Age had made her bitter and cold and doubtful of good in anything. But age always did that to women. Mr. Barton could not understand it. He himself had grown gentler and warmer as he grew old, as men did.

He made up his mind suddenly at this moment after dinner when he was alone with his son that he would speak. For the end of old age was death, and then there would be no more speaking.

"William," he said, "yours is a good talent. At one time I thought it was perhaps genius."

He looked about the walls of his library. In the far corner there still hung the small canvas.

"I used to dream of the day when I would hang one of your pictures in my gallery," he said. "I used to think I would hang it where my last Corot hangs. I was going to make a ceremony of taking it down and putting yours there instead."

William tried to laugh. "I never could be that good," he said.

"But why not?" the old critic asked. "Why not?"

"Mine is a secondary talent," William said ruthlessly and bled beneath his own wound.

"No," his father said, "no—a very superb talent, laid away in a napkin of content." He looked at William's canvas. "Soil too rich," he said; "the green's too lush. The essential form is lost. When there is no form, there is no meaning. A fine technique, William, signifying nothing."

"Speak out," William said steadily.

"I will," his father replied. "Go away somewhere alone and see if you can paint. It will soon be too late."

He rose and without drama he turned the picture toward the wall.

"Thanks," William said slowly.

"Shall we return to your mother?" his father asked.

"Yes," William replied.

. . . He did not leave his father's house until very late. His sister Louise came in with her husband and two friends, a dark young woman and a man with her. He saw Louise and Monty two or three times a year, often enough so that they were perfectly familiar to him, and yet today he felt isolated.

"There you are, William," Louise said.

"How are you?" Monty murmured. He held out his long languid hand.

William ignored it, suddenly realizing that he disliked Monty and had always disliked him. He was too successful, unreasonably successful. Monty was now a very rich man, by means which were not quite clear. International banking, it seemed, had given Monty his opportunity. He and Louise spent half their year in Paris. Old Mr. Barton, hearing rumors of Monty's wealth, seeing its evidences indeed in Louise's increasingly fabulous jewels, begged him to buy pictures.

"There is nothing like a fine painting as an investment," he told Monty gravely. "It brings pleasure and it is always salable."

But Monty remained cold, his pale, pleasant eyes resting inattentively upon the pictures his father-in-law loved. Monty contradicted no one, but he always did only as he liked. Against that pallid silent self Louise had battered and had not prevailed. She had come now to accept him as he was, and even to be proud of him, since success proved him right. His friends were her trial. He made strange friends, such as these two who were here today. Where had he found this dark young woman and this man who was neither husband nor brother?

"I say, Lou, would your people mind if we took a couple of people with us to dinner there tomorrow?" he had asked.

That was all she knew about them. "Mother doesn't like strangers," she had said coldly.

"Tell her they're my cousins," he said.

"But they're not, Monty!"

He gave her his sidelong smile. "Don't be like your mother, Lou," he said gently. "I'd hate to have to begin lying to you, too, my dear."

It was what she feared, that some day he would begin lying to her and then he would be lost to her. As it was, he told her, or so she thought, everything he did or was about to do, and he listened to her, or she still thought he did, when the margin for honesty was not too narrow.

"You must be honest, Monty," she said.

He smiled. "Of course," he agreed.

But the margin was so narrow that sometimes, when she sat alone, she was glad she had no children. Her only child had been born dead, and she had wanted no more of such suffering as childbirth. If she could hold Monty straight as long as her parents lived, perhaps afterward she could just rest. Though how she could rest, either with or without Monty, she did not know. But at least there were no children.

She looked at William. All these years, where had he been living? She had little curiosity. Most of the time she was too tired to wonder about other people. Besides, she had taken for granted what her mother said, that William's family was better forgotten.

"William knows he is always welcome here in his *own* home," her mother said. Louise had felt this was admirable.

But now, she thought, William looked tired too, and sad. Was everybody simply tired as soon as they stopped being young? Or did William have troubles? She could scarcely call Monty a trouble, and yet living with him was like living in the shadow of storm. One never knew—this war, for instance. Nobody was even thinking about war in Europe except Monty. But from somewhere or other he had heard it was coming and believed it.

"A war, Monty?" she had gasped. "But we don't have wars any more!"

"Not at once, old girl," he had said. "Say in three years or so."

"How do you know?" she had demanded.

He had not answered. He had got it, she supposed, from those queer friends of his, in Constantinople, in Vienna, in Berlin and Paris.

She sighed, and her faint curiosity about William died. She had her own troubles, living all over the world with Monty. When her mother asked her who these people were, she had said as glibly as Monty might have done,

"They're some sort of cousins of Monty's, Mamma. Of course if you'd rather not—but they're visiting us."

"If they are your guests, bring them," her mother said imperiously. She could see her mother's astonishment at the dark pair, but she had concealed it and summoned her strength as a famous hostess. She came out of her taciturnity and drew talk from them all. The drawing room became quietly gay. Even William roused himself to listen, but the talk was too quick for him. He found himself lost in its changes. His mother marked his silence.

"Ah, William, you should come out of your too green retirement," she said with a flash of malice. She turned to the dark young woman. "My son is bucolic," she said. "He married a farmer's daughter and paints whatever he sees out of her windows."

"Mother!" he cried suddenly. She had never spoken so directly before.

"Well, you do, William," she retorted, "and you've grown intensely boring to everybody."

Her sharpness was tempered with the willful mischief of pampered old age, but he felt her deep impatience with him, that impatience which when he was a child withered him like wind from a desert. It made him self-doubtful instantly, and he was bitterly humble when the young woman spoke to him.

"You should come to Austria. There is a life to paint there," she told him. Her eyes narrowed as she looked at him.

"I assure you, I am entirely second rate," he said, and smiled.

He could not stay long after this. The talk went away from him again and flitted about the world. He heard the names of places and of men in the swift narrative of the times that he had chosen not to share without exactly knowing how he had done so.

He heard Louise say in her high peevish voice, "Monty says we are going to have a world war."

They all looked at her when she said that, and the dark young man flushed suddenly crimson as though he were very angry. He and Monty looked at each other and Monty's long, pale face grew paler.

"Nonsense," Mrs. Barton said, "we're not savages any more. Whatever makes you think that, Monty?"

"One feels it," he murmured.

"I'd like to get a Raphael I've had my eyes on if anything like that were really about to happen," Mr. Barton remarked.

"Where is it, sir?" the dark man asked.

"It happens to be, of all places, in Spain," Mr. Barton said. "Almost no one knows of it!"

"Spain!" the young man repeated. "No, Spain is not safe, I feel sure."

From all this William felt himself infinitely remote. In a few minutes he rose and bade them good night and drove himself homeward. Had the life that might have nourished him most deeply escaped him?

"I wonder if Ruth would mind if I did go away for a while?" he thought. He suddenly felt the need of living very hardly. He wanted to go where crude people were suffering and bathe himself in their pain. His morning's agitation over a butterfly now seemed ridiculous. He found himself thinking of the sternness of war, of deprivation and danger and sacrifice of a plain physical sort. Through these ways the spirit was forced upward. How else could the spirit rise?

Moving through the unlit darkness of a countryside already long asleep, he felt for his own soul. It lay in him untouched, like a sword not put to use. How could he put it to use? There must first be a reason, an emotion greater than himself. He felt suddenly, though he was forty-seven years old, that he was young and unused, immature in his work because he was immature in himself. His brain was unwhetted.

"If I were just to go out of Ruth's house, not knowing whether I would come back," he pondered, "then where would I go?"

That house now rose before him in the soft, warm darkness. The windows in the kitchen were lighted. He put the car away and walked along the garden path which his feet now knew by instinct. He opened the door to the kitchen.

Ruth was there. She held a whip across her body, its ends in her hands. Hal stood facing her against the table, leaning backward on his hands upon it. She was speaking when William came in but she stopped. She turned her head to him.

"Go away, William," she said.

But he was sickened and cried out, forgetting everything

else, "No, I won't, Ruth. You—this isn't the way to manage a boy!"

He saw her face grow sterner than he ever dreamed it could, and for the first time it was ugly to him.

"I'll have to do what I think is best, same as I've always done," she replied quietly.

Then before he could speak again or stop her she stepped forward and with a swift fling of her hand she struck Hal three times across the back, three hard, cracking blows. Hal shivered and bent his head.

"Ruth!" William shouted. He leaped forward and snatched the whip from her.

"You leave her alone," Hal said suddenly. He was not crying, but the tears of smarting pain stood in his eyes. "She said she'd whip me. I knew it was comin' to me."

"I can't bear it," William said shortly. He threw the whip to the floor. "And I don't understand you, Hal—taking it like that."

"I wouldn't if it was anybody else," the boy retorted. Through his shirt a thin red stain appeared.

"Take off your shirt, son," Ruth said. "I'll see to your back."

"No," Hal said, "it's nothing." But he took off his shirt and Ruth fetched a basin of cold water and a soft bit of cloth and sponged the blue welt that had broken into bleeding.

"I had to do it hard, son," she said, "else it wouldn't have signified."

"I know it," Hal said. It was as though they had forgotten William. It was as though what Ruth had done had turned her son to her. He let her lave the wound until the blood stopped and then he put on his shirt.

"I'll have to sleep on my belly tonight, Mom," he said with a wry smile. "You sure have a strong right arm." He kissed her, and suddenly she hugged him about the waist.

"I've got to make a man out of you," she said.

"Sure," Hal said. "G'dnight, Dad."

He nodded toward William and went out, and they heard him going heavily upstairs to his room.

William picked up the whip and gave it back to her. "I never want to see that again," he said.

She took it without answer and put it on top of a cupboard. Then she went through the small round of preparing for the night and together they went upstairs, still without speaking.

He watched her while she undressed and washed herself and put on her cotton nightgown. He was in bed before her and he lay watching her loosen her long, uncut hair and brush it before she braided it. Her every movement fascinated him even after all these years, and in spite of what had happened tonight. It was not only that he loved her. She could be repulsive to him, too. He had never acknowledged this to himself before, but tonight when she was beating the boy he knew she could be repulsive to him. A more delicate woman could not have lifted the whip so steadily for three times, nor let it fall so hard that it brought blood. He could never feel the same to her again.

And yet he loved her because all she did was right and consistent with her being and therefore was without pretense. He compared her with the slender, black-eyed woman he had seen tonight in his mother's drawing room, and knew that beside the reality of Ruth that woman was emptiness. Wherever Ruth stood, she made reality. Thus the whole evening he had just spent became nothing, and this room lit by the oil lamp, the big bed, the old-fashioned furniture, the white curtains fluttering at the windows, were the center of reality. She bent over the lamp to blow it out, and he saw the full, smooth contour of her face suddenly clear and once more beautiful. Her face was calm now, and he compared it involuntarily with the way it had looked a little while ago when she had struck Hal. She could be incredibly hard, he thought, even cruel. Was that the base of her? Then the light was gone and she climbed into bed and he felt the smooth firmness of her thigh against his. She slipped her arm under his head.

"Did you have a good time?" she asked, and her voice was usual in the darkness.

"There were some people there," he said evasively. He

never told her of those disturbing visits to his home. She never asked and he was glad, for he dreaded the long explanation that he must make if he were to try to make her understand their effect on him.

"Were your folks well?" she asked. In all these years Ruth had never wanted to see his parents. Once, half-heartedly, he had tried to persuade her to go with him on one of his visits, but she had refused.

"Your mother and I wouldn't get along," she had told him, and then she had added, "We're both proud of our own ways, and she wouldn't give in and I wouldn't. So we're better apart."

He had not contradicted her.

"Yes, they're well," he replied now.

She yawned and they lay in silence a few minutes. She was healthily tired with her active day and could have fallen instantly asleep. But her only sensitivity was toward him. She knew, after all these years, that he was always different when he had been to see his parents. He was different tonight. She could feel it in the way he lay beside her, his body against hers and yet as though he did not know it. It always made her jealous, this difference in him, and yet he always came back to her and always would, she knew that now, though when she was young she used to be afraid he would not, maybe, someday. She used to wonder if he had ever loved somebody else not like her, a woman of his own people. She had been so afraid that she had never dared to ask. Now it didn't matter what he had done before he knew her. He belonged to her. She did not want to know what had happened before he knew her. It was too bad he had come in before she put Hal right. But it could not be helped. She turned to him, curving her pliant body to his. She loved him more and more as years went on, better than anything. But to her astonishment his body remained cold. He did not move. She was now suddenly intensely jealous of his evening away from her. All of the old jealousy she had forgotten was there in her again.

"What's the matter with you?" she said. She drew away from him.

"Ruth," he said, "my father thinks I ought to go away somewhere."

She could not answer for a second while she took this into her mind. Her body, stricken in its tenderness, grew stiff with terror. Now here was what she had always feared. If he left her he would know all he had missed in being married to her. For without knowing what those things were, in her mind she had grown increasingly afraid of them as time went on, lest he find them out one day. She remembered jealously the look of his old home in a photograph he had once showed her, and what she called its "style." She made fun of it. "I'd hate to have the cleaning of it," she said. "I'd hate to live there," she had said, "it's like a hotel." She waited to hear him say carelessly, "I like this house better, too." Most of the time she believed him, because hers seemed the only right way to live since it was the only way she had ever lived. But sometimes she remembered that he had grown up in that other house.

"What for?" she said at last. "You ain't sick, William. Besides, where would we go and how could I get away with thrashers due here any day?" she asked, her throat dry.

"My father thinks I should go alone," he replied.

"What for?" she demanded again, angered against his father.

"He thinks my work has gone stale and that I need something new," he said.

He could feel he was hurting her but he was more able to hurt her tonight than he had ever been, because of Hal. He could not forget how resolutely she had lifted that whip three times while he stood in all the protest of his being, watching what he could not help. He could not yet forgive her, partly because she had gone on to do her own will against his, but mostly because she had shown him that she could be cruel.

"If you leave me you'll never come back to me," she said.

"Yes, I will," he said, "of course I will."

"No, and I know it, already," she said. She had almost ceased to use her old Pennsylvania ways of speech, but when she was deeply disturbed she went back to them, and he was a little touched.

"Don't be silly, my dearest," he said gently.

"Everything I do is for you," she said. "I don't hardly care for anything else. If you've give up everything for me, so have I for you, William."

"Now, Ruth, you're making something very big out of nothing. Why, most artists travel everywhere and their wives have a terrible time. I've been a very faithful fellow, I think." He tried to be playful.

He felt her quivering strangely, this steady, strong, middle-aged woman who was his wife.

"Why, my dear!" he cried and turning he took her in his arms, shocked into a tenderness which was unusual only because it was protective. She had never seemed to need protecting before. "Why, my—little girl!" he muttered. He had not called her that once in his life.

And then suddenly she began to weep and to pour out all he had never known of her soul. "Oh, I know it's because of me you want to go! I'm not good enough for you. That's why your father wants you to go away. I knew when I married you I oughtn't to have. I've always been afraid I oughtn't to have. I ought to have married somebody my own kind as I could have helped and not hurt. I've spent myself trying to make it up to you, trying to have everything the way you wanted and not so much as asking myself what I wanted. If you leave me, it'll all be no good!"

"Hush," he whispered, "hush, Ruth! The children will hear you."

"Oh, I don't care!" she cried. He let her cry then, holding her, but strong enough not to say he would not go. He was deeply shaken, but he would not let her see how much. He did not indeed know how much. For his father had shaken him, too, and which one the more, his father or Ruth, he did not yet know. This morning would tell, when alone he could walk up the hill and think for himself.

And when she had wept all she could and had waited for him to promise he would not go, and when he did not promise, she grew terrified. And out of her terror her passion clamored for possession of him in the deepest way she knew.

"Oh, love me," she whispered, "love me—love me—"

But even in love he did not promise. He held doggedly to his determination that he would wait for the morning and only for the morning. Even as he gazed at her, tender and beautiful to him now, he could not forget how she had looked when she had lifted the whip. For that one moment she had made herself alien to him and hateful, and one moment was long enough for him to see himself separate from her.

Ruth lay awake long after he slept. He was different, and she was frightened. She was always frightened when his mood varied in the slightest from what she knew best. His mind she did not know and she was not able to know it, but his body she knew utterly and by his body she measured the content of his soul. When he ate and drank and slept, when he came to her gusty with passion, then she was pleased. His work she secretly could not imagine was work. He sold a few pictures a year, but not enough to pay for more than his own needs. She made their living upon the farm, made it proudly, too, knowing that plenty of people were sorry for her that she had a man who could not provide for her. To them she found ways of saying what she had forbidden the children to mention.

"William's father is a very rich man. William'll be a rich man when the old man dies."

Their pity was tempered with this possibility, and with a curious respect, too, for what they could not understand about artists. They stared at his pictures, wondering why he had chosen a particular lane, muddy with spring flood, to put upon a canvas forever.

"Seems as if there was sightlier things," they murmured.

And Ruth herself had this same respect and contempt for his painting. Still, she knew he must paint if he were to be happy. She herself was easiest when he was beginning a new picture, because then he was so happy. He was always excited and hopeful when he was beginning a new picture. Then he worked hard, and then the more he worked the less hopeful he was, and she had come to dread the finishing of a picture. He was never satisfied at the end, and when he was not satisfied he was restless. And nothing she could say was any use.

"I don't see but what it's just as good as your others," she had said only this morning. She couldn't, herself, see much difference in his pictures.

"Oh, Ruth!" he had groaned, and then she knew she had said the wrong thing again. It was so hard to know what he wanted her to say.

His restlessness she could cure only by love. Many a day she had endured, hoping for the night. But tonight for the first time love had not been enough. She felt him still far from her. Even in his sleep he had turned away from her now. She lay thinking through her fears in her direct practical fashion.

"There was too many things coming together against him today—he finished his picture and he went to see his folks and then he come home and he never can understand anything about Hal. I'll have to make it up to him somehow tomorrow." She turned carefully and put her arm over him. The late moon had risen and shone into the room and she could see his shape in the pale light. She looked at it fondly. How she loved him! It didn't matter that he hadn't been a good provider or even that he hadn't been good about helping with the children. She could always ask Henry Fasthauser about anything she didn't know on the farm. He had bought the next farm and was a fine neighbor, though he had married a poor do-less girl who couldn't keep his house clean, nor bear him a healthy child.

"You and me should ha' married, Ruth." She was used to his saying this time and again when they were discussing the sowing of a crop or the way to plow against rain wash.

"Shut up, Henry," she always said exactly the same.

"I mean it," he said yesterday. "Your do-less man and my do-less woman."

"Shut up," she said again.

She could never have loved that great, rough fellow, not after she had seen William. And no woman could have loved William as she did. Oh, other women must have loved him, women like those she had seen long ago in New York! Was it a woman now who made him want to go away? It must be, for only a woman could make his body cold to hers. She had heard wives talking together. "When he don't want his reg'lar, then look around and see what's goin' on."

Her heart beat to pain with jealous love. Oh, they could look around and see, but how could she? He had come down like an angel from heaven to live with her, and if he went away how could she follow him?

"My dear," she whispered. He called her lovely names but that was all she could say. When she had said even so much, her heart swelled and she was suffocated with love. She would not let him go.

The next morning, which was Sunday, they waited at the breakfast table for Hal. The girls were in their fresh muslin dresses ready for Sunday school and Ruth wore her tan linen, with an apron to keep it clean. William would never go to church. He loved his Sunday mornings in the farmhouse when the others were away. This morning he had waked, instantly clear, to the decision awaiting him, and was grateful for the hours of loneliness ahead. This morning he would make up his mind. He faced calmly in himself a probability, growing with the rising of the sun, that he would take his father's advice and go away.

"If I am ever to be content any more with what I have," he thought, "then I must know what I can do elsewhere."

Ruth had got up early as she always did and gone downstairs to the kitchen, leaving him asleep. He was alone in their room but the house was alive about him. He was fond of it now, he realized. It was safe, comfortable, beautiful in its simplicity. The smell of bacon and coffee was its fragrance at this moment, and he heard the girls' voices, muted until he should appear.

He lay in the wide old bed, feeling light and aloof and free. A bond had broken. He knew it last night. For the first time in their life together he had not turned importunate to Ruth, but she to him. There was a difference so deep in this that he could not at once fully comprehend it.

It made him free to consider to the utmost possibility what his father had said to him. Had his father said it was time for him to return to the world in which he was born, he would have angrily denied it. But his father had said it was time for him to return to himself—before it was too late. What he must consider was not one world or another, but his true self. Yesterday that self had risen at his father's words, like a ghost from the dead.

He got up at last, bathed and dressed and went downstairs to the breakfast table. Ruth and the girls were waiting for him. However late he was, Ruth always made them wait for him. It was one of her little determinations that they must all sit down together at meals. "Families mustn't eat just anyhow," she always said. But Hal was still not there.

"Where is that boy?" Ruth said impatiently. "Mary, run upstairs and call him."

"He's tired after last night," William said pointedly. He sat down and Jill sat down and then Ruth. She did not answer him or meet his eyes. "Why don't we let him sleep for once?" he continued.

"He didn't do anything yesterday to make him tired," Ruth retorted.

In a moment they heard Mary's shriek. "Mother!" she cried.

Ruth leaped to her feet and ran into the hall and up the stairs.

"What is it now!" William muttered. He rose and followed her, Jill at his heels. He could hear voices upstairs.

"He's not here!" Mary gasped.

"He's got to be!" Ruth said loudly.

They were in Hal's room when he reached them. The bed was untouched. Ruth threw open the door of the closet where Hal kept his clothes. It was empty.

"He can't be so foolish!" she cried. But her face went the color of cream, and her lips were grey.

"I'll see if his bicycle's here," Jill cried, and raced downstairs. She was back almost at once while they waited. "It's gone," she said.

"Oh, the silly boy," Ruth groaned. Her eyes flew about

the room, looking for a message from him. But there was none. They went downstairs and William tried to think what they should do.

"We ought to notify the police at once," he told Ruth.

But she had the farming folk's fear of police and of public attention. Besides, she was growing angry at Hal as she comprehended what he had done.

"He'll be back by night," she said. "Mark my words— when he's hungry, he'll come back."

But none of them could go to church. She went upstairs and put on her old blue working dress, and when the girls begged to stay at home she let them.

They stayed together all day, working at desultory tasks. William could not paint, but that he might be busy he cleaned his palette and box. He moved a small table to the window, saying that he must have light, but actually because from that window he could see the road.

"Boys often run away from home," he told Ruth cheerfully.

But as a boy he himself had never thought of running away. He had gone dutifully from one day to the next, obeying the regime that his mother had set for his training. Then it occurred to him that he really had run away that day when he first saw Ruth. All his long subdued instinct for escape had accumulated into one great leap that had lasted until now. That was the way his parents regarded it, he knew. Some day, they doubtless still told one another, William would come home.

"It's better to get the impulse out of one's system young," he told Ruth, without telling her what he had been thinking.

"Hal had no call to run away from his good home," she said curtly.

She polished the furniture and cleaned the stairs and she went upstairs to clean the attic, because from the high windows she could see a long way. William went with her to look over the piles of old magazines. He did not reproach her, knowing, as though she could tell him in words, how she was reproaching herself.

Her reproach began to crush her as the day drew on to

twilight. He did not need to make it heavier. Her anger faded under it, and by night she was trembling with terror. He had never seen her as she was when at last the darkness had covered the road and the boy had not come home. She turned to him in the attic she had made spotless and crept to his breast.

"I'm a wicked willful woman," she whispered. "I didn't whip him for his own good yesterday. I whipped him because I was so mad at him and God has taken him away to punish me."

He stripped his heart of everything except the great rush of new protecting love he felt for the cowering, clinging woman he now held in his arms.

"Nonsense, my darling," he said. He comforted her, smoothing her hair and laying his cheek against her forehead. "We haven't begun to try to find him yet." No use to argue with her against God, he knew. All his easy rationalism had never disturbed Ruth's belief in a God relentlessly just. "We'll call the police," he said. "They have all sorts of ways of finding lost persons."

He led her downstairs and left her in the rocking chair in the sitting room. "Rest a little," he told her. "You've worked hard all day and eaten almost nothing and been so anxious." Then he went to telephone the police.

He was a good deal shaken when he had to tell them how Hal looked. He had never seen his son so clearly, "—tall for his age, reddish brown hair and brown eyes, freckled across his nose, red cheeks, and his mouth full" —"like his mother's," he all but added until he checked himself. He went back to Ruth with his own lips quivering. She had the family Bible on her knees and was staring at it.

"William!" she cried, "he's written in the Bible."

He strode to her and looked over her shoulder. And there in Hal's childish handwriting, under the date of his birth, were these words: "Left Home July 13, 1913."

"I took up the book to find some help in it," Ruth sobbed, "and it turned to this!"

The heavy book slid to the floor and she wept aloud. And he knelt beside her and held her while she wept.

For a month the police searched the county and state for a brown-haired, brown-eyed boy. For six months and then a year they searched the country, but he was not found.

William never left Ruth for an hour. If he painted he went up on the hill and if she did not come out of the kitchen and wave her apron, he came down and hunted for her through the house until he found her.

"Are you all right, dearest?" he would ask her.

"Why, yes, William," she always said quietly.

He knew of course that she meant she was as right as she could be until they found Hal. Secretly William feared and sometimes believed that Hal was dead, but he never said this to Ruth, and she spoke of him always as living. Never, even in the depths of her secret heart, did she consider the possibility of his death. She kept his room waiting and ready for him, airing the bedclothes, washing the sheets from time to time as though the boy had slept in his bed. Some day he would come walking in, smiling his mischievous smile. She would smile, thinking of it.

"What are you smiling at, Mother?" Jill asked. She had grown quickly since Hal had run away, her emotions forced by her awareness of the suffering in the house. She had changed even her manners, even her speech, imitating her father in her new awareness.

"Nothing," her mother replied, absently.

Ruth seemed outwardly much the same, but inwardly she changed. She grew gentler to William than she had ever been, and more dependent on him, but she was sharper with the girls. She was sometimes so sharp that William could not bear it but he did not reproach her again as he had reproached her for whipping Hal. For she had never forgotten his reproach. Sometimes in the night he woke, feeling her awake at his side.

"Can you not sleep?" he asked.

"I've got to thinkin'," she said. This meant always that she was thinking of her son. "If I'd ha' listened to you," she said heavily. "If I'd only ha' done what you told me that night and held back my hand from him—"

"Ruth, you mustn't keep going over and over that

night," he told her. "Besides, the boy wasn't angry with you. I remember being impressed because he was so—so understanding of why you felt you had to punish him."

"That's why he left me," she groaned. "If he'd been mad, he'd got over it and been all right. But he went to bed and figured it all out that he was one way and I was another and that we couldn't ever get along."

He was astonished at her perspicacity. Had Hal been as shrewd as this? He could scarcely believe it of that heedless boy. But perhaps she was right.

"If he understands you as well as that, then he knows how much you love him and he'll come home again. Dear Ruth, dear wife, don't grieve. I need you." He held her to him. "Darling, this is the best part of our lives. If we are not happy now, when will we ever be happy?"

"You never loved Hal like I do," she said.

He released her. "I think that is true," he said. "I don't believe that I have loved any of the children as much as you have. But perhaps I have loved you more than you have loved me. All my capacity for love has been used in loving you."

She listened to this and grew frightened as she always did when he talked beyond her understanding.

"I don't hardly see how a body could've loved a man more," she said. She found it so hard to say directly that she loved him that he was suddenly impatient with her. He sat up in the darkness and bent over her.

"Say that you do love me!"

"William, don't be so—"

"Do you love me or not, Ruth?"

"Of course I do."

"Why don't you say it then? I tell you a dozen times a day."

"I wasn't raised to talk."

"Do you think it's only talk with me, Ruth?"

"No, but—"

"Then say, 'I love you, William.' "

"If I didn't, would I slave for you like I do?" Her voice trembled as though she were angry. "There isn't a woman anywhere as has so much to do as I have! Home and farm

and children, they're all on me. Would I do it if I didn't
—want to?"

"You mean, I'm no use to you!"

"No, but you're not like the menfolks around here."

"You mean I'm not like Henry Fasthauser." He wondered at himself. He was not in the least jealous of Henry.
For years he had known that Ruth turned to Henry for
advice about the farm. But the man was such a clod, he
was bald and thickened and coarse, and from very fastidiousness William would not have stooped to jealousy. He
never saw Henry Fasthauser without being pleasantly
conscious of his own slender and alert figure and his own
thick, handsomely greying hair.

Ruth answered with dignity. Her voice was steady
enough now. "William, I'm ashamed of you. You know
I'm not a woman as would think of any man except her
own husband."

He was instantly humbled. He put his cheek upon her
bosom. "I know it, Ruth."

But he felt her heart beating quickly, and she did not
put her arms about him.

"If you think that of me," she went on, "then nothing
I've done for you is any good, though everything I do is
done for you. I make the house the way I think you want
it. I never stir up cake or put the bread to rise without I
think, 'It's for William.' Night or day, that's my thought."

In all their years she had never said so much as this.

"I know it," he whispered. "Dearest, don't say any
more. I understand you. I'm so unreasonable. You give me
everything."

"I mind to," she said, "but if it's words you want,
too—"

"Don't, darling—don't say any more!"

"If it's words you want," she repeated resolutely, "why
then—" she went on with such difficulty that he suffered
with her, shy and ashamed, "I do—love you."

It was as though she had wounded herself for him. He
put his hand under her breast and felt her sweat. But he
was exhilarated and excited, too. He had made her say it.

He had forced her out of herself, out of her silence. He had made her come to him. He laughed aloud.

"Oh, you sweet!" he cried. This middle-aged, reserved woman, busy about her house and her children, was a shy and lonely girl, and he alone knew what she was. He lit the lamp by the bed and stripped off her high-necked gown. And she lay so beautiful in her prime, so much more beautiful than she had been as a girl.

"Your thighs are beautiful," he said, "and your breasts."

She did not answer, but he saw her body begin to arch and quiver towards him.

"I had rather it were so," he thought. And with all the symbolism to which he was so sensitive, he proceeded to his triumph.

If she was strong, so was he. If she was in her prime, so was he. He thought of the passion of their youth as small, weak flutterings of this mighty thing that now was theirs. Together they plumbed the abyss and found its depth. Together they sprang up again.

"Good?" he demanded.

"Good," she said.

In peace, at midnight, he laughed in his heart to think that he had ever thought of leaving this house of hers to wander upon the earth in search of—what? Himself, he had said, himself, he had thought. But had he gone, he would have left himself behind. He had not left her the day that Hal ran away because he could not. Now he knew that he would never leave her because he would not. This, this was he.

Another two years and more passed without a word of rumor or a letter or a card from Hal. William took it for granted now that the boy was dead, but he said nothing to Ruth. Mary and Jill had almost forgotten how their brother looked. They knew only their father thought him dead and their mother did not.

"What do you think?" Jill asked Mary.

"I think like Mom," she said.

"But I think like Father," Jill said. She wanted to think like her father in everything. She worshiped him and was afraid always that she was not nice enough to please him. She wished she were pretty. Neither she nor Mary was really pretty, but Mary was prettier than she was. She wanted to be pretty for her father, because she knew how much he saw her mother's beauty. Sometimes in the middle of a meal, or when they were sitting around the fire at night, he would say suddenly, "Ruth, you're beautiful." They all looked at her then and saw how beautiful she was, her brown hair curling around her forehead and her little ears, and her cheeks red and her eyes blue. Then she would feel them staring at her and her neck would turn pink.

"Stop it, all of you," she would say. "William, you ought to know better."

"What?" he would say laughing.

"Before the girls!" she cried.

"But they know you're pretty!"

"I don't mean that," she said, blushing more than ever.

"Then what?"

"Oh—*William!*" She was always tongue-tied when he forced her to say what she meant. And then he went on, to tease her.

"Do you mean they mustn't know I'm in love with you? But they ought to know it—it's good for them to know it. They must begin to know what being in love means."

"William!" Only when Ruth's voice reached a certain agony would he stop his teasing.

But it was not only teasing. Oh, they knew that, she and Mary! But Mary always took her mother's side. They would discuss it afterwards.

"Dad oughtn't to talk so. She doesn't like it," Mary said.

"I think it's lovely! Other men are so stupid. Look at that fat Henry Fasthauser! I'll bet he never talks about anything except cows and corn."

"Ellie said he was in love with Mom, too," Mary said slyly. Ellie was Tom's wife.

Jill's little gray eyes stared at her sister. "You mean— he might have been—*Father?*" Mary nodded. "Oh, it would have been *horrible!*" Jill cried.

"We wouldn't have known it."

"Oh, *I* would! Not to have our real father!"

But secretly she was never quite sure of William as her father. She examined herself sadly in the mirror to discover if she could see any likeness to him. But there was none.

"Don't any of us look like Father?" she asked Ruth one day over dishwashing.

"Only Hal," her mother said shortly. "But he wasn't like him, really—only in looks."

But none of them were prepared for Hal's shocking likeness to William when suddenly one day he stood at the half-open Dutch door of the room William had made into a dining room. It was a Saturday and they were at their noon meal. They happened at the moment to be silent. Ruth was cutting a cherry pie. A lazy voice spoke.

"Got a meal for a tramp?"

They looked up. A young man stood there. William felt faint. He was looking at himself. That face—it was more familiar to him than the one he now saw in the mirror every morning! Ruth screamed for the first time in her life.

"Hal!"

Hal put one long leg over the door and then the other.

"Oh, Hal!" Ruth half-rose, and then sank down again, her brown face ash-colored. She began suddenly to cry. William leaped up.

"Look to your mother, girls," he cried. He lifted his glass of wine and held it to her lips. "Shame on you," he said angrily to his son, "coming on her like this after all these years!"

He was suddenly raging at Hal for everything, for the grief he had caused in the house, for coming back to make Ruth look like this, above all, he knew sharply, for looking so exactly as he himself had looked thirty years ago. Oh, he was very angry at Hal for that!

But Ruth cried out against him. "For shame yourself, William! What does anything matter now! Oh, Hal, Hal, you've come home." The tears were still streaming down her face and she moved away from William's arm and put her hand to Hal's cheek. He patted it.

"Sure I have, Mom. You knew I'd come home some-time. Why, Mom, I wouldn't go away forever."

"You might have sent a letter to tell her so," William said dryly. The boy was taller than he was and too hand-some. Had he been so handsome when he was young? He remembered out of some forgotten year Elise saying to him in her bold direct fashion, "You're too handsome to be so good, William. What's the matter with you?"

"Oh, well, I'm no great hand at writin'," Hal laughed. "I was always goin' to write and somehow I just didn't get around to it."

"Hal, where have you been?" Ruth cried.

"Everywhere," he said. "Don't get me started on that till I'm fed."

The thought of his hunger brought her back to herself. "Sit down," she commanded him. "Mary—Jill—get a clean plate and cut some meat—and get whatever we have. I'm glad I made the pie. It's your favorite, too, son. When I made it this morning I kept thinking of you. But oh, Hal, not to let me *know!*" Her red lips were quivering again.

His mouth was full of bread but he stopped chewing. "I know, Mom," he muttered, and swallowed. "I see now 'twas awful of me. But gee, the time went so fast—so much was happenin'." He pulled another piece of bread from the loaf.

"What has brought you home now?" William asked. He sat down again at the head of the table and his voice was stern. He could not make it otherwise. But Hal looked up at him with frank, unclouded eyes.

"The war, sir," he said; "we're goin' into the war."

Three years, Monty had said. It had been less than that. Nearly three years ago war had begun in a small European town and had spread like cancer over the na-tions. But that war had never been real to William, because all that was real to him was here in Ruth's house. He glanced at headlines two or three times a week in the county newspaper and sometimes he bought on Sundays the Philadelphia paper. With no special feeling he read one familiar name after the other capitulating to Germany. He had enjoyed Germany. A month's journey on foot through the Black Forest had been one of his greatest pleasures. What if Germany did extend her borders? The war remained a shadow play on the other side of the world and the years slipped over him like a stream of clear water, flesh warm, so he had neither seen nor felt them.

Now he looked about the table, startled, and saw their mark upon his children. Hal was a man, and Mary a woman, and Jill a tall girl of fourteen. He turned to Ruth, and instantly the comfort of her surged over him again. She had not grown older. The years had left her alone. Her hair was as brown as ever, her eyes as blue.

Just now those blue eyes were full of bright alarm. "It ain't our war, Hal?" she asked.

"Might be," he said. His plate was heaped before him and his fork filled. He used his thumb to push back a fragment of meat that fell from it.

"I don't believe it," Ruth said. She put down her fork.

"Might be, though," Hal said again. "That's why I come home. I've volunteered."

"Hal!" Ruth's cry was sharp.

He looked up and saw her face and put down his own fork.

"Mom, they'd have got me anyway. There's goin' to be conscription."

"That's no reason to go before you have to."

"Yes it is, Mom—besides, I want to go, I've always liked goin' places."

"Not to your death!"

Hal laughed. "I ain't agoin' to die, Mom! You don't die unless a bullet's got your number on it!"

William broke in. "But what have you got against the Germans, Hal?"

"Not a thing," Hal said cheerfully. "Not a thing in the world. I'm goin' for fun." He laughed and Mary and Jill, swept with irresponsibility, laughed with him. But Ruth and William looked at each other, grave.

"Why do you laugh?" William asked them sharply.

They stopped, chidden, and looked from one face to the other. Why were their parents so solemn?

"It's no laughin' matter," Ruth said.

He told himself that Ruth would be herself again as soon as Hal had gone. He tried to be patient with her. This was a woman preparing to tell her only son good-by, for months, for years, and there was the shadow of forever beyond. He was ashamed of his own contrasting impatience to have Hal gone and the house and his own life just as it had always been, and he hid his selfishness from Ruth with guilt as he acknowledged it. He knew that he resented in a foolish fashion Ruth's division from him. He was jealous of her attention fixed upon this tall, too-handsome fellow who was his own son. He wanted to send him out of the house, to separate him from their life, and take Ruth back for his own, entire. He wished, his impatience quickened by disgust, that she would not laugh so much at his silly jokes and pranks. Hal was a practical joker, a tease, a heckler, and only Jill resented him. William drew near to the sensible Jill.

"Let's take a little walk this evening," he said to her one evening after their supper. He felt restless with restraint before Hal. What did a man do, he wondered, when he discovered that he particularly disliked the sort of man his son was proving to be?

Jill's plain face lit. "I'd love that," she said.

They walked across the lawn and down the lane and he was touched by her anxious effort to be companionable to him. She walked carefully, holding her steps to time with his leisurely stroll, though her usual gait was a sort of dog trot.

"Am I too slow?" William asked.

"Oh, no," she said fervently. "I love to walk slow—you see everything. Sometimes when I walk by myself now I go slow, just so that I can see everything."

He found it hard to talk and was sure that she found it harder, though she tried bravely one subject after another. He let her try because she was revealing herself to him. He had never felt curiosity about any of his children, and yet he knew by an instinct that this was the only one of the three whom it would be worth his while to discover. She fell silent at last, depressed, he could see, by her lack of success in amusing him. He decided to startle her.

"I suppose you know I'm rather fond of you—as a person, quite apart from my being your father," he remarked.

She looked up at him, her face bright with unbelieving joy. So she would look, some day, he thought, when the young man she loved said to her words not too different from these.

"Oh," she gasped, "do you?" She caught his arm. "I've often wondered. Because we—Mary and me, I mean—we've thought you didn't, maybe. Not that you aren't grand to us, but then, you're grand to everybody."

He was amused by this. "I'm not committing myself beyond you," he said. "It's a principle of mine that you oughtn't to have to like somebody merely because he's a relative. I shouldn't like you to think you had to like me just because I'm your father. It's pure chance that I am."

They had reached the fence and beyond it they saw Henry Fasthauser turning his cows into pasture for the night.

"That fellow, for instance, he's as much right to be your father as I—only chance didn't happen that way," he went on.

She pressed against him. "If old Fasthauser were my father, I'd die," she murmured.

"He's no older than I am," he said.

"You'll never be old!" she cried with passion. "You'll always be just what you are now, the handsomest, best man I ever knew!"

He laughed. "Don't commit yourself, my dear. Save that for the young man around the corner of tomorrow. He may not be a bit like me."

"Then I won't have him," she declared. "He's got to be just like you."

He laughed again, warmed, amused, touched, and now curious, a very little, about this young girl who was his daughter. Her small grey eyes worshiped him in the twilight and her mouth was tender.

"I wish I could tell you how I feel about you. You're different from everybody. You make me feel different. I don't want just to be like everybody else—because you're my father. I'm terribly proud of that."

He pressed the hot young hand in his arm. "Sometimes I think I'm not much," he said.

She would not have this. "Oh, but you are! Everybody looks up to you and—and thinks about you the way I do. They all know you're—different."

He sighed. The difference! It separated him. He felt suddenly a little lonely.

"The twilight is chill," he said; "let's go in and find your mother." Then because he felt her taken back, he patted her hand again quickly. "You're a nice girl," he said, "a very nice girl."

But he knew that no child of his could ever be part of him. He entered the house, shouting, "Ruth, where are you? Ruth—Ruth!"

"Here!" her voice cried very faint from the attic.

He tramped up the stairs, swearing a little, and came upon her kneeling by a trunk. A candle set in a saucer flared beside her.

"What on earth are you doing up here at night?" he demanded. "You'll set the house afire with that candle."

"I'm emptying this trunk for Hal," she said.

"Trunk! He can't take a trunk to camp!"

She sat back on her heels. "Can't he?"

She looked so beautiful kneeling there before him, the candlelight from beneath, that he leaned and seized her and lifted her up and held her hard.

"I'm about tired of all this," he muttered, "it's time you gave me a little attention." He felt her hand on his cheek, his neck. "What do you think I married you for?" he demanded, and kissed her once, twice, fiercely, delicately.

"I don't know," she said, half-laughing.

"Not for brats," he said, "only for myself—" He let his lips rest on hers long and hard for a moment. Then he lifted his head and gave her a slight shake. "I want a woman who's my wife," he said.

"What would the children do?" she asked.

He laughed down at her. "What's that got to do with you and me?" he said, and went downstairs again.

But that, she thought, kneeling there alone in the attic, was the difference between men and women. A woman felt responsible. Suppose she only thought about William, then who would look after the children, or the farm for that matter? But the farm was only because of William. If she had married Henry she wouldn't have had to bother about the farm, only about Henry. But Henry would have wanted her to tend him first, too, and she could not have done it.

"I'm glad I married a man as I want to put first," she thought. " 'Twould be terrible to have to do it not wantin' to."

When she went downstairs to the kitchen again, for no reason at all she was sharp with Hal, idling by the stove. She saw William pacing the grass outside as he smoked his evening pipe. His figure was clear against the evening sky, just now bright with afterglow of the sun.

"Go and turn on the light in the sittin' room for your father," she said. "It's gettin' damp out there and he'll come in when he sees the light."

In their room the two girls prepared for bed. Whether they were silent or not depended on Jill. If she talked, there was talk. If she did not, Mary undressed in drowsy silence, yawning softly now and again. Tonight Jill was silent. She undressed quickly, washed her face and brushed her teeth and took down her long, looped braids and folded the red ribbons with which they were tied. Then she got into bed and pulled up the covers. Mary was twice as slow. Jill glanced at her sister's plump, pretty figure, clad only in a chemise. Mary was in love with Joel Fasthauser, old Henry's second son. She knew, because Mary had told her so. Mary was only waiting for him to propose to her. They had discussed that proposal and wondered when it would come and how.

"Mary, you must tell me when he does!" she had cried. "You wouldn't be so mean not to tell me when we've talked it over so much!"

But Mary, peony red, had refused to promise.

"Maybe I wouldn't feel to tell even you just what he'd say," she said.

"That's downright mean," Jill retorted. Mean she felt it would be until tonight. Somehow tonight she understood. For she could not have told Mary about that walk with her own father and how she felt, not about her father exactly, but about somebody, someone she had never seen, who would be like her father but much younger, though otherwise exactly like him. All through her being she felt a delicate, deep longing and aspiration to be better, finer, more clever, more beautiful than she now was.

"I ought to do everything to make myself ready for *him*," she thought—not her father, but that other one like him, only young and eagerly looking for her. "I could never, never marry anybody like that Joel," Jill thought. But how could she tell Mary that?

Between William and Ruth the war became personified in Hal. William was aware of it, but Ruth was not. The transformation took place the last day that he was at home. They had never seen him in his uniform. At home he wore an old blue shirt always open at the neck and a pair of trousers whose original color had long been lost. His red-brown hair was as rough as it had been when he was ten, and he went barefoot in the house. Thus he sat at the dinner table the last day. None of them could imagine him different from this lounging, smiling, careless young man, whose humor was in pinching and teasing his sisters and even his mother. William controlled in himself an impulse of real rage when Hal leaned across to his mother and pulled her small, close-set ear.

"Leave your mother alone," William said suddenly.

They all looked at him in surprise.

"That's no way to treat your mother," William said with unusual sternness. He was aware of the same astonishment in Ruth's eyes as in the children's. "I wouldn't have dreamed of such familiarity with my mother," he said.

"I don't mind it," Ruth said, amazed. "I know what Hal means—he don't mean nothin'."

"That's right, Mom," Hal said, laughing, "except I think you're all right." He spoke in his lazy way, his big voice amiable. That voice came with a shock upon William's ear. When Hal had left home his voice had been the half-quivering, uneven voice of a boy. There had been a quality almost pathetic in that uncertainty. There was no uncertainty in this big, coarse-timbred voice. It was the voice of a man, and, William knew, of a man forever strange to him.

After dinner Hal went into his room to put on his uniform. He was to leave in less than an hour, and there was to be a parade in Hesser's Corners. Two other boys were leaving for the war, one of them a chum of Hal's, and the third a chum of the second. Each had been led by the others to volunteer.

"The Three Musketeers, eh?" William had said affably, hearing of it.

"Sure," Hal had replied, his eyes blank.

William had refused his instinctive irritation. Hal who never read a book, who never even inquired of a book, who had not so much as glanced at the shelves William had put about the house, did not know *The Three Musketeers*. Why did he not say so? He had all the rustic's determination not to give himself away. William had turned away from him.

"That's a book, Hal, so I suppose you don't know what I'm talking about."

"Thought maybe it was," Hal had said, acknowledging nothing.

None of them were prepared for the Hal who emerged now from his room. Ruth was in the kitchen putting it to rights after the dishwashing. Jill had gone upstairs, and Mary was sweeping the crumbs from the dining-room floor. William was at the half-open door judging the quality of the afternoon light over the lawn that he was painting. The door opened and Hal's voice said,

"Well, how do you like me?"

They all turned to him, and William saw his son as he had never seen him before, a strange young man, neat, smart, sharply outlined in his new uniform, his hair brushed smooth, his healthy-colored skin ruddy and clean, his broad shoulders square.

"Oh, Hal!" Ruth cried. She went to him, her blue eyes

bright and warm upon her son. She could not keep from touching him here and there, making sure that everything was right, though she knew it was right already. Then she put her hands on his shoulders and looked into his eyes. He was a head taller than she.

"You be a good boy, Hal," she said. Her voice trembled. "Remember all the things I've told you and be good."

"Sure I will, Mom," he said. He bent and laid his cheek against hers. "You smell so sweet, Mom—just like you always did. I remember it from when I was little and used to smell your dresses hangin' in the closet."

"Oh, Hal, but will you remember to be good?" she moaned.

"Sure I will, Mom," he said.

And suddenly William could bear no longer the spectacle of Ruth's love for this man so young, so strong, who was nearer to her than any other because he had her own blood in him. That was why men were jealous of their sons, it now occurred to him, because the sons had blood access to their mother's hearts, and a husband was always an alien in his blood. And blood was woman's bond.

He went over to Ruth and drew her gently to himself. "Hal must go now, Ruth," he said. "It is time for us all to go if we are to see the parade."

He had before this made mild fun of the parade and had never meant to go to it himself. But now he made up his mind he would. He wanted to be with Ruth until Hal was gone.

"You goin', Dad?" Hal asked.

"I am, after all," William said.

"Good enough," Hal shouted.

William did not answer, enduring a sense of dishonesty in silence. "You look very well, Hal," he said at last.

"Not too bad, I reckon," Hal replied.

So they had gone to the parade and in a mood of intense though unexpressed cynicism he watched the little parade of the fire department, headed by the town band, march through the single street of the village. Ruth wept and he put his arm about her as he stood smoking his pipe, and he was aware of Mary winking back her tears.

Jill's face was calm. He could not tell her thoughts. They saw the three soldiers herded off on the train and then walked home, silent. It was Ruth who broke the silence.

"Hal was handsomer than the others, wasn't he?"

"Yes, he was," William replied. They were entering the lane and the heavy-set, solidly built house was just at its end. He still entered it sometimes, as he did now, with a sense of shock. How strange it was that years ago he should by merest chance have come here, hungry for a single meal, and then stayed to be fed for the rest of his years! He had made an accident his life, and out of the moment's chance he had shaped Ruth's life and created the three new lives of the children who would in their turn carry on the widening ripples of that chance. When chance was thus the true beginning of all these lives, who should ever demand reason for their being?

"What are you thinking about, Father?" Jill's fresh voice, which was her only beauty, recalled him. He looked at her and looked away again. She was at that moment, young and different as she was, so piercingly like Ruth's father, old and dead, that it was ghastly. The young ought not to have to wear the looks and ways of the old. They should be born like no one. What was that but chance again? If he had married Elise, there would have been simply the choice between Elise's father and old Mr. Harnsbarger.

"William!" Ruth's voice came from a long way. "Did you hear Jill?"

William smiled slightly. "I was trying to think whether a Roman nose was better than a potato nose," he said.

They looked at each other, mystified.

"Father, you couldn't have been thinking so silly!" Jill cried.

"I was," William maintained. "And if you think I wasn't, you don't know how silly I am."

The girls laughed, but Ruth was grave. Her mind slipped off as it always did when William began such talk. She tolerated it, though it was foolishness, because it meant he was feeling happy, and when he was happy she needn't worry about him. She could put her mind on the hundred and one things that needed doing about the house. She sighed, thinking, as she often did, that she could have done with another son, Hal being what he was. She often wished that she had insisted on another child. But William was so queer about children. He could never understand that a woman had to love her children not best, but some, and she could not always keep herself in two clear parts. Actually she did, but in sheer time and thinking, she had to give more to the children. It was natural. Only when she was scared about William did she forget the children altogether because of him. He could still scare her, though he had never spoken again of going away. She had to thank Hal's running away for that. She sighed again, thinking of Hal all those years away. What had he seen and what had he done? She had tried to pry the years out of him, but they had seemed to leave no mark on him. He had knocked around some, found work easily enough all the way to the coast and back, staying nowhere very long. He had even gone to Alaska for a year.

"I had a real good time of it," he said.

"And missed all your schoolin'!" she had cried to reproach him.

He had looked at her out of mischievous red-brown eyes. "Learned a lot, though," he said, and would not tell her what.

Well, anyway, he was never in jail, he had told her that much. And now he was in the army. The army was as safe a place as you could get for a boy like Hal. They kept them busy, and told them how not to get diseased from bad women. No use to expect William to speak to the boy, though she had asked him. William had only said, "He's never learned anything from me—why that?" So she had let the boy go, only saying to him he must be good. They would tell him in the army, anyway.

It reminded her suddenly that the next thing she had to do on the farm was to get three of her Ayrshire cows bred. Henry Fasthauser had told her he was getting a new Ayrshire bull any day now and if she liked she could bring the cows over and he would help her. It would save her the cost of hiring a bull. If she had had a man to help her on the farm, she would have kept her own bull. But she managed with seasonal help and what the girls could do. They did well, especially Jill, though they had to go to school. She wondered sometimes if William had any idea how much work there was to do, even when she share-rented most of the land. She glanced at him. He was whistling softly a tune she had heard him whistle before but never could remember. He grew handsomer, she thought, as he grew older. Hal got all his looks from William.

"What's that tune?" Jill asked and put her arm through his.

"My Heart at Thy Sweet Voice," he said.

"But what's that?" she persisted.

"Samson and Delilah," he said.

"In the Bible?"

"The same pair, but outside the Bible—I must take you to opera one of these days."

"Will you, honest?" Jill squeezed his arm.

"Maybe."

What would it be like to drop back into New York? Like Rip Van Winkle, doubtless, that old Rip who had soon died when he discovered how the world had gone on without him. Probably he was sorry he had ever waked up. A cow bellowed suddenly in the night.

"What's that damned cow roaring about?" he asked. He hated cows.

"I'll see to her tomorrow," Ruth replied. Both the girls would know what the cow wanted, but not for anything could she have told William before them. Nor, indeed, could she have told him anywhere. He did not like to see animals in heat. It was queer, she thought, seeing how it was only nature. But so it was. Once he and she, walking in the orchard, had come upon the dogs and he had hurried away in disgust. A moment before he had been loving her and then suddenly he seemed disgusted with that, too.

"A little lower than the angels," he had said, whatever that meant. But he had to have everything exactly as he wanted it.

She pondered that, as she went about getting supper. He had to have everything delicate-like. Sometimes at night she wanted to be hearty and straight and then go to sleep. But she had learned that this was impossible for him. The light had to be so, not too dim, not too bright, and she must give him plenty of time and not think about being sleepy.

The cow bellowed again through the silent twilight, and Ruth turned to Jill.

"You take that cow and tie her to a tree way across the orchard. She'll turn your father's stomach with her bellerin'."

And Jill ran to obey.

. . . William had begun work again with unusual eagerness. The house, now that Hal had gone from it, seemed easy and free. After breakfast one day William kissed Ruth and left her, intent that day upon painting a canvas full of blue sky and white clouds, the landscape a strip of brilliant green, miniature fine in detail of houses and spires as tiny as doll houses beneath it. So he had seen the world as he looked out of the window that morning.

"Here's the universe," he had thought, "all sky above a strip of green and dolls' houses."

Painting this universe upon the hill behind the house, he looked down at midmorning and saw Henry Fasthauser's lumbering figure halfway up. He put down his brush. He heard a roar. Then he saw that Henry was motioning him to come down.

"Why doesn't the damn blockhead come up?" he muttered. He was loath to leave his picture at this point. The new flexible paint would dry and he would have to work it all up again. But there was nothing else to do. Henry stood there, hooking the air violently with his arms. Only when he saw William moving downward did he begin to climb again to meet him. Within the carrying distance of voice to ear he shouted, and William heard Ruth's name—Ruth? He began to run.

"What's wrong?" he shouted.

"She's hurt—hurt bad!" Henry roared.

Then he did run and in a moment they were running together toward the house. William, slender and agile, easily ahead. Behind him the thick-set farmer was panting.

"She brought her cow over this morning. If I'd ha' knowed it, I'd ha' brought my bull over. I don't know a woman anywheres around does what she had to do—" He was so angry with William that for once he had made up his mind to tell him what he thought of him, letting a woman bring a cow over to be serviced by a bull! Ruth had been ashamed of it herself.

"If 'twas anybody but you, Henry, I couldn't do it," she had said. "I hadn't counted on the cow gettin' ready quite so quick. Hal could have helped, if I'd only thought yesterday. But she didn't start bellerin' until night, and William can't stand—"

"She said you couldn't stand the noise," he shouted at William's back, "so she brung it over herself, the pore thing. Didn't want her girls to—and she knows she can count on me."

"Damn you, what's happened?" William turned on him, blazing at him.

"She's gored, that's what!" Henry roared back. "I told her to get out of the bull pen quick, but she didn't get out quick enough. The bull caught her in the back and tossed her clear up and she fell hard. Then I picked her up."

"Oh, God," William groaned. He sprinted as he had in track days in college, down the hill and through the orchard and garden, through the kitchen. There was not a sound in the house. "Oh, damn," he groaned again. "Ruth— Ruth!"

Jill came clattering down the stairs, her brown face pale. "Mother's hurt bad," she said. "The doctor's here. He says if it had been a half-inch to the right, her kidney would have been tore."

He paid no heed, dashing up the stairs to the bedroom. There she lay upon the bed, his Ruth, face down, and the doctor was probing the horrible wound. Mary stood holding a basin, her face pallid and her hands trembling. The doctor did not glance up when William came in.

"Is she—in danger?" he cried.

"I can't tell yet." The doctor, a fat, middle-aged fellow,

was probing with two stubby fingers. Ruth groaned and William bent over her.

"Oh, my darling," he whispered.

"Don't speak," the doctor ordered.

So he stood there gazing at Ruth's eyelashes and her drained white face. Suddenly she was unconscious. He was glad for that, but what did it mean? He could ask nothing until the doctor had cleaned and sewed the wound. Then he followed him downstairs. Henry Fasthauser was still there, waiting in the hall, but William faced the doctor.

"Exactly how serious is my wife's condition?"

"Not as serious as it would have been if the horn had gone right or left. By luck it's muscle and not spine or kidney that was gored. But it will take watching. She'd better go to the hospital or have a nurse."

"She'll want to stay in her own house, so send a nurse—two, if necessary. Is she in danger of her life?"

"Not if everything goes right."

"I'll see to that."

Henry Fasthauser growled, "Kind of late, I'm thinkin'."

William felt his anxiety for Ruth explode in him. "Will you get the hell out of here?" he cried.

Henry's yellowish grey eyes glittered in his round face. "Me? Not till I've said my say, mister! If you'd done the man's work around here this wouldn't have happened in the first place! A woman oughtn't to have to do the things Ruth's done. If she'd been my wife—as she'd ought to of been and would of been long a'ready if you hadn't come walkin' in all dressed up with your picture-paintin' and your fine city ways of livin', to live on her the rest of your life— Why didn't you take her to your father's big house and look after her and give her some pleasure?"

William's voice cut coldly across this fire. "I should have been delighted, but she has always wanted to live here. Now will you mind your own business?"

The doctor was busy looking over the bottles in his medicine case. He had lived in the valley for thirty years and there was nothing he did not know about everyone. He had been in and out of this house on children's ailments and one thing and another—all small, for it was a healthy family. He had wondered sometimes if William was happy. The woman was, of course. Women didn't look like Ruth if they weren't happy. He had known her when she was a little girl, healthy and pretty, but determined to have her own way. He could imagine her saying she was going to live right here and doing it.

"Well, I'll be going," he said placidly. "I'll send a nurse —one'll be enough. Our nurses are used to work. Give your wife three of these pills every hour. It'll ease her if she has any pain. Don't believe she'll have much. A thing can go deep into a body's vitals and the mind hardly seems to know it—queer thing! Mind and body aren't as close as some think."

He went away, with a nod exactly alike to the two angry men. "Hope I don't have to come back to sew one of them up," he thought. He speculated a little on them as the speedometer of his old car trembled around seventy. "Always did know Henry was in love with that woman," he thought. "Well, God'll have to go easy on him for coveting his neighbor's wife. He thought Ruth belonged to him. 'Twould have been more suitable, certainly."

He stopped at a village to telephone for a nurse and then rushed on to a small, unpainted farmhouse and went in to deliver a round-faced baby boy. He had long ago lost count of how many times he had done this. Nowadays he said, "Reckon we'll need 'em all if this war goes on."

In the house that in so short a time the doctor had left far behind him, William regained his control. He hated this thick farmer, and it disgusted him that probably the man in his dull fashion was still in love with Ruth. But he was not jealous. He knew Ruth was his. Who could prefer Henry Fasthauser to him? The man's hands were horrible, lumps deformed out of all human shape, not fit to touch a woman's flesh. He put his own very beautiful hands into his pockets and lifted his head proudly.

"Mr. Fasthauser, I doubt it will profit either of us to talk to each other any longer."

"I'm not doin' it for profit—I'm doin' it for her. What're you goin' to do about the chores?"

"We usually hire a man in the spring anyway. We'll manage."

"If you mean that drifter, Gus Sigafoos, he's not due here 'till next week."

"We'll manage, thank you. I am capable of a little, perhaps, in spite of your opinions of me."

"I'm not botherin' about you. I'm thinkin' about her," Henry said heavily. "And what I'm goin' to do for her is to send my boy Joel over here every day till Gus Sigafoos gets here."

William longed to say, "It is not necessary." But he was too honest to deny the necessity. He smiled suddenly, capitulating to reality.

"I'd like to say I won't have Joel around, but I'd be a fool if I did," he said. "I wish my university education had included the milking of cows and the feeding of pigs, but it didn't."

And Henry, who had resisted so instantly William's anger, found himself unable to say a word when William smiled and stood at ease, his hands in his pockets and his tall, slim body relaxed. He stared at William and slowly the perception of their difference came over him. Women wanted men to look like this man, and Ruth was a woman. She'd use men like himself and come to him for help with seeds and crops. But this other one was the man she wanted in her house. Anger went out of him as though it were his strength. He felt tired and weak.

"Well, I'll be goin'," he muttered. "Got a lot of work waitin'."

"Thank you for all you have done," William said gracefully.

"It don't matter," Henry said. "I'll send Joel over."

"Thank you," William said again.

Henry wanted to say, "Let me know how she does," but he could not. Of her own will Ruth had chosen this man. She chose him still. "Well, g'by," he said.

"Good-by," William replied. He watched this rough good man lumber out of the house with pity in his heart and triumph. When he was gone he leaped up the stairs and knelt at Ruth's side. Her lashes fluttered and she opened her eyes and saw him.

"What's happened?" she whispered.

"Dearest, be still. You shouldn't ever have gone over there alone—you should have told me, at least."

"I didn't want—to bother you."

"Dearest, how could it have been bother?" He caressed her hand passionately. "I'm such a bad husband to you, poor darling."

She smiled, a faint, white smile. "You're the—one—I want."

He bowed his head over her hand. Yes, it was true. By that strange chance which had first brought him to this house and then kept him here, each was still the one the other wanted.

Outside the house the world circled into war. Ruth measured its speed through Hal. She lay upon her bed, thinking over his brief letters. The war was a long way off because Hal was still in a North Carolina camp. It was nearer because maybe he would be in the next regiment to go abroad.

It came very near on the day he sailed. She was well again, out of bed, but the doctor would not let her walk downstairs for another few days. She was straightening her white cotton underwear in her bureau drawers when Hal walked in on his final furlough. He was wearing his new uniform and the tears came to her eyes when she saw him. He bent to kiss her and she put up her arms in a rare gesture of love.

"Hello, Mom—cleanin' again! Always cleanin', ain't you!"

"I got to do something. Oh, Hal, do you have to go?"

"I want to, Mom—"

William, watching them together, knew that they were one flesh in a manner that he and Ruth could never be. He left them and went off alone. He could not work because he felt himself alone. Strange that a man could in love bestow his son upon a woman and rob himself in doing it! Hal was his flesh made in his own image, without that part which in William was alien to Ruth. Hal was a William born and reared in this house, in Ruth's own ways. All that she did not understand in William was not in Hal. She comprehended wholly this youth that had William's body and her mind.

It was evening before William came back to the house. At the barn Joel was milking the cows and Mary was carrying in the buckets of milk. William met her, a foaming bucket in each hand. Her placid face was stirred into a smile unusual to her. She did not see William until he called to her.

"Mary!"

She started and the milk slopped over the edge of the bucket. "Father! Where have you been? Mom's been asking for you. She's that worried about you."

"I thought Hal was here."

"He's gone long a'ready. Where was you?"

"Just walking about."

She stared at him with her round blue eyes. "What for?"

"Trying to see what I wanted to paint next."

"Oh! Want supper?"

"I'll get something."

"Mom's had hers."

"All right."

Her eyes lost interest and she went on with her buckets. In the barnyard Joel suddenly began to whistle as loud and clear as a mocking bird. William went into the house and up the stairs. Jill met him at the top.

"Father! Oh, where have you been?" She wound her thin, brown arms around him eagerly and he put his arm about her for a moment.

"Nowhere—just walking."

"Mother's asked me twenty times. She's gone to bed again. Hal's gone."

"I know." He tiptoed into the room and Ruth cried out, "William, is it you?"

"Yes, dear."

"William, where have you been?"

He sat down on the bed beside her. "I thought you

wanted to be alone a little with Hal. Dearest, you aren't feeling worse, are you?"

She gazed up at him out of clear blue eyes, as young those eyes as the first time he looked into them.

"I'm tired, that's all. But why for should I want to be alone with our son?"

"I thought you did."

"I missed you. You'd ought to have been here when he went."

"He didn't miss me."

"But I did." Her full lower lip quivered and the tears came into her eyes. They looked up at him, out of the depths, bluer than ever. "Oh, William, what if he's killed? I can't help thinkin'—maybe I've kissed him for the last time. Oh, this terrible war! I wouldn't mind so much even if it was to fight for somethin' on our own soil, but to go off to them foreign countries!"

"The countries our forefathers came from, darling, so not quite alien to us."

He held her hand in both his. This hand of hers, grown firmer with the years, lay warm and powerful between his two encircling ones, his always so much more flexible than hers.

"I don't care for 'em," she said rebelliously. "What do I care what happens to a lot of strangers? What I care is what happens in our own house. He'd no call to go."

"Dearest, every young man is going to have to go very soon. It's war." He saw her beautiful face quiver and break, and leaned to take her in his arms. "Don't, darling!"

But she was sobbing into his breast, wordless with sorrow, and he held her and let her weep. In sorrow she returned to him. She was so strong for life, and the day's work, so seldom was she weak or did she weep, that there was a sort of ecstasy in this moment which gave her to him again. She sobbed a while, then lay still, her cheek against his shoulder.

"War's come into this house," she said at last, her voice broken like a child's.

"War has come into many a house," he said gently, "and it will come into many more."

"I only think of mine," she said stubbornly. Then she seized him passionately in her arms. "I've got you, though," she cried. "Nothing can take you away from me, William!"

"Nothing," he said gravely, "nothing in life."

"We aren't going to die!" she cried. "I reckon we'll live forever and ever."

"I reckon," he agreed, taking her word for his own. He held her and felt her holding him and perceived through every vein and nerve and muscle of her the gathering again of her passion for him.

"Sweet!" he murmured.

She put his hand to her breast and lifted her eyelids. That slow upsweep of dark, thick lashes was whip to his heart. He bent and crushed her mouth with his. This union of flesh to flesh, how infinitely richer it was now than it had ever been! Once there was mere hunger to satisfy, first body hunger, blood hunger. Then there had been hunger for children. Body to body they had created the children. But now there was no more such simple hunger. The flesh was long since satisfied, and there would be no more children. This—this was for communion, body to body, heart to heart, spirit to spirit, symbolic and significant of two beings fused in one.

It was long past dark when at last he rose and slipped the wooden bolt of the door and went out. The house was dark. The girls had gone to bed. No, under Jill's door at the end of the hall he saw a thin sreak of light. But he did not go to it. He wanted to see no one. The house was his. He went downstairs to the kitchen and lit a lamp, and found wine and bread and applesauce and cheese, and he ate. Then he rose, yawned and stretched. He blew out the light and went to the open kitchen door and stood looking out into the soft black night. The summer nights were always soft. The river kept the air damp and mild and good for sleep. The air was still. Impossible to believe that anywhere in the world was committed the folly of struggle and noise and dying! None of that was life. Life was here, in this house, between him and Ruth.

He went upstairs softly and softly let himself into their room.

"Asleep?" he asked.

"No," she said. "I was waitin' for you. We'll sleep together."

. . . When Ruth was well again and outdoors, she saw in a moment what in a month William had not seen. Mary and Joel were in love with each other. She was well satisfied when she saw it. She liked Joel, his father's son through and through. The do-less mother had been nothing but a tool in his creation, a cradle for his body. He was born of her and free of her and had no more to do with her. A sturdy, plain-faced boy, with none of his mother's foolish, pale prettiness, he was handy at everything that had to do with land and beast.

"That boy of mine—he gets a crop no matter what," Henry boasted. "Nothing goes wrong that he has the watchin' of."

So as Ruth was able she walked about the garden and the barn, her eyes sharp on everything, stables and fowl coops, and the fields as far as she could see. Everything was better than she had left it. The cows were clean and placid. Those to calve were healthy, and two more were started. That left only the two they were milking now. Three of the sows had farrowed and only two piglets were lost. Small jobs she had not been able to get done were done, the coops cleaned, the woodshed filled, the water troughs scoured, the two horses re-shod.

When Joel came over in the evening to milk, she went out to him.

"You've done wonderful, Joel," she said. "I'll never forget it, and I shall tell your father so."

"That's all right," Joel said. He dug his forehead into the cow's flank as he milked. "I only did what I'd a mind to."

"Then all the better of you," she said.

It was at this moment that Mary brought out the pails, and Ruth saw Joel lift his head quickly and watch her as she came. She knew then that he loved Mary. Yes, but what of Mary? She saw her daughter walk shyly near her.

"Mother, had you ought to be out so long?"

"I can't bear to just sit," she replied.

Mary laughed at Joel. "Mother's that hard to manage!"

"Be you the same?" he asked, laughing back at her.

The laughter, the quick, flying looks of the young eyes told the older Ruth. "She loves him back, I reckon," she thought.

"Well, I'll be goin' in," she said suddenly. This was enormous knowledge. Would William want it? Yes, he must want it, for it was right. Mary and Joel, there was rightness in the marriage. She had not been able to marry Joel's father because William had come by one day, but now there was not another William for Mary. Strange how like her Mary was in looks! But that was as far as the likeness went. Mary would never have seen a young William anywhere.

"Rest a little, Mom," Mary begged.

"Well, maybe," Ruth replied.

She went back to the house and lay down on the couch in the dining room and waited for William to come in. Jill was in the kitchen, getting the supper. Did Jill know? But she would speak to no one before William. She lay there thinking of Henry. Curious and queer it was how blood came back to blood in the generations! Part of her through Mary was going to be married after all to Henry. She didn't mind. Mary was the part that could have married Henry anyway, if William hadn't come.

Through the open door she now saw William strolling down the path, his knapsack over his shoulder. So he must have looked that day when he first walked that path. But now his dark hair was silver. She watched him, content with him. For years he hadn't left her, not even to go to the city. That his father, and others, too, sometimes wrote to him, she knew, but she ignored those letters. Sometimes she found them in the pockets of his clothes when she turned them out to clean them, but she felt no temptation to read them. They had nothing to do with her. Letters! They meant so little. It was living with people that made them real. She remembered suddenly what she had not thought of for years, the letter William had once written her. She had worn it around her neck until her wedding night.

He came in and she drew him to her with her smile.

"What are you smiling about?" he asked.

"A queer thing!"

He threw off his knapsack and came to sit beside her. "What queer thing?"

"Do you mind a letter you wrote me once when you was in New York?"

"The only one I ever wrote you, and you never answered it!" he replied.

"I was afraid to!" She considered for a moment telling him why. To this day he had never seen her writing. She had never written to anyone but Hal. "You know everything about me, so I reckon I'll tell you—I was plain scared to write back."

"Why, darling?"

"You wrote so beautiful, and I couldn't, and I was afraid you'd think less of me."

"Ruth!"

It was pathetic to him to imagine that humble young girl afraid of him because she loved him!

"I couldn't even read all you wrote."

"Couldn't you, dear? What did you do?" He touched her cheek, her neck, her eyebrows with his paint-stained fingers. He knew the noble shape of this head so well by his touch that he felt sometimes he had molded it as a sculptor molds clay.

"I folded it into a piece of red ribbon and made it into a good luck piece." She laughed at that girl she had been and was still, half ashamed of her, and not quite sure he would not be ashamed of her, too. But he was only moved.

"Why didn't you tell me about it? You've kept something all these years! I'll never know you—what else haven't you told me?"

"I'd half forgotten it."

"What made you remember it now?"

"I don't know. Yes, I reckon it was Mary and Joel. William, they're in love!"

"They are!" He drew back his hand quickly. He had seen nothing. "Did they tell you?"

"No, they didn't need to!"

He considered the matter, staring down at her. "I don't know that I care to be tied to old Fasthauser."

"It's not him—it's Joel."

"He looks like his father."

"Mary looks like me."

"I don't like it the better for that!" He rose and began walking up and down the room, his hands in his pockets.

"That's how you get your pockets full of paint!" she cried.

He took his hands out of his pockets. "That clod!"

"Joel's a real good farmer," she said.

He did not answer. It had not occurred to him that Ruth's children and his would be marrying—anybody.

"Who'd Mary marry if it wasn't a boy like Joel?" Ruth asked. "Where would she see anybody different?"

He could not answer this. If he himself had been different, if he had taken Ruth away from here instead of coming here to live, his daughters might have met young men not like Joel.

"I suppose you're right," he said. "Well, it can't be helped."

He went into the kitchen to wash, not knowing what more to say at the moment, and there he found Jill, her face red from the oven from which she was taking out a deep apple pie.

"What do you know about your sister and Joel?" he asked abruptly.

She set the pie on the floor, closed the oven door and looked up at him on her knees. "It's terrible!" she said. "I'll never understand Mary, never! He smells so—like cows! And his hands, his hands make me sick!" She lifted the pie to the table and turned on him. "Father, can't you stop them?"

He began scrubbing his hands at the sink. "What have I to offer Mary that's better?"

"But he's so repulsive!"

"I suppose she doesn't think so. And your mother says he's good."

"Oh, Joel's good! But *marrying*—" She hesitated, and he saw her struggling to put into words the delicacy of her flesh. He was startled at the sudden comprehension of this delicacy. What was the use of delicacy in this plain frame? What useless thing had he bestowed upon this daughter?

"Jill, what about you?"

"Me? What do you mean?"

"What do you want to do?"

"I don't know."

"I want to help you to do whatever you want."

"I knew you would, Father. My trouble is, I don't know. Mary's always known."

He saw her tremble a little. She turned her face away and looked out of the window beyond the table by which she stood.

"You mean Mary's doing now what she wants but you're not?"

"Well, she's always said she'd marry a farmer. But I'm different."

He went to her and put his arm around her thin, narrow shoulders. "Different, Jill?"

"Yes. I don't see things so clear."

"What things?"

"Maybe—myself." She turned those small, disconcerting grey eyes of hers upon him, and his arm dropped. How curiously unmingled Ruth's blood was with his in these children of theirs! One could sort them out, this child's eyes and Mary's face Ruth's blood, and Mary's shape his own, and his mind, or part of it, in Jill's skull so totally different from his own, and Hal's body his except his hands which were Ruth's, and in the boy that restlessness which was all that William's blood had been able to do in him! If only he could have sorted them all out and put them together again to make whole human beings!

In his pocket at this moment was a letter from Elise. She had not written to him in all these years. Now she wrote to say she had two boys in France, and his boy would be going, too. Perhaps they would meet. Would he give his son the names of her sons? She sent their pictures. He had looked a long time at little snapshots of two young men, one fair, one dark, both very English and very gay. He would not send them on to Hal. Better if they did not meet, his son and Elise's.

"I want to help you," he told his daughter Jill.

Adoration blazed in her little passionate eyes. "I know you do," she said. "I always know you do."

. . . War grew and spread but Hal was alive. As long as he was alive the war could be endured. Ruth did not ask who was winning in those foreign countries far off. She cared nothing who won or lost. All the outcome of war in which millions of men were wounded and died and in which nations sank like ships, all was bound up in the shape of the one man to whom she had given birth. Hal was still alive. Then she was winning the war. If Hal were to die, for her the war would be lost.

Joel must go now, too. All young men must go. The wedding must be first, so that he and Mary could have a week together.

"We want it right here," Mary said. "We don't want to go away. I'll just go over to his house, that's all. I'll stay there with his folks when he's gone."

Once again there was a wedding in the farmhouse, and William stood as a father in the room in which so many years before he, too, had stood as a bridegroom. By some chance Mary's wedding dress was blue and she looked for the moment startlingly like Ruth on that earlier day. He had the odd discomfort of feeling that he was giving Ruth in marriage to the stout young farmer in a tight new black suit. But he went through with it gracefully and a little humorously. When it was done, he felt that something had cut clean between him and Mary. That bond of her daughterhood, always tenuous and frail, was gone when from among the little crowd of guests in the house he saw her standing beside her husband. She was thinking of no one now except herself and Joel. She would never think of anyone else again. He had a sudden, clear perception of this young woman who had been his daughter all these years—a narrow little heart in the body he had helped to make, a little heart that could be devoted to nothing but its own. Mary would defend her husband, right or wrong, because he was hers, she would love her children, not because they were children but because they were hers. All the little allegiance she had to him and to her mother would now be transferred to what was only hers. Without a word his heart bade her farewell and relinquished her.

It was not too easily done. There was the loss of a child who might have been, though she had never been. He had a twinge of longing for a real child of his own, one to whom he could speak out of mutual comprehension. His imagination fluttered toward Jill. She was bringing in wineglasses and plates, her wide, thin mouth drawn tight in the task, but he did not move toward her. People were coming up to talk to him hesitantly. They were still shy with him, these people among whom he had lived as a foreigner all these years. But he had learned how to behave himself with them, how to listen, to smile, to answer a few quite common-place words. Cleverness frightened them, so he had learned not to be clever.

"Hello there, Mr. Sieger! How is that fine grandson of yours?" This was the butcher, whose scarlet face cracked into smiles.

"Swell! He's walkin' six months a'ready. Hope you'll get so good a boy for your first, Mr. Barton!"

Grandchild! William had not thought of grandchildren. He and Ruth with grandchildren! But it was inevitable, of course.

"I hope I'll be as lucky, Mr. Sieger."

"Don't know why you won't be," Mr. Sieger chuckled. "They're a hearty-lookin' pair, I'll say."

William smiled. His glance followed the butchers bright blue stare. Yes, Joel and Mary were a hearty pair. There would be nothing complex in that mating. But what if his own blood, subdued in Mary, broke free through the child? That was Nature's wicked way, Nature always laughing behind the backs of her copulating human beings!

In the midst of the strongly colored, strongly smelling country crowd he suddenly felt himself intolerably alone.

Ruth was at the far end of the sitting room, busy with the wedding cake Mary was about to cut. He saw her face, flushed and concentrated upon the task. She had baked the wedding cake herself, as her mother had baked hers long ago. The recipe was the same, but would the result be as good?

He slipped through the crowd unnoticed until he reached the stairs. He mounted them and went to the room he used for storage of paints and new canvases. He had a desk there, and he sat down to it and searched the world for someone to whom to speak. Then abruptly he drew a sheet of paper toward him and began a letter to Elise.

. . . Hal was gone and Mary was gone, and the house closed about the space as though they had never been. Joel went away to war and Ruth and Mary had long talks together that no one else shared. But however often Mary came back to the house, she never was a part of it again, as William knew she would not be.

"How are you, Father?" she said when she saw him.

"Very well, thank you, Mary," he said calmly.

The months went on and he saw she was pregnant, but it was no more to him than if any farmer's wife had so appeared before him. It was the sort of thing that Ruth would never mention. Some day she would come in and say calmly,

"Mary's had a little boy."—Or a little girl.

And he would say as calmly, "Is everything right?" and that would be all.

He was scarcely aware of Jill because he was painting very fast this year. He felt especially well and full of energy, partly, perhaps, because the year was unusually dry. He was writing regularly to Elise, too, and his mind was stimulated and made alert by her long, closely written letters. The one he received the end of that April told of the death of her younger son, Reginald, the fair-haired one. He took out the little photograph he had never sent to Hal and studied it carefully. So quickly had that young life reached its crisis and passed! He had a strange sense of bereavement, because in her letters she had recently enclosed some of the letters from her sons, Don and Rex, she called them. They were, he thought, extraordinary letters, these young soldiers so brilliant, so fluent in thought and word, so aware of life and death, so conscious of every beauty about them. He saw sometimes Hal's letters to Ruth. The boy wrote only to his mother, short, stolid letters whose chief news was what he ate and drank, where he spent his last day's leave, and what he wanted sent to him. But they satisfied Ruth because they told her he was alive and had no wound.

William, alone in his little room, read over again all of Rex's letters. Now that the young man was dead he must return them to Elise. They would be precious to her. But he spent hours in copying pages from them, paragraphs and sentences that seemed to contain the young soul, though the body was broken and gone.

"Life, now that I know any moment brings death, is so wonderfully precious. It is worth so much more than anything else that I wonder sometimes why I do not throw down my gun and simply run away. I could do it. The terrain here is familiar to me. I could lose myself some night on sentry duty, strip off my uniform, speak French or German as the need arose. I speak either as well as English. I know that in my heart I value life more than anything, more than country or honor, or any of the big words. I value my five senses, my body, my physical being. And yet I know that the reason I do not desert is because there is something more to me than these. I do my duty not because I am a patriot—I am not—nor because I am honorable in the conventional sense, but simply because to desert would be to destroy something else that is me, as much as body is."

. . . "There's a sunset tonight, Mother. Nothing to see against it except ruins, but there it blazes just the same. It's the eternal in this universe—it goes on, just the same, whatever we do upon the earth."

. . . "I would have liked to be really in love before this war got me. I don't mean taking a fancy to some girl. I mean the real thing, love, marriage, children, going on forever and ever. I want something beautiful that lasts forever, beyond myself."

Over and over again in the letters was this longing for an eternity. William, copying the young man's fine, straight writing, pondered this need. Was he satisfied now in that endless darkness which was his? Who could tell?

He sent the letters back to Elise with a note of his own, impersonal as all their letters were impersonal, and yet he knew that what he said would comfort her. For they no longer needed the other's personal being. What they gave each other was the reassurance of mind to mind.

"I know you are able to encompass death, dear Elise," he wrote. "It is not necessary for me to speak of Rex's death. What interests me far more is the persistence of his being. The being does continue, I believe, when the mind has positive qualities beyond the body. How, I cannot ascertain any more than anyone else. But I am quite sure that some people—not all—do go on alive after the body dies, and of them I know your son is one."

He went downstairs that night in one of the peculiar fits of loneliness that beset him when he had wandered far from Ruth.

"Ruth, Ruth!" he called her through the house.

She was outdoors in the vegetable garden picking corn for supper.

"Well," she cried. "Where've you been, William?"

"Upstairs," he said.

She paused to gaze at him closely. "You feel all right? You look a little funny, dazed or something. You didn't get too much sun today, did you?"

"I need you," he said.

She never quite knew what he meant by that, but she knew how to deal with it.

"Help me get this ready to eat," she said. "I'm behind hand today. A hen stole a nest and I was bounden determined to find it."

"Did you?"

"Yes, I did. She'd gone around the pigpen in that old trough we don't use no more."

He sat beside her on a bench made of a split log on four

legs and tore the green sheaths slowly from the bright yellow corn.

"How beautiful this is," he said. The silk lay smooth against the kernels and he stripped it off, strand by strand and put eternity aside.

"Could I," he asked himself that night, "have slept with Elise like this, night after night, and found it good?" He knew he could not. The simplicity of Ruth was the fountain in which he refreshed himself. He sat beside her in silence that he might discover what was the exact quality of the repose which his spirit found in her. It was soothing and somnolent, it encased him, not with hard, exact substance, but with warm fluidity which gave itself to his being. With her he need not think or question or argue; he need not speak unless he wished to speak. They talked together very little, less and less as the years went on. When she spoke he listened without hearing, and what she said in her rich soft voice only deepened the restfulness of her presence. He had come to depend upon her for everything except the restless core of his mind. Now Elise had come back. The war had thrown her back into his life.

But in Elise there could have been no return from himself, as he returned from himself to Ruth, because he could not have left Elise. Where he went Elise would have gone, and they would have been together always, and he would have been she, and she would have been he, and there would have been neither rest nor release in the inevitability of their absolute unity. Better for them that the ocean lay between!

In a large, square English garden at the back of a square English house in Kent, Elise sat reading William's letter which had come that day enclosed about Rex's letters which he was returning.

She read his letter over and over again because it contained the only comfort that anyone had been able to give her since that second fearful moment yesterday morning. She had been in the garden just like this, because the house was unbearable when she was so anxious that she could not sleep or eat. The weather was glorious, had been so one day after another, windless, clear, mild. But if it had rained she would have put on a mackintosh and stayed outdoors. Was this partly also because Ronnie was in the house? She and Ronnie were fond of each other, but she had learned to share the silence in which he preferred to live and it was easier to be silent when she was outdoors, alone.

But no silence, no manufactured calm, no compelled tranquility in talk had been any use. She saw the maid bring the second telegram and knew when she saw it that she had always known it would come. Yes, she knew, even when her heart's first wild thought as she read the first telegram had been that at least then it was not Don. Now it was Don, too.

She read the telegram, the formal communication which notified her, with regret, that her son Donald had been killed in action. Her lips grew stiff and her chin began to quiver.

"Well, Minnie—" she tried to say.

"Oh, my dear," Minnie cried, "it's never Master Donald!"

She nodded, her chin still quivering, and began to walk to the house. Ronnie must be told. She had been the one both times to get the telegram. This time she need not speak. She would just hold it out to him. Rex had been his favorite, and that time she had felt she must comfort him. This time there simply was no comfort.

So she walked quickly up the terrace steps and across the flags to the open French windows of the library where he sat reading and handed the telegram to him. He read it. Then he rose, his book sliding from his knees, and put his arms about her. She laid her cheek against his tweed shoulder and held herself breathless and tight, her eyes closed. If she could tighten every muscle, every sinew, perhaps she would not cry.

"That's it, old girl," Ronnie murmured, "mustn't cry. Take it standing, won't we! We've reached bottom now—nothing more to lose!"

Yes, that was it. She had nothing more to lose. Both her sons were gone. There was no comfort in the thought, but it was bitter and tonic. She crushed down her swelling heart, and after a moment they drew apart, each aware that the other was able to go on without further communication. Ronnie took off his reading glasses and polished them slowly, his fair, aging face sad enough. She sat down, and stared at the rug.

"Now that this has happened," Ronnie said, "I think I must get into it."

"What will you do?" Her eyes picked out a little running thread of scarlet in the small fine Persian pattern.

"There's things I could do. But what about you? I don't like leaving you here alone in this big house."

"It is too big, isn't it?" she replied. "Would you mind if I went home?"

"Home?"

"To America."

"You don't mean—to stay?"

"Of course not—only for a while."

"It might be the best thing."

So it was decided, but because Ronnie could never do anything at once, they would not go for a few days. The house they would offer for a hospital. She put away a few things and decided to leave the rest because she realized that she cared for nothing. Then she sat outdoors in the garden again, reading and rereading William's letter. Could it have been written about Don? Rex wrote her often, and Don almost never, and yet she loved Don, her firstborn, better. Was Don the sort of spirit that would go on living? If not, then she had no use for eternity.

"I shall ask William," she thought to herself.

And then she sat there in the soft English sunshine, both her sons dead, and thought of William. When she saw William she would cry and cry. Ronnie would never let her cry, but William would. "William—William!" she murmured, and at the sound of his name the tears rushed to her eyes and brimmed there, waiting to fall.

Hal was not wounded. The first year of war had ended and the second year begun and one battle after another was fought and lost or fought and won and still he came through them whole. He wrote to his mother boasting that the enemy had not yet made a bullet that could get him. Joel was wounded and came home, his right shoulder hanging lower than the left.

"So long as there's enough of me left to make a farmer," he said, grinning.

There was enough for this and more and soon Mary was pregnant again. Her first boy was named Henry after Joel's father, and William watched him sometimes with quiet irony. Henry Fasthauser, his grandson! The old Henry he seldom saw, but when he did both were good-natured. Ruth had let most of the farm to Henry, who farmed it with his own and paid her for it.

"It's the best way I can help you," he had told her when Joel went away.

"Reckon it is," she said gratefully. They had looked at one another, each ready to say more, but neither did. What could she do for him in return? She had wanted to ask. But there was nothing she could do, and so she had kept silence. She loved William and would love him forever— why, she did not know. There was nothing he did for her that paid her for all her work, except that he was himself and made anything she did worth doing because it was for him. What she got from him she could never put into words but it was what no other man she had ever seen possessed. She had married above herself, but she had made William happy.

He seemed more than usually happy these days, she thought, that second spring of the war. It was early June and wild strawberries were thick and she had gathered a pailful, though they were tedious to pick, because William loved wild strawberry jam. It was mid-afternoon and she sat on the doorstep of the front door, under the shade of the crooked old sycamore that leaned over the house, hulling the delicate fruit. Her fingers were stained scarlet. The second summer of the wicked war, she thought, her mind floating away, and Hal was alive and William was well and happier than he had been in a long time. He had not left home for years, even to go to the city to see his parents, the last time, indeed, just before Hal ran away. He must have quarreled with his father, though she had never asked. But she remembered often that William had talked then of going away. Well, he had not gone, and though now he painted less rather than more, his pictures were better. Even she could see that there was something new in them. But he spent a great deal of time not painting, only walking, reading, thinking, writing. He had made the parlor into a library. Books covered the walls up to the ceiling. What her mother and father would have thought of the wastefulness of such a lot of books—a lot more than anybody except William could read—though now Jill was beginning to read too much. She worried about Jill. She was so plain. There wouldn't be many men who would see behind those sad little grey eyes and the big mouth. She had pretty hands, thin and fine like William's, but what man around here would notice a woman's hands?

And as always she did, Ruth turned for comfort to Mary. Mary was having a real woman's life, now that Joel was back from the war with only his right shoulder stiff. The rest of him was as good as ever and he could farm, and he and Mary would have a lot of children, but none of them smarter than little Henry. She and old Henry took mutual comfort in that sturdy, strong boy of theirs. She smiled, remembering what old Henry had said only yesterday in his shameless way—old they called him only because of little Henry, for Henry wasn't old by a long time, yet.

She had gone over to see Mary about a recipe and the two Henrys had been in the yard. Old Henry was trimming out a lilac bush and little Henry was playing in the dead branches. She had stopped a moment to watch the handsome, rosy boy, who, everybody said, looked like her. He did, too. She could see it herself, though she couldn't say it because he was so pretty a boy. And old Henry had given her a big grin and said,

"Well, you and me, Ruth, we got together after all in that boy, though by a long, roundabout way. I'd ruther have taken a short cut, myself."

"Shame on you, Henry Fasthauser," she said to him, though by now she had said it so often that it didn't mean much. So she added severely, "Ain't you ever goin' to quit that kind of talk? We're gettin' old, Henry, and it ain't decent."

"Long as I'm man and you're woman I'm liable to say things," he said mischievously.

So she had walked away. Nobody could say she hadn't always been a strict good woman, with thought for no man except her husband.

It was at this moment that she heard the sound of an automobile on the road. Tom said there were lots of them, but still they had never had one stop at this gate before. She looked up from the strawberry bowl and saw a tall woman in a tan coat step out. A wide, scarflike veil tied her big hat on so that Ruth could not see her face. But the woman walked with a long, foreign sort of stride and in a moment Ruth saw her face, a thin, dark face, the eyes big and black.

"Is this where Mr. William Barton lives?" the woman asked. She had a fine voice, rich and echoing, as though maybe she could sing.

"Yes, it is," Ruth said. She did not get up or stop hulling the berries.

"Will you tell him an old friend has come to see him?"

"I don't rightly know where he is, at the moment," Ruth said. She set the bowl down and rose. "I'm sorry I can't shake hands," she said, holding out her red-stained hands. The woman looked surprised.

"Oh," she said, "are you—"

"I'm Mrs. Barton," Ruth said gravely.

"Oh," the woman said again. She stared at Ruth, her black eyes big and intense. They felt hot on her face, Ruth thought.

"Come in," she said. "If you'll sit down, I'll find him." She led the way into the cool house, and into the sitting room which William had repapered and furnished not with new things but with some of the oldest things her mother had.

"This is William's house," the woman murmured.

"My own folks have lived here close on two hundred years," Ruth said.

She left the woman there and went to ring the kitchen bell for William. If she could honestly have not found him she would have been glad. She would have liked an excuse to go back to that strange woman and say that she could not see William.

But William, walking in a little grove of white birches near the creek, heard the bell clearly and a moment later Ruth saw him coming toward the house. She was at the sink scrubbing her hands when he came in.

"Anything wrong?" he asked as he stepped in the door.

"There's a strange woman to see you—says she's an old friend." Ruth did not look up. There was no getting the red stain off. It would have to wear away.

"But I haven't any old friends," William said, wondering. He thought of Elise at once, but the ocean was between him and Elise.

"Well, that's what she says," Ruth said.

"Where is she?"

"In the sittin' room."

"I'll go in and see." He strode past her and then, perhaps because he had thought of Elise so instantly, he came back three steps and put his arms around Ruth and kissed her firmly on the mouth. "You smell of sunshine and warm strawberries," he said. He took her hands and dried them one after the other on the tan linen towel, and kissed one stained palm and the other. "Do you know how I love your hands?"

She smiled and blushed and drew her hands away. "Go along with you, William—she's waitin' long a'ready. Shall I bring in some dandelion wine and little cakes?"

"Yes, do. Where's Jill?"

"Readin', I reckon. It's all she does nowadays."

"She ought to help you." He hurried away then. A dozen steps across the dining room and he opened the door of the sitting room and saw Elise. She had taken off her veil, and under the big hat she looked almost the young girl he had seen her last.

"Elise!" He sprang forward and took her hand in both of his. "I thought of you when Ruth said an old friend and then I said it couldn't be you."

"Don is dead, William."

She felt suddenly that she had come all the way to say only this. It was not what she had planned to say, but when she looked into William's unchanged brown eyes, she knew why she had come.

"Oh, Elise!" He sat down on the sofa beside her, still holding her hands. "Dear Elise! How long have you known?"

"Since just before I sailed." She had not cried at all, and now she knew she was going to have to cry. An enormous flood rushed up from her heart. Tears swam up to her eyes, gathered and began rolling down her cheeks. "Killed—in action," she said faintly. "That's all I know."

"And your husband?"

"He simply had to go into war work. The house is quite empty—" Her lips quivered and then with a loud cry she covered her face with both hands and bent over and began at last to weep in great clear sobs.

William did not speak. Gently he took off her big hat and laid it down. Her black hair was an even grey, he saw with a shock. But his own hair was white. Years had passed over them both. It was hard to believe, so natural did it seem to see Elise again. No, but a lifetime had passed. She had been a bride, and now her two grown sons were dead. Yet she was Elise and he was William and they had known one another as children. He put his arm about her shoulder.

"It will do you so much good to cry," he said gently. "Poor Elise, I can tell you've been bottling yourself up, and that was always hard for you to do, I remember."

"Do you remember me like that?" She looked up at him, her face wet. Now he saw that she was older. Tears revealed her. She would always be handsome because the lines of her bones were so good—her skeleton would be handsome when her flesh was dust. But her mouth was sad and there were lines about her eyes, and one deep line between her brows as though she were used to frowning. It was not a happy face, and life, not death, had made it so.

"I do remember you," he said simply.

The door opened and Ruth stood there, a tray in her

hands, and on the tray small old glasses full of the dandelion wine and a silver plate of the salt-sweet cakes she always kept to go with it.

Her blue eyes opened wide. "Are you ready, William?"

"Yes, of course," he said quickly. He was aware of his arm across Elise's shoulder and took it away too quickly. His impulse was to cry out to Ruth in self-defense, "She has lost both her sons—" but he restrained himself. To Elise Ruth was a stranger. "Drink a little of Ruth's good wine, Elise," he said. "It will make you feel better."

So without looking again at Ruth he took the tray from her and set it down and lifted a glass from the tray and gave it to Elise. But when he took another for Ruth, he saw to his amazement that she was gone. When he took the tray she had simply turned and left the room. He was angry with her, and surprised at his anger, because it was so unusual to him. He had never been angry with Ruth before! He sat down again and tasted the wine and put the glass down.

And Elise could not drink, either, for her sobbing. She wanted to talk, to tell him everything about Don, how he looked, and how strong a child he had always been, never any trouble and clever in school, and honors at Cambridge. He had planned to go into government—it was the tradition of Ronnie's English family. Now all of it was over before it was begun.

"Why, William? Why—why?" she sobbed.

"I don't know," he said. "If I could answer that—it's all chance, so far as I can see, chance when one's born, chance in everything that one does, and so, I suppose, chance when one dies."

"But—but in your letter about Rex," she said piteously, "you spoke of persistence after death, for some people, at least. Do you have anything to guide you—is there any way to know what sort of people—why Rex more than Don, for instance? Don was less delicate than Rex, that was all. He loved life more than Rex did, really—you know, physical life, eating, drinking, sport—he worried me terribly because he was always falling in love. But it was never serious—he used to say it was just defining for him the person he was really going to fall in love with some day."

He let her talk on and on, and slowly the image of a strong, vivid young male creature began to come back to life before his eyes.

"Do you have those little snapshots I sent you?" she said suddenly. "Have you them, William? I thought I had prints of them, but I couldn't find them. And I always loved particularly that one of Don."

"Yes, of course I have them," he said. "I'll get them." He rose to cross the hall to the room he had made into a library. The house was as quiet as though no one were in it except Elise and him. Where was Ruth? But he could not go now to find her.

Then when he opened the library door he saw Jill, her thin body almost hidden in one of the two deep chairs he had bought when he put in the fireplace.

"Hello," she said, looking up from her book.

"There you are," he said.

"Who's the caller?" she asked.

"An old friend," he said. He opened the drawer where he kept Elise's letters. He had put the photographs in this drawer with them, not in an envelope, but loosely. The one of Rex was there, but not the one of Don. He searched again, sure that it must be there. It was not, and he began to look through the letters. It was in none of them.

"Strange!" he muttered. "What could I have done with it?" He turned to Jill. "You haven't seen a photograph anywhere, have you? I may have dropped it. It was of a tall, dark young man in the uniform of an English soldier."

He was amazed to see her face turn a bright crimson.

"I took it," she said.

"You took it! But why? It was no one you knew."

"I—liked his face." She bent her head and fluttered the pages of her book. Then she shut it and looked at him bravely. "I was going to ask you—who he was."

"When did you take it?"

"Several weeks ago."

"You've had it all this time without asking me?"

"I was afraid you'd think I was silly."

Her lips were trembling with distress. He continued to gaze at her, incredulous.

"But it seems a very strange thing to do—to take a photograph out of my drawer."

She stood up quickly. "I was straightening your desk. Mother told me to, and I put your drawers in order and I saw the picture. I thought the dark one was you at first, when you were young, maybe in one of those foreign countries you told us you went to before you met mother. Then I saw it wasn't really you. But something about him made me want the picture for my own. I ought to have asked you—only I was ashamed to."

"Do you have the picture now?" he asked.

She nodded. "Shall I get it?"

"Please do, Jill."

He waited, leaning against the desk, while she was away. What did this mean, he wondered? A romantic impulse in a young and lonely creature, perhaps no more, and yet he never felt that any impulse Jill had was meaningless. He had a strange sense of tragedy hanging over her, something frustrated, something gone wrong. She came back, and held out a little packet to him. She had wrapped the picture in silvery tissue paper. He did not open it. He took it, and something in her eyes made him know that he must tell her this young man was dead.

"The reason I want it," he said, "is because the lady who has come to see me is his mother. She married an Englishman and she had these two sons. Both of them have been killed in the war. She happens not to have a print of this picture."

He saw that blushing face grow pale before his eyes. Even her lips were drained.

"How terrible!" she whispered. It was what any girl might have said, but he saw in her eyes and in the tightening of her body more than the commonplace words said.

"It is very terrible," he said gravely. He walked quickly to the door, leaving her standing in the middle of the room staring after him, taking in what he had said. Then in the hall he heard the door flung open and she caught his arm.

"Father, could I come in and speak to his mother?"

"Of course," he said.

So she came in with him. She was always shy, this Jill, and yet when they entered the room where Elise sat, she snatched the picture from William's hand and gave it to Elise herself.

"Oh, I'm so—*sorry!*" she said impetuously. She had a beautiful deep voice and William had never heard it so beautiful. She sank down beside Elise and took her hand. "I feel I know him. I did know him. I've looked at his picture every day. I wanted to know him. Now I never can." She looked at Elise piteously, uncertain of her understanding, and Elise looked back, and then as though they had known each other, the two put their arms about each other and wept together.

And William, amazed and confounded, left the room very quietly and went back to the library and sat there alone, to ponder upon the meaning of Elise in this house.

In the sitting room Elise drew a little away from Jill, but only far enough that she might see this girl who was weeping because Don was dead.

"Are you William's daughter?"

"Yes, I'm Jill."

"You cry as though you had known my son."

"I feel as if I had." Jill searched the tired, dark face. This was his mother! "I had the strangest feeling when I found his picture in the drawer. I knew him. I had seen him. At first I wondered if it could be a picture of my father when he was young."

"Did you see that he looked like William? Oh, no one ever saw that but me! I never dared tell anyone!"

"I saw it. Then I knew it wasn't my father but someone else. And I took the picture, thinking I'd find out. I've kept it ever since, and looked at it"—she laughed in sheer excitement, without mirth—"almost as though I were in love with him."

They looked at each other, trembling in the knowledge of what might have been. Then Jill whispered, "I couldn't have said that if he'd been alive."

"I know."

The strangest sweetest sense of certainty filled the two of them. Hand held fast to hand.

Elise spoke. "It's the first thing I've had to comfort me. I shall want to tell you everything about him, from the moment he was born. I want us to be together—you and me. Do you think your father would let you come away with me?"

"He would. I don't know about Mother."

"I forgot her."

Their hands loosened a little, then Elise clutched Jill's hand again.

"Try, dear! For my sake! I've been so sad. And I have nobody."

"I will," Jill promised. Her wandering, warm heart that longed to love someone with all its strength fluttered about this woman like a hovering bird near shelter. "I want to be with you," she said. "Maybe it's where I belong."

"No," Ruth said.

Elise was gone. Up in the attic Ruth had stood at a gable window watching the tall veiled figure get into the car. William helped her in, though a man dressed in a sort of uniform, not a soldier, was there to do it. But Jill was there, too. What was Jill doing there and why should the woman bend over the side of the car and take Jill's face in her hands and kiss her? Ruth felt a queer jealousy. A strange woman had no business to kiss one of her children!

She came downstairs, her face calm and her heart cold at the surface and hot inside. She met William and Jill in the front hall.

"Where have you been?" William asked. "I wanted you to meet Elise. But when I turned around you had gone."

"I went to clean the attic," Ruth said. "I hadn't time to stay downstairs. Jill, the strawberries are put down to sugar. You can make the jam for me this afternoon. Be sure you don't let it burn. Wild strawberries can't stand a scorch."

"All right, Mother." But she looked at William as though she wanted something. William looked back at her.

"What is it, you two?" Ruth asked sharply.

"Mother, could I go to visit that lady?" Jill asked the question quickly as though she were afraid to ask it.

"She's a stranger," Ruth said.

"No, she's not," William said. "She's an old friend, Ruth. I used to know her quite well. She wants Jill to come and stay with her a while."

"No," Ruth said, "no."

She had not meant to speak so flatly, but the word flew out of her mouth from somewhere deep in her.

"Oh, Mother," Jill cried.

"Wait, Jill," William commanded. "Let me explain things to your mother."

They stood there the three of them in a second's silence. Then Ruth spoke to Jill. "You go and get that jam started."

"All right, Mother."

There were the two of them left. William looked down into Ruth's eyes, those blue eyes that he had never seen hostile. But they were hostile now.

"Come, my darling," he said. He put his arm lightly about her body, marveling at its resistance as, without a word, she obeyed him and came with him into the library. He shut the door behind them. "Now," he said.

She stood in the middle of the floor, a woman defiant. Her bright chestnut hair, with its two white wings above her eyebrows, her strong, bare neck, her smooth, rosy face, her whole bold, resilient figure, he saw her entire and his heart leaped in admiration of her as she was. He knew her limitations now. There was nothing about her he did not know, her ignorance and her wisdom, her prejudices and her illimitable generosities, her health of blood and mind, and above all for him still, her robust and undying beauty.

"What do you want to ask me first?" he said quietly.

"Nothing," she said. "I don't ask anything."

He was too surprised to know what to do except question her. "Why, Ruth?"

"Long ago I said to myself that I would never ask you anything beyond what had to do with me." Her eyes, unfaltering, were as clear as day. "I knew when you first came in this house that you came from a world I didn't know—couldn't, because I don't belong to it. Maybe some day, I used to think, you'd want to go back to it. Well, if you did, I wouldn't hold you back. That's what first I said. Now I know—after we've been together so long—I'll do my level best to hold you back anyhow I can. If I let Jill go—it'll be partly letting you go. I can't."

"I'll never go, Ruth." But he did not at this moment want to touch her.

"You don't know what you'll do," she said. She did not want to go near him. She felt suddenly that she was not fit. This morning a handsome, proud-looking woman had come to see William, from where, why, she did not know, she did not want to know. But she would not let that woman take anything from this house.

"If you refuse this to Jill, you are denying her very much," he said indistinctly. He saw Jill in a new and solemn shape. What right had Ruth to forbid her a world for which perhaps she was born?

"I can't help that," Ruth said.

How unchanging she was, he thought, how stubborn in all her strength! He felt suddenly desperate for Jill's sake.

"Jill was born in this house and in this house she'll stay until she marries some good man," Ruth said.

"And if she does not marry?" His voice was cold.

"Then she can help me. We're gettin' older, William." The words held a hint of pleading but there was no plea in her voice. It was firm with refusal. "There's no use talking, William," she said.

He resolved himself. "Yes, there is," he said. "Yes, we will talk, Ruth. We'll talk again and again until you see it as I do. You've got to understand me this time."

In the night, when the house was still, he tried to bring back his old world for Ruth's understanding. He felt Jill lying awake in her own room, depending upon him. She had never longed for anything as she longed now to go away with Elise. She had taken William aside that afternoon, and clasping his hand with hers that were sticky with jam-making, she had tried to show him how desperately she wanted to go away.

"I've wanted to go somewhere for a long time. I guess all my life I've wanted to live somewhere else than here. I'm not like Mary. I can't just keep house and milk cows and feed chickens. There are other things—there must be other things, aren't there, Father?"

"Many other things," he said.

"Mother thinks she always knows best," the girl cried passionately, "but how can she know best for me?"

"She can't," he said.

"If I don't go away I'll die," she said.

"You won't die," he said, "but maybe you'll live more if you go." He thought of that strange chance whereby she had found the picture of Elise's son. In this quiet house the life he had avoided reached in long arms to entangle him. He sighed. Jill, frowning and thinking only of herself, did not hear the sigh. She cried out, "It seems as if a man I never knew—that now I'll never know, though I might have—I never saw anyone who drew me so. He's opened a door to me, and I won't have it closed."

"I don't believe in closing doors," he said. "I'll do the best I can, Jill, without hurting your mother."

"You always think of her first."

"I always have," he said.

She threw at him one of her dark, sidelong looks and so they parted.

Side by side now he and Ruth lay in the wide old bed where they had slept two-thirds of a life together, and he tried to make new again for Jill's sake a world he thought he had forgotten. She listened, tearing the world down as fast he built it.

"I can only see things when they're put plain, William. Would you have married that—woman—if you hadn't met me?"

"I did meet you, dearest."

"Would you?"

"I suppose I would, just as you would have married Henry Fasthauser if you hadn't met me."

She thought this over. "Well, I can see that," she said. She pondered a while again. Elise was different from any woman she had ever seen. Was she like William inside? What did they talk about?

"All those letters you get," she said, "are some of them from her?"

"Yes, some are," he replied.

Then when she did not speak he asked her, "Would you like to see them?"

She took this in and turned it over and over in her mind. "No, I don't know as it would do any good for me to see them." She did not say, but she thought, what if she could not make more out of them than she had that letter of William's long ago? She felt wounded somewhere deep in her and baffled because she could not discover where the wound was or who had caused it. She could not be angry with William, for he was gentle and patient with her and she knew it, and yet she was angry somewhere, somehow, because he thought he needed to be gentle and patient with her. She would have been glad to be openly angry at him so that she could focus this large hurt in her.

"If Jill goes away with that woman she'll never be satisfied to come home again," she said.

"Is that what you're thinking?" he replied. "But it might work just the other way. She might be glad to come back. Remember that I chose to live here."

"It was different with you—you'd had nothing but that other kind of life and it seemed good to you to get out of it. But she's only had this and the other'll seem good to her."

"But have we the right to refuse it to her?"

"If it's for her good!" Ruth cried.

"Can we say what is her good?" he asked.

"Yes, we can," she replied. "She's ours."

"No," he said slowly, "no human being belongs to another."

There was long silence. Then her voice came out of the darkness. "If you believe that, why do you stay with me?"

He hurried to her with all his being. "Because I want to stay with you, Ruth!" He took her in his arms, though she rebelled against him a while, refusing to be easily comforted. She so seldom needed comfort, but when she was hurt the wound went deep and she could not be quickly healed. He lit the lamp so that he might see her face and study its change from its present sadness to its usual calm. And he set himself to bring her back to him, to believe in him, to know that he would never leave her.

And in all the tender words, the soft, gay love-making words that he spoke, while he pledged himself to her as long as he lived, he had a sense that part of him was escaping her through Jill. Jill was to be set free, and with Jill, a little of himself went out of this house.

There was no mention of Jill again between him and Ruth, but in the morning at the breakfast table he said quietly, as though it were a matter of no great concern to him, "By the way, Jill your mother and I decided last night that you were to go." He looked up and met the impetuous blue of Ruth's eyes, and challenged them with his insistent affirming gaze. "We both believe you have the right to choose for yourself," he said to Jill, and went on, his eyes still on Ruth, "It's no more than we did in our time."

Thus he gave his daughter to Elise.

He was aware, after Jill had left, that he and Ruth were more than middle-aged. They were getting old. Nothing in the world about them mattered much to him. Elise's letters continued, but now they were not importunate for herself. They centered in Jill. Jill must have new clothes and Jill must be given lessons in singing. Had William never discovered what a fine contralto voice she had? They were in New York, and Louise was helping to outfit Jill and to find the best teachers for her. Monty was enormously rich from the war. The longer the war went on, the richer Monty would be. He was being very generous with Jill. And Louise said what a shame that William had kept himself away from all his family. His parents were very old and frail now. When Jill was all finished they were going to take her to Philadelphia. Would William meet them there?

He read these letters carefully, comparing them with Jill's letters. Hers, he perceived, were written for her mother's eyes. He could make out little from them except that she was working very hard at her voice lessons.

"Did you know she could sing?" he asked Ruth.

"I used to think she sang the hymns in church real nice," she said, surprised, "but I never thought nothing of that."

"Ah, now I see I should have gone to church," he said laughing. But an instant later he was grave. "What a fearful thing it would have been," he said, "if we had not let her go!"

But Ruth would not grant him this. "It's not such a good life for a woman, singin' on a stage before everybody."

"Good for Jill, though, doubtless," he maintained. He did not mention the matter of Jill at his father's house. There was time enough for that when he knew whether he himself would go to meet her there.

Then the war ended and Ruth forgot Jill because Hal was coming home. Would he be home by Christmas? She cleaned the house from attic to cellar and put fresh paper in his room. The house was full of a new peace that had nothing to do with the war. That war had for her been contained in the person of Hal. He had come through it without a wound and boasted that he had grown an inch and gained fifteen pounds.

"He must look wonderful," Ruth said. "What'll he want to do, I wonder?" She spent a great deal of time wondering this. "Of course if he should want to settle on the farm, 'twould be too good to be true."

"I am afraid it would be," William said. "Don't set your heart on children, darling. It's no use."

"I don't know why my children should be so different," she said sadly. "Other folks' children seem to just settle down as nice as can be. But only Mary is like anybody else."

He laughed. "Your children have a queer sort of father, my Ruth."

She threw him one of her rarely mischievous looks. "Pity I didn't think of that when you first came to this house!"

"Is it a pity?" Perhaps it was this deep uncertainty, he thought sometimes, which made them eternally lovers.

"Pity or not, I could've done no different," she replied.

They had in those few days before Christmas a span as sweet as a honeymoon. Alone in the house, they were not lonely, and Hal's coming, which signified the end of a world war, added a joyfulness beyond themselves.

He did not come before Christmas, but the gaiety held. New Year, perhaps, and then New Year did not bring him. Then spring, perhaps, and still the gaiety did not break. Jill was very happy, Mary's baby was born, a second boy, to be called Thomas, and Hal was due any day.

The gaiety snapped one day in April when a letter came in Hal's eternally childish script. He was not coming. He had married a French girl who had lived in Paris all her life and would not leave it. As for him, he liked Paris fine. Maybe one of these days they'd come over and see him and Mimi. If they didn't, he'd get over for a while somehow.

William had found the letter in the mailbox and had taken it straight to Ruth, unopened. She was in the vegetable garden, raking the ground for seeds, and with her earth-stained fingers she tore open the envelope and read the few lines in which Hal had put the end of all her hopes. She held it out to William and he read it. Then he saw she could not speak and he took her by the hand and led her in the house, and made her sit down. He fetched some cherry brandy for her and made her drink it. And all the time he tried to soothe her.

"Dearest, I told you we must not set our hearts on children. They will do what they want. We have each other."

She found words. "William! A French woman!"

He saw that it was not Hal's marriage that dealt her death, but his marriage to a stranger, a woman to whom she could never, even if she saw her, speak a single word.

"The French are just like everybody else, dear. I used to spend all my summers in France when I was a little boy and I spoke French as well as English. I liked the people. Don't mind that."

But she did mind. It was nothing to her what he had done in that other life of his. With a French woman she had no means of communication.

"What'll his children be?" she mourned. "They won't be ours."

"You'll see them sometime, perhaps, and you'll be fond of them."

But she shook her head. "I can't be," she said. "They won't belong to me." The tears filled her eyes. "I wish we hadn't papered Hal's room. He won't never use it now."

"Of course he will," William insisted.

But he could not prevail. From that day on she felt that her son was dead. She did not answer his letter. It was William who wrote to Hal finally, and sent him a small check for a wedding present, gained from a picture he had sold to a tourist passing by who had seen him at work upon it.

"Your mother minds your not coming home," he wrote Hal, "so I shall write until she feels better."

Thus began the letters between William and his son, and out of them began his letters to his French daughter law. For one day he ended his letter to Hal with a message to her, and Mimi, reading this in her little Paris apartment, was charmed with its correctness. "Here is a miracle," she exclaimed to her American, "that out of all your regiment I should choose you who have an intelligent papa."

"I didn't know the old man knew French," Hal said, amazed.

"You do not appreciate him," Mimi exclaimed. And she set herself to appreciate William, especially when she had drawn from Hal the facts of William's wealthy family. She began to urge William to visit them. She would welcome her dear husband's father as her own. Paris was so improved over what it must have been in his youth. She longed to exhibit all to him.

These letters William did not translate to Ruth. He read them with amusement. They were gay, selfish, and not always correctly spelled. He had a very clear vision of Hal's little French wife, and when a picture came of Hal in mufti and with him a small, dark, determined creature in a ruffled dress, he was not surprised. He must, he thought, prepare Ruth not to see her son again, perhaps, ever. He would not put it in so many words, but he would try to make her happy in every way he could because in Hal her happiness was now destroyed.

. . . So how could he leave her, to return to that old house in Philadelphia, even to meet Jill? Had his father been able to know him, he might have thought thrice, though to the same end. But Louise, writing to him now because of Jill, warned him not to expect that the aged man would know him. He knew no one at all now, not even his wife. Instead his companions were those with whom he had always actually lived, the great painters of the past. He carried on long muttered monologues to Corot and Titian, and argued with Velasquez the quality of certain of his paintings.

"Father won't know whether you come or not," Louise warned him.

Then, he thought sadly, his father would not know now or care whether a painting of his would ever hang in his gallery or that he had never followed his advice and gone away to find out what he ought to paint. In a mood of bitter self-appraisal he looked at all his canvases. He sold a number of them each year after his exhibition in the small Masonic hall of the village, and year after year he believed that more people came to see what he had done. But he had become known for Pennsylvania landscapes, and nothing more, though into every canvas he had ever done he had tried to put far more. However he reviled Americans in his mind for loving to ticket for their own cultural convenience the work of any creator, the fact remained that they were too much for him. What he had tried to teach, that a landscape was valuable not geographically but spiritually, remained unlearned. It was no satisfaction to him to hear himself praised as the best painter of Pennsylvania countryside. Scorning his own work, therefore, he concluded against his hope that of all the canvases he had, the one he had never put up for sale, his first picture of Ruth, was the best.

"Still the best," he thought sadly, because he had finished it thirty-five years ago. It was a grim thing to face, that his best work had been his first. Why should he go to see his father?

When he heard that his mother, very old, touched with palsy, but in complete mental health, still refused to see

Ruth, after she had seen Jill, he made up his mind that he would not go to see her, however old she was.

"You ain't sick, are you?" Ruth asked. "You're so yaller."

"No, I'm not ill," he said. He had told her nothing of all his struggle and indecision under Louise's letters. He was not even sure he wanted to see a very wealthy and successful Louise and Monty. They were "doing everything" for Jill, but he could see they were enjoying it. And she was taking it all gracefully, he knew. Her sincere, happy letters told him that. She wrote kindly of Louise, humorously of Monty who now wore a monocle and a Vandyke and was getting very deaf, generously of her grandfather, and always with clinging affection of Elise.

"I have the strangest feeling sometimes that she is my mother," Jill wrote.

"This dear child of yours," Elise wrote, "is now my own. I have a strange conviction that if Don had lived, somehow he and Jill would have come together. She feels it, too. I doubt she ever marries."

He grew anxious when he read this and wrote a long exhorting letter to Jill, begging her not to allow Elise to influence her against marriage.

"Marriage is so profound an experience," he wrote her, "I should be sorry if you missed it. It takes place sometimes between two who are unsuited but still it is profound. I had rather you married unhappily than not at all."

She replied, "If I want to marry, I will. But I think I shall never want to—I am going to try for the Metropolitan. Do you remember "My Heart at Thy Sweet Voice"? I am learning it now. If I sing it on the stage some day, you must come and hear me. You promised me we would go together to opera!"

But all the time he was not quite sure whether he would go to see his mother once more. If he did go, it would be for the last time, he knew, and only because Jill would be there again.

Willfully his mother had decided to like Jill. Elise wrote him, "Your mother clamors for Jill. Of course she can't live in Philadelphia."

The day was set for early September, before the New York season began. Louise and Monty and Elise and Jill would motor down. It would be easy for him to go. Tom's thriving service station was managed by his two sons, and they came and went to Philadelphia as in the old days they had gone to the next village. If he wanted to go, one of Tom's boys would drive him over and bring him back. He put the whole matter off in the way he found increasingly easy to do these days.

"I mustn't," he thought, "I'm not old yet."

But living in the house alone with Ruth, it was easy to avoid any crisis of decision for himself. She made life so rich when she was content, and his universe was darkened when she was not. He did not like to leave her alone in the house any more. When he used to go to his parents, there were the three children to stay behind with her. Now she would only sit waiting and alone while he was gone, and when he came back, what would he tell her, how to explain now all that he had never explained? For Jill he had made a cause and won it, but himself seemed scarcely worth it. He was not afraid of Ruth, he told himself, as he had been of his mother. He loved Ruth, and wanted her to be happy, that was all. And if he left her alone, even for a day, she would be unhappy. So when the fourth of September dawned in a soft, misty rain it seemed too great an effort to tell Ruth that today he wanted to go and see his old home. After all these years!

He lay in the early morning, watching the rain, hearing it gentle upon the slate roof, and it did not seem worth while to him to get up. All that he cared for was here in the house. Ruth was still sleeping. He rose carefully on one elbow and looked at her. She was a sound sleeper, and he slept so lightly and restlessly that she was used to his tossing about in the bed. She did not waken, and as he looked at her all that she was came welling into his being from all the little channels of their days and years together. Her youth had been his, and her middle age. He had not changed her, nor did he want her changed. She was complete, a creature who had fulfilled that for which she was designed. He put aside the question of himself.

"I have been happy," he thought. Happiness was a primitive, simple state of being, a state of body first and of mind only freedom. Well, Ruth had left him free to think, and to imagine and to dream. He had had a good life with Ruth. How few men of his age, their children grown and gone, could look forward with quiet ecstasy to the years ahead, with wives grown old beside them!

Was Ruth old? He saw no sign of age upon her except the two white wings of her hair. Her sweet sleeping face was smooth—not young, but never old. Her skin was fine, her lips were still red, her teeth white and sound. He bent closer to that sleeping face and caught the fragrance of her body, as fresh as it had been his wedding night.

He lay back again and felt her warm and strong beside him. He closed his eyes and heard the steady rain pouring upon the roof above his head. His house, his home—he had made it his. He knew now he would never leave it until he died.

PART III

"WILLIAM, I haven't hardly asked anything for myself all these years," Ruth said.

"But our golden wedding, my dear, belongs to us both —or does it?"

William added the last three words when he saw her rosy, stubborn face. They were sitting together in the living room, in the middle of a summer's morning. Ruth as an old lady was going to be still beautiful. Her soft, curly white hair framed her fresh face. She had put on enough weight so that she had none of the wrinkles of age. He looked at his own thin, dark face in the mirror every morning and saw a mapwork of wrinkles. He looked twenty years older than she. One of his brown wool socks was spread over her hand and she was weaving in a new heel. Her blue eyes were as clear as ever and she wore no spectacles.

He went on when she did not speak. "But weddings always belong to women, from the first one to the last one."

She answered out of her own thoughts, without heed to him. "I'll have everything yellow—tablecloth and all. We'll have yellow roses by then."

"Do by all means have everything yellow," he said with impatience, "but can't we have yellow things without inviting the countryside in?"

"Folk in the neighborhood expect to come to a golden wedding," she replied. "A golden wedding isn't common."

169

She went on darning, but he saw sudden tears hang on her lashes and he leaned from where he sat beside her on the old sofa and took her hands, sock and all. "My dear, do you really want this—this party?"

" 'Tisn't I want a party, William—it's our golden wedding."

"But Ruth, why should we share our wedding with all the neighbors?"

"It's a thing to be proud of, William—a golden wedding."

He laughed, dropped her hands, and got up. "Oh, all right, my dear. I yield! I'll try to go through with it for you, Ruth."

"William, I don't think you ought to laugh at the folks. They all look up to you so."

"I, laugh? I assure you I hadn't thought of laughter."

He stood before her, restless and vaguely irritable as he often was these days. Perhaps this was old age, this restlessness to get on to whatever came next, impatience with what had continued for so long.

"I think I'll go now, Ruth."

"You still goin' to climb the hill? In all this sun?"

"The sun is good for me. It'll warm me."

She looked up instantly anxious. "You feel chilly, William?"

"No, no—don't fuss over me!"

"I don't see what you want to climb that hill for, yet," she said sharply. "You ain't fit for it."

"I'll never be more fit for it," he replied.

"Well, don't say I didn't tell you," she called after him as he left her. That was like William, she thought. When he didn't like something he just went away.

"William!" she raised her voice.

Out in the entry he stopped. "Well?" he called back.

"You ain't takin' your paintbox!"

"Maybe!"

"You'd better not lug that heavy thing up to the top of the hill—your heart won't stand it!"

He did not answer this. She heard him fumbling in the entry for his stick and resisted the impulse to go and help him. He did so little for himself nowadays—let him do what he could! He never so much as offered to wipe the dishes and she always had to ask him. She did now ask him to help her as she never used to do when the girls were home. It wasn't as if he had anything else to do, and besides she was old herself. She went on brooding over the lone grievance of his painting—the idle pastime, she thought, which had kept him from ever getting a real job and doing a man's work. What was the use of painting more pictures when there were nearly a hundred still stacked in the barn, not sold? It was little enough to show for a lifetime spent.

But then life was a disappointing thing, look at it how you could. She had had one disappointment after the other. There was Hal who had never come home from France, and now would never come home. She had almost forgotten how he looked. He had two children, both girls, both dark and thin. She kept their photographs on the mantelpiece in the parlor.

"Though I don't feel a mite of kin to them," she always thought when she dusted them once a week. She sighed, pursed her lips together firmly, and quickened the speed of the bright needle, weaving in and out. "For a man who doesn't work," she was thinking, "William wears out his socks wonderfully."

. . . William was not sure whether he could get to the top of the hill, but he wanted to try. He had an intense longing to see above the level of the green trees which now shadowed the farmhouse so heavily. In the years that he and Ruth had lived here together, the trees, already large when he first saw them, had grown enormous. They spread over the sky, and under them he felt smothered.

"Let's cut them down," he had said to Ruth again and again.

"What—the trees my grandpop's father put in?" she always cried horrified. "Why, my own pop would rise from his grave!"

"Then leave them, by all means," he retorted with a willful humor that he knew would be quite safe because it would escape her.

. . . There was only one person in this family of his whose perception of humor could not be safely trusted as obtuse, and that was Mary's youngest child, Richard. He saw sometimes in that child's dark eyes, only recently at a height, it seemed to him, to be well above the Sunday dinner table, something which was at all times so understanding, so quickly mirthful, even over the small, dry jokes of an old man, that he wondered if some germ of his own soul, swept along in the strong stream of Ruth's blood, had lodged in the boy. But he did not know. Richard was, when he spoke to him, aloof and mature. Actually the child was ten years old and Mary was almost past bearing any more children, he hoped. Six was enough. That was the way life went headlong on, these days. Already Mary was fat and at her menopause, and Joel was gray, and old Fasthauser was dead—dropped dead in a fit of anger six years ago, and young Henry had finished college and gone into law. It was he who had insisted on their sending Henry to college. Joel had done well with the two farms and there was no use in his holding the boy back. All of William's battles were now for his grandchildren, that they should not be held back.

He began to climb the hill. . . . Jill of course belonged entirely to Elise, an old bediamonded woman, until a year ago, when she had been killed in a motor accident in London. After she had got Jill, she had never gone back to Ronnie. There had been no divorce and scarcely a separation. Ronnie still came over now and then. He said continually these days that there would be another world war, but nobody would believe him.

"Nothing is being done about peace," Ronnie kept insisting, but still nobody listened to him. Most people thought the last war had left him a little mad.

And Hal was still in France. He drove a taxicab in Paris, it seemed. It was an odd thing to have one's son do. But none of his children now were very clear to William. Far closer and dearer were his grandchildren, particularly the little ones, and most particularly Richard.

"How do you do, Grandfather," Richard said invariably.

"How do you do, Richard," William as invariably replied. They shook hands, and that was all. But he was pleased that out of the six children Mary and Joel had, Richard at least remembered how he liked to be addressed. "I will not be called Grandpop," he had often said indignantly to his grandchildren. But only Richard always remembered.

He was climbing now and he paused a moment on the hillside, not to sit down yet, but merely to catch his breath. He still could not see beyond the giant trees. But the question of their remaining where they were was settled, for there was no one able to cut them down now. Joel's shoulder had grown worse as he grew older, and none of his sons could wield an axe or saw as he had. Ruth had not had a hired man since Gus Sigafoos was killed in the World War—poor old Gus, who had scarcely been able to read and write and who had no notion of what the war was about, had been among those who had fulfilled the letter of the law and, compelled to go on fighting after the armistice was signed, had died for nothing, at the last minute.

William could not himself now so much as contemplate the cutting down of trees. Even to hold his paintbrush tired him these days. He scarcely painted a picture a year, though this was not only because he was tired. He knew what he painted. They were an old man's pictures. They did not deceive him. He knew long ago that he had lost the tricks of depth and luminosity which had been exciting to those who had once perceived them. How he had lost them he would never know, or even when. But his pictures now were commonplace. The country school children were still brought to see them, and the county took pride in him. His canvases hung in country parlors. Sometimes he got as much as a hundred dollars for one, but usually he could ask only twenty-five or thirty dollars, and he sold most of them at ten dollars. Still, the people around were proud of him. "Our county artist," they called him. He had painted the seasons faithfully as they passed over the landscape in which he had lived. But he knew now that he was getting old.

He worried a little sometimes because he knew he would always be poor—not for himself, of course, but for Ruth.

He had forbidden the children to think of his inheriting money, and yet he had expected something. But his father, by an old will dated soon after William's marriage and never revised, had left almost his entire fortune to the founding and maintenance of a museum of art, the center of which was his own collection. There had not been enough to put up the great marble building for which he had left careful plans by a famous French architect. "The estate is much less than we expected," Louise had written. "Ever since the railroad was taken over by the government during the war, it's been worthless. No wonder they wanted to hand it back to private capitalists!" She and Monty thought of little else these days except how to circumvent a government of which they wholly disapproved.

To William, after his mother's death, his father's will had left only enough barely to feed and clothe one person —nothing for a family. Ruth's brother Tom had wanted him to fight the will, but he would not, though he could not tell them why.

"I did enough to disappoint my father," he had thought with sad, secret tenderness. "I won't rob him of his pictures, too."

He was still climbing and now, halfway up the hill, he knew Ruth had been right. He should not have come. He plodded upward again for five minutes. It was all he could do to get himself from step to step. He sat down to rest, gasping for breath. His heart was beating so hard it shook his body. If it had strength enough to beat like that, why could it not serve him better? This hill he had once scarcely thought of as a hill. He had gone leaping up, laden with easel and canvas and paints, eager for the day's work. But now he had come back to the perspectives of childhood. The hill towered above him. He waited a little longer.

Even as he now sat, he was barely above the treetops. But it had been so long since he had climbed to this height from which to gaze that he felt very high. He could see the long, soft roll of the green countryside—"flat," a tourist from New England had called it last summer, and he had been angry to hear his landscape misunderstood.

"It's not chopped up in little round-headed hills as your country is," he had said coldly. "It has far more majesty. It has the sweep of the ocean in it."

Now he felt its long, undulating richness, which the farms divided solidly into centers of human living. He could see the farm next door where Mary lived. All the farms looked alike, big barns and compact stone houses, like Ruth's and his. Seen from another hill this place at his feet where he had spent his life with Ruth would look like the others. There was no difference to tell that his life was not like any other. Nor was it, except as he was always, unalterably, different in himself.

That difference he felt, as he grew old, when he appeared in the little town which was also the county seat. The slightly jeering voices which he used to hear about him when he was young were dead. The men and women living now in the village had been born after he came here to live in Ruth's house. He was to them a part of the countryside. Still, having learned of their parents, when he went to the fair, when he sauntered in at the firemen's carnival, or at a meeting of the school board, they gave him greetings which were not quite the same as those they gave each other. Sometimes he liked this difference; sometimes it made him feel lonely.

Today, on this hillside, he felt lonely. In a way he had missed the world. He was aware of that world. Jill wrote of it because now it was hers. Her letters came to him from all over the country and half of Europe. Now she was going to South America. People were talking about South America, she wrote him, because in case of another world war, the United States ought to have allies toward the south. Jill had never married, even after Elise had died. Everybody was riding in automobiles nowadays, though he and Ruth had never bought one. Ruth went to church every Sunday in Joel's car and he was miserable until she was home again.

"A silly way to die," he thought. He thought a great deal about death now when he was old, yet not so much death as whatever was to come next for him. He believed in death as a part of life, the end of one thing and the birth of another. Anyway, Elise now knew more than he did about it, although she had drawn such comfort from something he had written to her once when her younger son was killed in the war. He could not now remember the name of that boy. The older one he remembered because Jill talked of him exactly as though she had married him. He was sure she told people that she had at least been engaged to Don, now that she was middleaged and, so far as he knew, had never had a lover. She had been a very successful woman and was still, if he could trust the newfangled machine his grandchildren had given him for Christmas. Only last Sunday afternoon he had turned a button and heard an announcer introduce his own daughter as the greatest American contralto, and then Jill's deep voice had poured into the room—overtrained, he sometimes thought. She called herself Judith, because there was no dignity in Jill, she said. Judith suited her better, he had to grant. She was slender, but tall, and full of poise and grace, and if one trusted things one saw in papers, her temper was not too good.

She came home once in a few years, and the last time she had worn a solitaire and a gold wedding ring.

"What's that?" he asked.

"Elise's," she said. Her cheeks turned a dark red. "She asked me to wear them, when she knew her back was broken and she couldn't get well."

It had helped her to make more real that tenuous imaginary marriage to Elise's dead son. And then he had discovered that Jill spent a fortune on spiritualists. She believed, she said, that she had established communication with Don. Perhaps she had. He would be the last to say it was impossible, now that the persistence of his own being had become a matter of interest to him.

He sighed and rose to climb higher. Somewhere near the top he heard behind him a rustle in the grass and he stopped, glad of the excuse. A pheasant, he thought, and then he heard it again. It was too heavy for a pheasant. It might be a fawn. He looked in the direction of the wind that carried the sound upward and saw beneath him not a fawn but the black head of a boy, and then the face and shoulders of Mary's son, Richard.

"Well!" he said, panting. "So you're here, too, today!"

"Yes, Grandfather," Richard said. He came leaping up through the grass.

William gasped a moment. "Can I carry your paintbox, Grandfather?" Richard asked eagerly.

"If you're careful," William said, and would not acknowledge that he was glad to give it up. Then he was struck with a suspicion of Ruth.

"Did anybody send you after me?" he asked.

"Nobody did," Richard answered. He slipped his hand into his grandfather's. "I was playing in the orchard and I saw you and came by myself."

"If anybody had sent you, I'd have told you to go home again," William said. But he was glad the boy was here because to his alarm he could not see clearly. The boy's face was blurred.

"What are you going to do, Grandfather?" Richard asked.

"Climb—to the top of the hill," William replied. He would, too, though he knew now he ought not to go on. Lightnings of pain were darting about his heart.

"I have a nest up there," Richard said eagerly. "Will I show it to you?"

"Shall I—shall I," William grumbled. "Learn to speak your words properly, child."

"Shall I," Richard repeated. "Shall I, Grandfather?"

"You come up here often, do you?" William asked.

"Every day, just about, but I didn't know you did," the boy replied.

"I used to every day, too," William said. He felt very badly, indeed, but if he did not go on now he never would reach the top again. He gathered all his strength together. "Come on," he said, "let's finish the last bit. I'll lean on your shoulder, and you can help me up."

"All right, Grandfather," Richard said.

They went up, step by step. The child was proud of his responsibility, and tried to temper his energy to the slow old steps. Under his hand William felt the slender body,

restrained, but springing ahead in spite of the child's will
to subdue it.

"Steady, Rick," he muttered. "Steady's the only way I'll
get to the end now."

Ruth paused in her dusting to go to the door. The postman was there.

"There's a letter for you—from Hal," he said. "I
brought it up. He don't write so often now, does he? Hope
there's nothing wrong."

"There wasn't, last we heard," she replied calmly.

"Queer he don't come back from that foreign place," the
postman went on.

"He's a wanderer," Ruth said. She would not open the
letter as long as he waited.

"Ran away first when he was a kid, didn't he?" the postman said, laughing.

"Yes, he did," Ruth said. Against her wish not to talk
she could not keep from saying proudly, "—and managed
somehow to keep alive and going for years and came home
looking as fat and healthy as you please, and he'd been
clear out to the west coast and even to Alaska."

"Hal's smart that way," the postman agreed. "Well, it's
sort of too bad he can't help you folks out a little now
with the farm. Mr. Barton don't feel so good these days,
does he?"

"He's frail," Ruth said. "It's his heart. He eats and
sleeps real good, too."

"People with heart trouble don't have energy," the postman said. "Does Hal know?" he asked solemnly. "You'd
ought to tell him, Mrs. Barton. Maybe he'd come home."

"Mr. Barton never wants I should tell the children about
him," she said. "He doesn't want them to think he's got
any claim on 'em."

"Yeah?" the postman said. "Well, so long, Mrs. Barton,
I guess I got to be goin' on."

She sat down the moment he had gone to read Hal's
letter. It was from Paris, France. He was still living there
with his wife, and the two little girls, Germaine and Angèle.
He wrote seldom, only at Christmas or Fourth of July or

some special day. This was written on Mother's Day, he said. He enclosed two small square snapshots of the girls, thin, timid young creatures in ribbons and ruffles. Ruth examined them, the one after the other, without any feeling that they were even alive. She could not pronounce their names and had never tried to do it. Mimi's regular monthly letters she never answered. What was the use when Mimi could not read English? They were addressed to William and he read them and told her what was in them and then he answered them.

She thought sometimes with bitterness that it was William's blood in Hal that kept him restless and never willing to come home. Even now when William was old and half sick he was restless. Climbing that hill now! Though goodness knows she had done everything to make his life easy! "William's had an awful easy life," she muttered to herself.

She took up Hal's letter and unfolded it and began to read it carefully.

Dear Mom:

Well, I sure am having one swell time. I gave up the taxi business and am chauffeur for an American big shot. We drove all over England then drove through Belgium France Switzerland Italy. This is Spain. It didn't make me feel too good to see the old battlefields and the cemeteries full of white crosses when we went to find the bosses son that fell in action. I sure was lucky to get out of it alive. There's lots of talk over here now about a new war but I guess this time it wont get me. I had enough last time and wont go Mom you don't need to worry. I guess war is hooey anyway.

Well, Mom, we are all swell. The kids are swell. Mimi is a swell wife and mother. Wish you could come over to see us. Maybe with this new job we'll get over to the States sometime. Would like to see the old place again and everybody in it. Well so long Mom and look after yourselves,

Hal.

"Now that's real good news and I'll tell William," she murmured half aloud. She went to the door and looked out. William was still toiling up the hill in the sunshine. He had Richard by the hand. Where'd the child come from?

"William!" she cried. But her lifted voice could not reach him. "He's so foolish," she thought with anxious anger. "He'll come back dead beat, and for something he didn't need to do." She sighed and went back to her work. She had better get her work out of the way. He'd have to be taken care of as soon as he got home, like as not.

"Don't be so cross with me, Ruth," he begged her faintly. He was in such physical distress that the added weight of her harsh, angry, frightened love was almost enough to send him over the edge that was always near him now, beyond which was darkness.

"I'm not cross," she retorted. "I'm just sayin', William, that if you'd only listen to me—"

"I do listen to you," he whispered. "I have always listened to you."

"Well, I certainly told you not to try to climb that hill," she retorted, "and carryin' that paintbox too!"

He did not answer. He closed his eyes and braced himself for the new attack upon him of the strong fresh pain. He must remember what the doctor told him, that he would probably not die in pain. Death would come stealing upon him in the night when he was asleep. He would simply not wake. That was his comfort.

Ah, here was the agony! He groaned out of the depths of his being, a groan that was a retch from his soul.

"Here, hold to me," Ruth commanded him. She took his hands in the way that long experience together had taught them helped him most, and he clutched her hands. Sweat broke from his palms but her hands did not slip. The crest of pain passed.

"You're strong—as ever—" he gasped.

"I have to be," she retorted.

But she was kind in her passionate way. She knew the habit of his pain. At just the right moment she gave him the tablets, at just the right moment she moved his arms and legs so that he could feel his body alive, and rubbed his flesh and then gave him a little hot milk and covered him against the inevitable chill that came over him when the pain was gone.

"Now you go to sleep," she said more gently than she had yet spoken. This attack had been worse than usual, she thought. "Maybe someday you'll believe your old wife," she said with scolding tenderness. She bent and kissed his ash-white cheek, and felt the tears come suddenly to her eyes. She loved him still, though he made her so angry and though she thought sometimes she had never been really happy with him, after all. He seemed so gentle but at bottom he was stubborn. It didn't matter what most men did around a place, he would never do anything. He wouldn't even drive a nail or mend a shutter that the wind blew loose. She had had to do everything. Once she had wanted him to learn to milk the cows. But he had refused.

"I couldn't do it," was all he said.

"Somebody has to," she had retorted.

"I'm very sorry." It was all he ever said when he refused her anything. He was sorry, too, she knew, but he never seemed to think he could not help being as he was. And she had learned to manage without his help because she loved him, always with that deep uneasiness that perhaps her love was not enough for him. But it was all she had.

He opened his shadowy eyes, as though she had spoken her love.

"You could let me die, if I'm too much trouble," he said with faint mischief. It was good to know himself alive again. He died in every bout of pain, no matter what the doctor said. Death was toying with him, keeping him alive for its pleasure. He might fool death and die, if Ruth would let him. But her hands, holding his, still would not let him loose.

"You're plenty of trouble," Ruth retorted. "But you're all I've got and I'll have to put up with you."

He smiled, knowing this was her way of love.

"Now you go right to sleep," she said sharply.

"I can't," he said apologetically. He never could sleep at once. "Turn on a little music, Ruth."

"You'd ought—"

"Oh, please!" he whispered.

So she turned the dial of the radio he kept by the bed. Out of the air there came a voice booming into the room, "War between England and Germany was declared today. The French armies are massing themselves behind the Maginot Line—"

"War again!" he whispered, aghast. He had been expecting it for days, knowing it must come, but forgetting it as he forgot so much now, for hours at a time. Now it was here again, this supreme folly of the human race, ready to take boys like young Henry!

"Oh, God—" he moaned, and fainted with new pain.

. . . No one in France would say he believed that Paris would be bombed seriously. In the last war, of course, but there was the Maginot Line now. Nevertheless, Mimi, fifteen years old on the day when bombs were dropped over Paris and she and all the other girls rushed into the convent chapel with the nuns to pray until it was over, was not entirely easy this bright September morning in the clean little flat which was her pride and occupation.

She hid this uneasiness, however, from Hal, who was home for a two days' leave. She believed that women should keep men happy, and devoted herself to her husband when he was home, reserving her tempers, her attacks of nerves, and her explosions of anxiety until she was alone with her daughters. Hal looked robust and cheerful as a consequence, but Germaine and Angèle were pale and weary-looking young girls with apprehensive grey eyes. Neither of them was pretty, to Mimi's not too secret woe, and she tried to atone for this by making their clothes very *chic*. Since she spent a great deal of time on these garments, she was easily angry if they were soiled or torn, and the two girls guarded themselves continually lest they make their mother angry. In consequence they moved about as little as possible.

A plane soared over the city as the family sat at their

breakfast near a sunny window. Mimi's heart jumped. Now that Germans were actually attacking France, she could never hear a plane again and not feel her heart jump. But she would not allow herself to get up and see. Instead she spoke sharply to Germaine.

"Take care how you eat that honey, or it will spill upon your front."

The girl stopped at her mother's voice and the honey dripped from the spoon upon the tablecloth.

"Oh, heaven," Mimi moaned, "I knew when I allowed honey!" She dashed for a cloth, and sidewise she glanced from the window. Thank God, it was a French plane! But she felt intolerably restless. Was this a premonition? She wanted to get out of the house, out into the open where she could see what was coming. She hurried back to the table, her dark face tense. She scrubbed at the cloth. "I knew if I said honey—"

"Be quiet," Hal said. "What does it matter?"

He spoke a simple, rough French that somehow served his needs. He gave a bit of his bacon to Germaine. He had eggs and bacon for breakfast, but Mimi and the girls had only their milky coffee and rolls. The honey was a treat because he was at home. The girl smiled through her tear-filled eyes, and took the bacon on her plate. Then she looked at her mother.

"May I eat it, Maman?"

"Certainly, since your papa so generously gives it," Mimi said sternly. She sat down again. " 'Al!" She could never pronounce his name otherwise.

"Eh?" He scraped his egg from his plate without looking up.

"Let us celebrate by a picnic in the country today, instead of the theater."

"I've seen country day after day," he objected.

"Ah, yes, but we have not! And it is still so hot today, is it not? The air—it is like the inside of a trunk! Think of the country, and a little stream where we can wade, and picking flowers! And the sky above us—so clear!"

He looked at the children. "What do you say, infants?"

They looked at their mother.

"Picnic," Angèle whispered.

"Then," Hal said, "picnic it is." He dipped up a spoonful of honey. "That's to make a sweet finish," he said, and licked the spoon.

. . . Who could have foretold that day? The hours of the morning passed so quickly, so happily. The stifling about Mimi's heart eased. She forgot for a little while the deep memories of German planes diving over the city, over the convent chapel, forgot the frantic prayers to God who lived above the sky full of evil. The lovely summer day moved on, so gentle, so tranquil. They ate their lunch under a tree and afterwards she slept a little, and then they waded in the brook together, and Hal had just slipped upon a wet smooth stone and had fallen. She screamed with laughter, it was so amusing, his rueful round face.

"What the heck," he shouted, he who always returned to English when he was disturbed!

" 'Eck—what is it?" she had just cried, still laughing, when out of the sky something dived down, black as an angry bird. Oh, she had heard airplanes roaring high above them all day, now and again, but so high and so she had not looked. She would not look.

Now she looked and her laughter froze. Above her was the swastika, black against silver and blue.

"Oh, my 'Al!" she screamed. "They come again!"

That was all. That was the end of her life and Hal's. The two young girls who had run like partridges escaped by a few yards the volcano of water and earth. Barefooted, hand in hand, they stood motionless while the young man in the sky, who had stopped for an idle moment to spoil a little picnic, went darting on to his real business.

Hand in hand in the terrible silence the girls stole to the edge of the crater to see if their parents were there, and saw what was flung into cruel dismemberment outward from the violence of its center. Speechless, they sat down and put on their stockings and shoes and tied them. The picnic basket was there unhurt, and so was their mother's handbag. Angèle turned to Germaine.

"Should we take back the things?"

"Certainly," Germaine said. "Maman wouldn't like us to leave her things behind."

They picked up the basket and the bag and trudged to the bus line. In the purse was money and they bought their tickets back to Paris. The city was very quiet, very peaceful in the late afternoon. People were sober. The news from the front was grave, very grave. They sat outdoors, drinking and eating, to talk about how bad it was. No one paid particular heed to two pale, very neat young girls carrying a basket between them.

They returned therefore to their house, and only at the familiar door did it come to them all that had happened. They looked at one another.

"Alas," Germaine gasped, "we have no parents!"

Angèle's pale grey eyes widened and seeing the terror in her elder sister's face, she began to cry loudly, as her mother had never let her cry. The concierge came waddling out.

"What is it?" she cried. Then she saw who it was, the two well-behaved young daughters of the big American. "And now?" she asked, and stood as they sobbed out the impossible truth, the sweat pouring off her as she heard it.

Obviously, she said to all the neighbors assembling to hear her crying and calling, obviously there was but one thing to do. The children had a rich grandfather. Their mother had said so continually. She wrote to him regularly, being a prudent woman. She boasted that his French was perfect, Parisian in fact. And obviously, therefore, the little girls must be sent straight to this rich old man, who would give them love and every luxury. The things in the flat, if sold, doubtless would provide enough for the tickets third class. Germaine, a big girl, could look after Angèle. The neighbors approving, the thing was to be done.

Meanwhile, a letter of course must be sent, announcing the sad affair. Voluble French voices, contradicting and interrupting, settled the fate of the two listening girls, and crying out how fortunate they were to have a rich American grandfather, kind French people took care of the children until they could be sent. Madame d'Aubigne, who lived in the flat above them, took them in with her and dyed their frocks black, and Monsieur Albe undertook the sale of the furnishings. In less than a week all was ready and the two little girls were put on the train for Calais.

"Do not forget us when you become rich Americans," they said, pressing kisses and bonbons upon the black-frocked children. "Do not forget!" They were all at the station and saw them off, and Madame d'Aubigne sighed.

"To live in America, far from the enemy—it is not a bad fate, that," she said.

"Not too bad, certainly," Monsieur Albe agreed.

They trudged home through strangely silent streets. Assuredly today the war news was bad. It was as well that the two girls could not hear it.

William, in a big chair under the sycamore, read the letter again. Hal's daughters were being sent to him, Germaine and Angèle. Hal was dead, with his wife. He had known it for nearly two hours, but he had not called Ruth. She had come to the kitchen door now and then, and he had pretended to be asleep, the letter in his hand. When she came to tell him dinner was ready, he could no longer put off telling her what was in the letter. Two young girls in the house, French, speaking only French, probably! Everything said to them, he must say. He must help them in every way he could, for he was responsible for their being. If he had not walked down the path, past this very tree, one summery day very like this one, all those years ago, none of this would have happened. Hal would have come home as Joel did, doubtless, and these little girls would have been born here.

"Germaine and Angèle!" he murmured, his eyes closed in one of the moments of sleep that fell on him these days.

"Are they all right?" Ruth's voice, coming unexpectedly, startled him. He opened his eyes and saw her standing before him, her brown and red face full of health beneath her white hair. "Dinner's ready," she said. "Any news of Hal?" she said, glancing at the letter.

He debated whether to tell her now or after dinner. But how could he eat? And when he did not she fretted.

"This letter," he said slowly, picking up the thin lined sheet, "has bad news in it."

He looked at her. Her face took on the firmness habitual to her when she made herself ready for a task.

"What's happened to Hal?"

"A terrible, terrible accident, dear."

She sat down quickly on the garden bench. "You might just as well tell me, William."

So he told her, translating sentence by sentence the anguished French words. Then he folded the letter and put it in his pocket, and looking at her saw for the first time that she had become an old woman. He leaned over the arm of his chair and took her hand in his and held it, trying as he did so to control the slight palsy of his own hand.

"My dear!" he said.

But she said nothing. She sat in the absolute stillness of the animal wounded, staring across the valley and the river that lay a broad bright band along it. He thought, half wondering, half abashed, how much less he felt Hal's death than he had the death of Elise's younger son, years ago in the first world war. World wars! There would be nothing but world wars from now on. The world had become a neighborhood, what with fast trains and automobiles and airplanes, and the innocent would be involved with the guilty. But if life had any meaning it was simply that the innocent were always involved with the guilty— God who sent rain on the just and unjust alike! Not that he believed in God at this late hour of his own life. He was able to contemplate his own death calmly enough as an incident too infinitesimal to be of importance, even to himself. Its persistence did not interest him. He thought a great deal about it, however, and if he were given the choice afterward he was inclined to think he would choose eternal sleep. "I've had a long good life," he thought. "There's no use in having it all over again."

But Hal was another matter. Hal had been cut off in midlife, without knowing old age. William considered the value of these last fifteen years. No, he would not have missed them. They were as valuable as childhood, and he had enjoyed them far more than his childhood. Childhood had been insecure and bewildering. He had not known then from day to day what life might thrust upon him. But in old age life could play him no more tricks. He knew all about life, and death was no terror because it was simply an end. Yes, he would choose it to be an end.

"What'll we do with those girls?" Ruth asked. Her voice was so sudden that he jumped. His mind, always busy in the distances of eternity, came back to earth.

"Why, they're ours and I suppose we'll have to keep them." He had forgotten Hal again, but now he had to remember again these two young French girls who would be able to speak to no one in this house except him.

"I shan't ever feel they're ours," Ruth said definitely.

"Oh, but—Ruth!" He was distressed at the thought of the two children, bereaved of all they knew, coming here to such a Ruth. "Dear, they're Hal's children."

"I can't feel them," she said.

He pondered this slowly, his distress deepening. Mary's house was full, and besides, to whom could they speak in Mary's house? And he was so old. Even if they came here, how could he look after them? He had never been good with children. And, yet, he thought in sudden clarity, why should he blame Ruth? He was thinking of Germaine and Angèle not as Hal's children nor his own grandchildren, but as two lonely French girls alien in an American farmhouse. Ruth would never understand them. But he had been in Paris.

His mind wandered peacefully away from the children back to the Paris he had known fifty years ago. He saw it so clearly, the bright streets, the gay people, talking, laughing, eating in the sunshine, the pigeons with their rainbow breasts. Paris was full of pigeons.

"I won't have them here," Ruth said.

His mind raced back into his body. "What shall we do with them?" he asked, bewildered.

"I don't know." Her voice was somber with angry grief. "Hal ought never to have stayed there in that foreign place. He ought to have come home. Then none of this would have happened. People ought to stay where they belong."

He laughed silently. "You're a nice one to talk," he said.

"Where would I be if I'd stayed where my mother said I belonged?"

But she refused to smile. "That's different," she said.

He meditated contradicting this, and decided against it. He did not often feel strong enough to contradict her. He began instead to think quite clearly what could be done if he accepted what she said. His mind had moments of surprising agility, and one of these came to him now.

"Jill can help. She's been to Paris a dozen times."

"What would Jill do with children?" Ruth asked. But relief was in her voice.

"I have an idea she might enjoy them. She hasn't anything of her own."

He did not want to discuss Jill too much, because he and Ruth saw her so differently. The distance between Ruth and this second daughter had grown greater and greater as the years passed. But to him Jill had grown very near. She had become a part of the world that he used to know. He talked with her as now he talked to no one. And Jill had plenty of money. When his mother died ten years ago, a very old woman, she had left all her money to Jill.

"I don't think she could remember who I was," Jill told him when she came back from the funeral. "I mean, she always forgot I was your daughter. Somehow she thought I was Aunt Louise's child. She used to say to me, 'Your mother—' and she always meant Aunt Louise."

"I suppose she forgot me long ago," he had said rather sadly.

"I don't think she had forgotten so much as she wanted to think she had," Jill said. "She was a vain old thing. Partly she left me her money because I was a success."

"Ah, well," he had said, "I don't want it." No, he wanted nothing but what he had chosen to have.

"I'll write to Jill," he said drowsily. The sunshine always made him drowsy.

But he was not quite easy until he heard from Jill. Her large, square envelope reached him on the day the children's ship was due. "Of course, dear—of course, of course!" That was the burden of the letter. But not for Hal's sake, he saw that. Jill was taking them because they were French war orphans. Her handwriting was illegible. "Poor children! Oh, this war! It is the least I can do. I can't go abroad. My doctor won't hear to it. But I can do this. I'll meet them myself—don't worry, my dear."

. . . Germaine and Angèle, tightly hand in hand and terrified lest there be no one to meet them, stood waiting upon the ship's deck.

"I knew them at once," Jill wrote him. "Two tragic thin young things in black, waiting to see if anyone wanted them. I put my arms around them. They have nothing but black frocks. I am going to buy them everything new, from hat to heels."

He read this letter to Ruth one night in the kitchen. They sat there by the stove instead of in the library now, partly because it was easier in the brief interval between supper and bed, partly because she was happier in the kitchen. And in a way so was he. Here in this smoke-browned room he had first seen her for what she was, all woman.

"I think Hal's two girls are cared for," he said.

"Children have to look after each other," she said. "There comes a time when the old ones can't."

They sat side by side on the old settle by the stove, and soon he began to nod. The room was so still.

"Come to bed," she said. And he rose at the sound of her voice and followed her.

But by midnight he was awake again, as wide awake as though it were dawn. He had fretted once against this nightly wakefulness, thinking something was wrong with him, until hearing him complain one day Ruth had said placidly, "I reckon you're just gettin' old, William. I never saw an old person yet that didn't go back to being a kind of baby, sleepin' in the daytime and layin' awake at night."

He had complained no more after that. Yes, he was getting old, and he lay patiently awake in the great double four-poster bed. A hundred years ago this bed had been brought into the room and never moved again. He had come into this house and found here his place to sleep.

He ought to be glad he slept very little now. There was so much for the old to think about and so little time left in which to think.

Around him the night was wonderfully soft and deep. Long ago he had learned to love the country night. It had been one of his many compensations. He heard Ruth breathing gently in her sleep at his side. She slept as peacefully as she had when she was a girl. All the processes of her being were full of health. She was sound and ripe, not old as he was old. Why did he think of compensations when he had had so rich a life? He remembered her as she had been on their first night together. The memory of that passion was only sweetness, now that passion had passed from them both. They did not need it any more. Their flesh had long since been made one. If his spirit was still solitary, it was his fault, not hers. He understood so well that her flashes of temper, her irritations with him which had grown during the years until sometimes they made him, momentarily, really unhappy, were because their spirits had remained separate while their bodies were one. He felt humbly that this was his fault, because Ruth had put her whole being into their marriage. But there had been that part of him which she had not needed, and so it had been left in him, unused. It went winging out of him now through the night.

All the world for him to wander in was outside this quiet house. He lay dreaming not of anyone he knew but of things he had never seen, or seen but once when he was very young, and now would never see, people, places, pictures, friends he had never had, companionships he had not found. But there was no pain in any of this. Once in his strong middle age there had been. He had groaned then under the bondage of Ruth's need of him, though it had been full of a suffering sweetness, too. When her need passed, it was too late. For now he had needed her more than ever she had him, and now he was utterly dependent upon her.

He brought his wandering spirit home to her again and felt the comfort of her presence. She was so strong, she loved him, and it was long since too late for anything except their love. Their love had been the reality of his youth.

"I couldn't paint, that year in New York," he thought in one of his flashes of clearest memory. "And I couldn't have painted if I had left her during the years that Hal was lost." He pondered on, "I should have been racked with her misery if I had not been here to comfort her. She needed me then—or Jill would have suffered."

And now what had he but this tender, clinging love of his for her, and her strong love for him? Even if he often made her angry, he knew it was because she loved him. She had taken him into her being and he could disturb her as no one else could because he was in her being and yet not wholly hers, however much he tried to be and longed to be. He wanted in nothing any more to be alien to her, for there was a comfort in their love now vaster than life itself. He moved a little and felt a piercing pain, and for a second was frightened.

"Ruth!" he whispered. He did not want to waken her, but if he needed her he must. He could never go through a bout of his pain alone. But the pain did not return. He waited, but still he was free of it.

"I can sleep," he thought gratefully. But he was a little cold. He turned and curved his body against the warmth of Ruth's body and put his arm about her. They had slept thus so many years that she did not wake. They had slept thus so long together that almost instantly he fell asleep.

When she woke, his arm was fast and hard about her. She could not move from his clutch.

"William!" she cried to waken him. But he did not waken.

"William!" she screamed.

She forced his arm away, then, strong with sudden terror. "William, William—William!"

She flung him on his back, and he lay there before her, his face full of peace, unanswering, dead.

"Oh," she moaned. "Oh, my dear!"

She leaped out of bed and ran to telephone the doctor. But it was no use, of course.

"It's happened just as you said it would," she gasped over the telephone. "He's gone from me, in his sleep."

"I'll be right over, Mrs. Barton," the doctor said. "Don't bother about anything—just rest."

But she was not able to rest. She must tend William. There must be something to be done for him. He must be made neat and his hair brushed and the bed straightened.

She fetched water in a basin and put it on a chair by the bed, and sobbing all the time, she washed his hands and face as she had done every morning when she got up.

"Oh, my dear," she moaned. "Did you call me and I didn't hear? I'm such a wicked sound sleeper. Oh, William, William!"

She hung over him, knowing it their last hour together alone. Once the doctor came, once they—they began— She laid her head down upon his breast.

"I wisht I hadn't been so cross with you a many times," she murmured. "I wisht it now, something terrible! Oh, to think we couldn't see our golden wedding day, William— William!"

. . . They took him away in such a cruel little while. She stood watching as they lifted the tall figure from the bed. Other people had dressed him while she put on her own clothes.

"Go into the kitchen, Mother," Mary said. "There's nothing more you can do for him." Both the girls had come at once. Jill brought the two little girls, but Ruth scarcely looked at them.

"My life's over," she thought. "I've lost him."

She had tried to prepare herself for this moment ever since she knew it must come, but she was not prepared. Nothing could really prepare her for the end of all that for which she had worked and lived. She could not remember what it had been like in this house before William came that day to dinner, nor could she imagine what it would be like now.

"I can remember exactly how he looked that first day in this very room," she thought, looking around the kitchen.

She sat down, gazing at the walls, the furniture. She had loved him the moment she saw him. She loved him now.

"Though why I've been so crotchety cross with him lately I don't know and can't think," she said to herself. Tears gathered in her eyes and rolled down her cheeks. "I wasn't good enough for him," she thought, "I was never good enough for him and all along I knew I wasn't."

This was her grief. She had kept it down all her life but now it rose up, now that William was gone.

"He was better'n me. He wasn't even cross with me, ever," she thought wretchedly. "Oh, William, I wisht you had been, sometimes!"

Mary came in and found her sobbing aloud. She put her arms about the old woman.

"Now Mother, don't," she said. "It had to come, Mom. We knew it had to come and it came so easy, in his sleep."

Ruth shook her head. "I ain't cryin' just for that," she said. But she could not explain to a child what had been between her and William. So she wiped her eyes. "I guess I better get myself cleaned up," she said.

"Yes, folks'll be coming," Mary said.

Young Henry came in, pencil and paper in his hand. "Grandmom, there's a reporter here from the county paper. He wants some information about Grandfather. They've got the—the obituary but they aren't quite sure about his family. Wasn't his father the Harold Barton who had the big railroad company?"

"Yes, he was," Ruth said. "But you tell that man to wait. I'll come and give him the straight of it all myself. I want it right."

She hurried upstairs and washed herself and put on her best black dress and came down to the parlor where the young man was. Jill was there, too. She had never seen her mother so handsome, she thought. Ruth entered the room with a plain dignity.

The young man rose. "You are Mrs. William Barton?" he asked.

"I am," Ruth replied. Yes, she was that. She would always be Mrs. William Barton.

. . . She went through three days in a stately dream.

Again and again the doorbell rang and she always answered it herself. Her children let her, and her neighbors, too, who had come in to help, when they saw it was a comfort to her.

"Mrs. William Barton?"

"I am Mrs. William Barton," she said proudly.

There was a wreath of white flowers, or a telegram, or a little group of school children, or a stammering, halting man.

"I used to see Mr. Barton, ma'am," one said, "used to fit his shoes. I thought maybe—"

To them all she said, "Would you like to see him?"

She led the way into the parlor. The center table had been taken away and there William lay on his bier. She had the best of her potted plants about him and all the other flowers that had come. Sometimes those who gazed at him did not speak, but more often they did.

"He looks wonderful, don't he?"

"He looks what he was," she always said.

She was calmer now because there was so much to do. Sometimes, planning with Mary about sandwiches and cakes for the meal after the funeral, or telling young Henry how to take care of the relatives who filled the house, or reading a telegram Jill brought in, she forgot why all this was. It was almost like any big family gathering—almost, indeed, like the golden wedding party she and William had argued about so often. Though if she'd thought—but she had no time to think. All the relatives were hers today. William had nobody but a sister, and she was not coming. Jill said Louise could not bear to come, because she never went to funerals.

"It's funny she can't come to her own brother's funeral," Ruth said coldly.

"She never does anything she doesn't want to, I'm afraid," Jill said. She would never be able to explain Aunt Louise to her mother. There was no possible plane of understanding which either could reach. Old people were so definite, she thought, half sadly. They made such different worlds for themselves out of what was really only one world. Her father alone had belonged to every world.

How desperately she would miss him! No one, no one could take his place. What would she have done if he had not seen how lonely she was and sent her Germaine and Angèle to be her children? They were over at Mary's house, safe, she knew, and yet she kept thinking about them, and seeing their faces, just now beginning to lose the look of anxiety, and their thin little hands. Were Mary's hearty, plain children being good to them? In a moment she would slip over and see. She had decided against black frocks for them even at the funeral. There had been so much black in their lives already. Instead she had chosen white.

"Well," her mother was saying, "let his sister stay away from him now. His folks never meant anything to him when he was alive. Though I can't understand—" She went away fuming. What would William have done without her, alive or dead? She had relatives enough for them both. They kept up with each other as families ought, and they had always liked William and in later years had respected him, too. They were proud of him. Her brother Tom was buying all the newspapers and making a scrapbook of the clippings about William.

"There's even pieces about him in the Philly papers," he said proudly. He read aloud, "William Barton was at one time regarded as one of the most promising of the younger American artists."

There was nothing in the New York papers. They could hardly expect that. But every newspaper in the county carried long columns about him. Ruth found time to read them all, down to the last paragraph. "He is survived by his widow." That was her. She was William's widow.

Upon the strength of this dignity she passed the hours until William was taken from the house on the morning of the third day to return no more. She followed him then, Tom driving her slowly in his bright new car. Behind her came the long line of slow cars moving down the country road to the cemetery that stood around the church to which William had always refused to go. But here he came now, to rest at last in her own family lot where her father and her father's fathers were buried. And here he would lie, and she would lie beside him, to all eternity.

The house was very quiet. She had insisted that everybody go home. It had been easy to persuade the girls. After the big funeral feast was over and the relatives gone and everything cleaned, she had said to them, "Now you both run along home. The children will be needing you. Besides, there isn't a thing you can do here. If I want anybody, I'll keep Tom."

"Sure," Tom said.

So Mary and Jill had gone. Uncle Tom, they told each other, could stay perfectly well. There were plenty of people to look after the garage. But it was easy to persuade Tom to go, too. Ruth said plainly, "I want to be by myself, Tom."

"You'll be lonesome," he objected.

"No, I won't," she told him. "A woman don't get lonesome when she's been married as long as I have. The end of her life meets the beginning again."

But he was afraid he ought not to go, and she had to make him at last, before he put on his coat and hat. She had to walk with him to his car. Even then, with his hand on the wheel, he hesitated.

"Sure you're all right, Ruth?"

"Sure I am," she replied. Oh, be gone, be gone, her heart cried at him, longing for freedom to mourn.

But he lingered, being a kind-hearted old man, seeking for some last word of comfort for his sister. It had been so hard for her, the relatives had all said when she was not in the room, because William had "passed away" in his sleep, without a last word to her. They put great importance upon last words, and they repeated solemnly the last things that others had said. Tom searched his memory and found some words which he remembered because at the time William had spoken them he had not understood what he meant. William was always talking queer. He did not understand them now, but maybe she would.

"Ruth," he said, "that last time I talked with William he said something about you I was going to tell you."

"Did he?" she cried. "Oh, Tom, what was it?"

"He said he wouldn't know what to do without you. 'Member that day last autumn when I ran the car up with a box of books for him from the express office?"

She nodded. William was always buying books with his picture money. She used to be angry about it, because books were so useless, but now she was glad he had done what he wanted—though what she would do now with all those books!

"You brung a shawl out for his legs—'member?"

She nodded.

"Well, after you was gone in, he said you was his daily bread or somethin' like that."

"Did he, Tom?"

He watched her face to see if she were comforted. And he saw she was. She understood then what the old man had meant.

"I thought maybe you'd like that," he said, pleased with himself.

"It was a wonderful sweet thing for William to say," she replied.

When he was gone she went back to the kitchen to eat her supper. Bread! William had been so fond of good bread. And he always said hers was the best in the world. He had talked like poetry about her sometimes when she stood kneading bread at this very table. Bread meant something special to William. That first picture he had painted of her had been with a loaf of bread in her hand. She sat remembering all she could of what he used to say about bread.

"If I have good bread to eat, I don't care what else is lacking," he used to say. "Bread is my real food," he used to say.

"He couldn't have said a more meaningful thing about me," she thought gratefully. Somehow it eased her for everything. She had always been proud to be his wife, and still always there was the inner discouragement of knowing she was not good enough for him. But if she was like bread to him, then it meant he could never have done without her.

"I guess he didn't mind my being a mite cross once in a while," she thought. "I guess he knows there just wasn't anybody but him nor ever will be. And I did everything for him."

Her eyes filled, but she kept on eating. This was the first of many meals she must eat alone and she might as well get used to it first as last. The house was so still she could have been frightened if she had been a woman like that. But she wasn't. She could always do what had to be done. So she sat, finishing her meal.

About her there was not a sound, inside the house or out. It was the time of evening when even the birds were still. Then suddenly she was overcome with longing for him. This was how it was going to be, still, like this, day and night, all the rest of her life. She could eat no more and she put down her spoon and sat staring out into the bright evening. The house was empty. She had a queer feeling that it was altogether empty, that even she was not here.

"Oh, *William*," she said heavily. Her voice was loud in the emptiness about her.

He was really gone.

Then suddenly in the stillness she heard a noise. She heard a clatter in the barn. Something had fallen. She jumped up.

"My goodness, what's that?" she cried. She hurried out of the kitchen and across the grass to the barn bridge and up to the open door. "Who's there?" she called sharply. A tramp, likely, she thought, but she wasn't going to be afraid.

"It's me," someone said. The voice came from the room under the hayloft where William kept his paintings.

"For pity's sake," she said, and went quickly across the rough old floor and looked in.

There among William's tumbled paintings stood Mary's youngest boy, Richard.

"Rickie, for pity's sake!" she repeated. "What you doin' here?"

"I wanted to see his—his pictures," the boy faltered. He had been crying and his cheeks were streaked with dust from the canvases he had been turning over as he wept.

"Well, why didn't you ask me to show 'em to you?" Ruth said. She sat down on William's old chair. He had sat at his easel in later years when standing tired him. Then she pulled the boy toward her.

"Mercy me, look at that face! Here, I'll wipe it with my apron." She wiped his face and he was comforted by her scolding tenderness, since there was no one else to see her babying him. She gave him a hearty kiss. "Now then, want I should show you your granddad's pictures?"

"If you don't think he'd care."

"He'd love it," she said briskly. She put a picture on the easel. "Now this here one he painted one day—I can remember like anything—when they was making hay. A thunderstorm come up—see, there it is, you can see it just as like—"

One by one she lifted the paintings, remembering. "Now this one he always said just wouldn't come right."

"I think it's good, though, Grandmom," Richard said eagerly.

"So do I," she said. "Wonderful! He was a grand wonderful man, Richard, and we mustn't forget it, shall we, you and me?"

"No, never."

They looked at all the paintings and then she said, "Now it's time for you to be going home, dear. Your Mom will be worryin'."

They stacked the paintings carefully and walked away together, hand in hand, out into the clear twilight. Then he gathered his courage.

"Grandmom!"

"Yes, Rickie?"

"Can I have his big paintbox?"

She was startled, and he held his breath, waiting.

"Why, I couldn't—I don't know as he'd want me to give that away," she said. "What would you do with it?"

"Paint pictures. Please, Grandmom—anyway, when I'm grown up—like Grandfather!" He was clutching her waist.

"My goodness," she said, amazed. "Where'd you get such a notion? Nobody else in our family paints pictures!"

"I don't know—it's been inside me always. Please, please!"

Inside him! Then it occurred to her for the first time, looking down into the pleading face at her breast, that of course William could be inside this boy. But somehow she had never thought of it before. She looked at him solemnly.

"You'll have to be awful good," she said.

"I will," he said gravely.

He dropped his arms from her waist and stood, a little figure haunted, William's spirit looking out of his eyes.

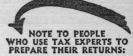